TRADING BY FIRELIGHT

TRADING BY FIRELIGHT

THE MAGIC BELOW PARIS™ BOOK FOUR

C. M. SIMPSON

MICHAEL ANDERLE

TRADING BY FIRELIGHT TEAM

Thanks to our Beta Readers

Nicole Emens, Charles Tillman, Larry Omans, Daniel Weigert, and Mary Morris

Thanks to our JIT Readers

Jeff Goode
Dorothy Lloyd
Diane L. Smith
John Ashmore
Misty Roa

Editor

SkyHunter Editing Team

DEDICATION

This is for all those who believed in me enough that, eventually, I had the courage to believe in myself.

Thank you.

—C.M. Simpson

*To Family, Friends and
Those Who Love
to Read.
May We All Enjoy Grace
to Live the Life We Are
Called.*

— Michael

MIKA'S OUTLET ESTABLISHED

Mika's Outlet was secure. Marsh took a long look at the clearrock the rock mages had grown to block the opening and the massive set of iron-bound gates that sealed it from the outside and turned to where Roeglin, Gustav and Master Envermet stood beside her.

"It's done."

"Way to state the obvious, Marsh."

Marsh pivoted to face the direction of the voice. She saw nothing but a darker patch of shadows and imagined herself stretching to take them in her hands.

"You *like* digging latrines, Tams?"

Marsh tugged on the shadow but it would not yield. Damn! The boy had gotten stronger in the last few weeks. She tried again, coaxing the shadows apart, trying to get them to thin and show what hid beneath. As she did, she felt them resist her attempts and knew Tamlin was working just as hard to hold them together.

A small giggle escaped the densest section of them, then Tamlin gasped.

"Stop it, Aysh!"

The giggle came again, and Marsh felt the shadows wriggle beneath her hand.

"Aysh!"

More giggling followed, then an exclamation of outrage, and the shadows dissipated to reveal Tamlin squirming away from his little sister as she tried to tickle him.

"Thanks a lot, sis! Now, c'm'ere!"

Marsh watched as Tamlin made a grab for the mischief-maker, only to have her slip into the rock she was leaning against.

"Cheater!"

"Am not!" the rock said.

"Get your tail out here!"

"Uh-uh!"

"You have to sleep sometime!"

Aisha stuck her head out of the rock.

"Yeah? You and whose army?"

Beside Marsh, Roeglin started to laugh.

"Remind you of anyone?" he asked, nudging Marsh in the ribs, and Envermet snorted.

"Every damn day," the shadow guards' captain said and walked to where the rock mages were inspecting their work.

Marsh stared after him, not sure whether to be insulted, shocked, or entertained. Envermet's parting comment didn't help.

"I told you to watch the examples you set."

Marsh turned to Roeglin, ignoring the amusement dancing in the dark-haired mage's eyes.

"I can never tell if he's mad at me or joking."

Roeglin smiled and clapped her on the shoulder.

"Join the club. Come on, let's go see how Master Petit-feu's latest batch of cookies came out."

"Cookies!"

At the mention of the word, Aisha came out of the rock and shot past them, with Tamlin in hot pursuit. There was a flurry of movement, and Scruffknuckle emerged from a nearby cluster of shrooms and grass. He bounded after the two children, two hoshkat kits racing in his wake.

"You think he's still bent on revenge?" Roeglin asked, but Marsh shook her head.

"Nah. He's just trying to beat her and the pup to the cookies."

Roeglin broke into a trot.

"Boy has a point," he said as he bolted past her. "If those two get to them before the rest of us, there won't be many left."

Laughing, Marsh sprinted after him.

Her laughter died, however, when she entered the community center that was acting as a temporary barracks in the small town.

"You!" Brigitte scolded, brandishing a ladle at her.

Before Marsh could reply, the mage swept her hand toward where Aisha was sitting and sipping a cup of hot chocolate, her hand curled protectively around two very large cookies.

"I thought things would change when Envermet elevated me to master, but *no*. Instead, I get assigned not one but *two* pestilential apprentices—and one of them has the appetite *and* all the manners of shroom-muncher!"

"Hey!"

Clearly, Aisha's lessons with the rock mages had extended to include *all* the lifeforms in the caverns. She knew enough of the shroom-devouring beetle to know what Brigitte was referring to and be offended. Across the table from her, Tamlin said nothing.

"Shut up and eat your cookie!" Brigitte scolded, but Aisha was way ahead of her, so she couldn't do anything but chew and roll her eyes in reply.

The ex-journeyman looked at Marsh and Roeglin.

"I suppose the pair of you thought you'd get to test these too?"

Marsh looked at Roeglin, feeling her skin heat as she blushed. At least the shadow mage looked just as uncomfortable as she felt. Brigitte raised her eyebrows.

"I see," she said, and reached behind her for two small baskets. "Then you can take these out to the mages working on the wall. The Deeps know they need the energy far more than either of you."

She watched as they took the baskets and gave them an impish grin.

"And you can have one, too…as thanks for your help."

"Hey!" Roeglin began, but Marsh grabbed him by the arm and spun him around before he could say more.

"On it!" she said, and she had the shadow master out the door before he thought to resist.

"What did you do that for?"

"What? She gave us a whole basket of cookies each, and left us unsupervised to deliver them…" Marsh started, and let the words trail off.

Roeglin's eyes widened when he caught where she was going.

"You wouldn't…"

"Oh, I don't know. New mage master giving orders to her seniors…it might be fun."

"Right up until I give you both latrine and stable duty for a week." Master Envermet's disapproving rumble interrupted her before she could go any farther. "Make sure my mages get their cookies before I fine you yours for being more of a pain in the ass than usual."

And he brushed right past them, heading for the kitchen.

Marsh watched him go, her mouth open in surprise.

"That was humor," she managed after a small pause, and it was Roeglin's turn to hook his arm through hers and guide her toward where the rock mages were resting beside their wall.

"It was," he agreed, "and aren't we just lucky he was in a good mood today?"

"I wonder why…" Marsh mused, but Roeglin didn't reply, and neither of them spoke until the cookies had been delivered.

The answer became clear on their return to the dining hall.

Shadow guards were hurrying back and forward, some packing their bedrolls into backpacks, and others clearing the tables and chairs from the center of the room. At the same time, several Mika's Outlet locals were lining up before a short, round man with a balding pate and curly gray hair. Master Envermet was standing beside him and looked up as they entered.

"Good to see you back so soon," he said, but whether he was referring to them delivering the cookies or genuinely glad to see their rapid return, Marsh couldn't tell. "I'm leaving twenty guards to train the Protector's here; the rest of us are moving out in the morning."

He looked at Roeglin.

"It would be helpful if we had more mind mages," he said. "I don't suppose…"

Roeglin shook his head.

"Only Felicity so far, but I'm hoping there will be more."

Master Envermet's face clouded, his good mood evaporating as he glanced down at the man at the desk.

"Everyone has the ability to do magic, don't they?" he pressed, clearly repeating a question he'd been asked. Roeglin sighed, realizing he'd have to explain the whole magical ability thing again.

"That is what the first wanderer told us, but we have found that the ability varies…like other human abilities. Some find magic an easy thing," and here he glanced at Marsh before continuing, "and others find it difficult to the point of near impossibility…and then there is the fact that not everyone can access the same kind of magic, or more than one kind. It's just a matter of people trying to see what they can do—and knowing and believing that they will be able to do something."

Roeglin delivered that last bit like he was delivering a speech, but Marsh didn't mind; she knew why. She recognized the gray-haired man now. He was the village leader, the mayor, and Marsh knew he'd be looking for a way to get his people to embrace the need to discover and use what magic they might have.

She didn't envy him the task. Ninetta's farm wasn't the only place they'd discovered a bad attitude toward magic. Of course, they hadn't arrived in the nick of time to save the farmers from a band of raiders, but they *had* done that when they arrived at the town—and the rock mages and shadow mages had been the only reason Mika's Outlet wasn't a ghost town like so many others before it.

Things like that had a way of turning attitudes around —for most people. She had no doubt that there would still be some who needed more proof... and others who would *never* be convinced. The community would just have to find a way to deal with it as they developed. From what she could see, magic had always been inside them, and it was there to stay.

She studied the mayor's face, watching him digest the news. From the little she knew of him, he'd already be trying to work out ways of getting his people to try what Roeglin had suggested—trying to see what abilities they had that he could leverage. Marsh cleared her throat, looking around the hall, and drawing Envermet's attention.

"Yes, Shadow Mage?"

"I was just wondering how many of the rock mages were staying," she said. "There's a wolf pack looking for partners, and..."

Master Envermet waved for her to stop.

"I'm leaving a contingent of twenty shadow guards, and a half dozen of the rock mages have asked to stay, something I will agree to as soon as I've cleared it with the Masters of Beast and Stone."

He said this last with a glance toward Roeglin that was as good as an order.

"When?" the shadow mage asked.

"When we're done here," Envermet told him. "The mayor needs to know as soon as we are able."

The mayor, for his part, was looking at Envermet in puzzlement.

"Yes?" the shadow captain asked, no doubt knowing what was coming.

"I don't mean to be rude," the mayor began, and Marsh sensed genuine concern behind his words, even with the "but" hanging in the air between them.

And sure enough, it was there when the man continued.

"But how can rock mages help us with wolves? Or crops," he added after a moment's hesitation. "I don't understand how workers in stone can be of any help with the plants and beasts…and I don't see any druids here."

He cast an apologetic glance toward Marsh.

"With the exception of the shadow mage here, and the child, of course. No offense intended."

"None taken," Marsh told him, but left it to Master Envermet to explain why the rock mages were so much more than their name implied.

The shadow guard captain gave a heavy sigh and walked away from the table. Before Marsh and Roeglin could do more than draw a breath in protest, he'd collected a nearby chair and returned to sit beside the mayor. Marsh and Roeglin hurried to do the same.

"The rock mages," Master Envermet began as soon as they'd seated themselves, "are only called that because that is how they served the Caverns when they showed themselves at all. If they'd lived on the surface they would have been called druids from the start, but, just as the shrooms and their creatures are a part of the natural world around them, so too are the rocks, and most work with more than one of those elements."

Marsh listened as the shadow captain described the different things the rock mages could do, her eyes tracking the movement in the room. She saw when the last of the Mika's Outlet recruits arrived and gathered around the table. These men and women listened intently to what Envermet had to say, their gazes drifting across the room as though searching for these "rock mages."

Marsh saw some frowns when they didn't see any of the druidic mages and watched as their attention was drawn by something else. She followed their gazes and found that, having cleared the packs and bedding from around the hall, the shadow guards had moved the tables to the edges and stacked the chairs on top of them before forming into squads in the room's center.

She had to admit they looked impressive in their Protector uniforms. They looked even more impressive when they started their first set of katas, drawing their swords and going through the standard moves before pulling shadow from the edges of the room to coat their blades. Marsh saw the Mika's Outlet recruits' eyes grow wide as Master Envermet finished his explanation.

Without a word, the shadow captain got up out of his chair and carried it over to the edge of the room, with Marsh and Roeglin doing the same. They came to stand behind him as he positioned himself beside the table, watching as his troops brought their final kata to an end, saw him waiting, and came to attention.

"Recruits," he began, and all eyes turned toward him as he addressed the locals.

When he had their attention, he indicated the guards in the hall.

"*That* is how skilled you will become," he told the recruits, and Marsh saw several eyes widen.

The mayor looked impressed and pleased, but interrupted what Master Envermet was about to say next.

"And will they learn *other* types of magic, Master Envermet?"

Marsh suppressed a sigh as the man continued to push his agenda, but she left the response to the shadow captain. Envermet paused and shot him a look that said he was interrupting, but then he replied.

"Yes, Mayor Hulin. We will help them tap their natural ability to use magic and teach them how to use it to protect the town."

"And how to use it for other things?" the mayor urged.

Master Envermet frowned.

"What the Masters do in their own time and who they train outside of their Protector duties will be a matter for the Masters of Stone, Shadow, and Beasts to decide, but *no one* will undertake non-Protector training without reaching a minimum standard in their Protector training first."

The mayor frowned.

"And who gets to decide that?" he challenged, and Master Envermet smiled.

Marsh suppressed a shiver. She knew that smile. That smile meant the person asking the question was about to make a discovery they truly didn't like. Apparently, some of the men and women gathered at the recruiting table also recognized that smile, because looks of apprehension flitted across their faces and they grew very still.

"It's taken me some time to decide who I will leave in charge of the Protectors here," he told the mayor, and Marsh tensed as Envermet continued, "but I have decided to leave Masters Faudree and Foye in command."

Marsh released a breath she hadn't realized she'd been holding. While she would have been glad for any of her friends to be given the promotion, she would have missed them when she left them behind to start on the next leg of their journey.

Envermet thinks you're hilarious, Roeglin told her, which only went to prove that the shadow mage had absolutely no boundaries when it came to his mind-walking abilities.

Marsh knew that if she looked, she'd see a sheen of pure white coating his eyes. She also knew this was why he'd closed them. There was nothing that gave away what a mind mage was doing more than the color of his eyes.

He also says to tell you he'd never break up a team that works without a very good reaso... Roeglin's mind-voice slowed to a standstill as he realized how the shadow captain had been able to interrupt without speaking, and Marsh bit back the urge to laugh.

Sprung, she thought, then wondered how Master Envermet had even known that Roeglin was in his head.

Maybe it's a skill he thought he should have, Roeglin answered, and he sounded very put out.

However, whether or not Master Envermet thought he should have any skills in mind-walking was not a question he chose to answer. Instead, he focused his attention on introducing the two shadow guards to the mayor and turning the recruits over to their keeping.

After that, he excused himself to other duties while they got to work. Marsh and Roeglin took the hint and left as well, spending the day in training of their own. That evening, Envermet took the two mages he'd just promoted aside, giving them the instruction they needed to run the outpost and bring it to a point where it could defend itself.

And, of course, he called on Marsh to note down the proceedings and update the recruiting records. Apparently, such duties were something "every shadow mage should know." She didn't argue but used the time to study the new appointees more closely.

Master Faudree was one of the shadow guard commanders, and she looked very surprised to be chosen to lead them. The other commander, however, looked just as pleased that it had been her who'd been chosen instead of him, and she said as much when he congratulated her.

"I am so pleased, Tilla. I was terrified he was going to choose me. I'm just not ready."

To which Tilla had only one response.

"Don't worry, Brey. I need a second, and you need a learning opportunity. It's a match made in the most glorious of Deeps."

The look on Brey's face had been enough that Marsh had fled the room to "fetch kaffee" so that she could let go of the laughter she'd been holding in.

On her return, she discovered that Master Foye was an entirely different matter.

"But I don't want to be a commander," he protested, confronting Envermet while he thought he had half a chance of changing the shadow captain's mind. "Faudree is more than capable. Why can't she…"

"Because I need a rock wizard to make decisions on matters only a rock wizard would know—and because you are the most senior druid here."

"But I will be out in the cavern most of the time."

"Then you'd better choose a representative capable of handling the decisions for training and strategy as well as I expect *you* to."

Foye had relaxed at that and left shortly thereafter—and Master Envermet had looked at Marsh.

"Not everything I do is perfect," he'd told her, "but Foye knows his people better than I do, and he *is* the most senior among them."

"So there will be no hard feelings when *he* chooses who represents him," Marsh said, and Envermet nodded before changing the subject.

"How are those records going?"

"Almost done."

They'd worked in silence after that, and when they were done, Envermet had risen, saying, "We move out the day after tomorrow. Make sure your team is ready."

He didn't tell her why but left for his quarters, leaving her to lock the office behind him. Marsh completed the last of the recruitment records and filed them before following suit. They had a busy day of preparation ahead of them, and she was looking forward to seeing her uncle and Daniel again.

WAYSTATION INTERLUDE

For their parts, Per and Daniel were glad to see Marsh when they arrived back at Kerrenin's Ledge late the next day. From the way he greeted the kat, Marsh had a hard time telling who her cousin was happier to see: Mordan or her. Not that the kat was complaining. She rubbed her head along Daniel's trouser leg before taking the small haunch of mouton from him and retiring to her place in front of the fire to eat it.

Daniel followed her progress with a look of contented pride, then turned and gave Marsh a brief, perfunctory hug.

"It's good to see you, cuz," he told her and headed back to the kitchen, leaving Marsh to stare after him.

"Well, he seems happy," her uncle said, watching him go.

"Really?" Marsh asked. "How can you tell?"

"He hasn't thrown anything yet."

Marsh had to admit her uncle had a point. If Daniel was feeling angry or sad, they'd have heard the sound of skillets and kitchen utensils landing. Instead, all they could hear was a contented humming and the usual clatter involved in cooking.

"Hmmph," Envermet said, arriving in time to overhear their exchange. "So I should tell him they're moving out in the morning *after* dinner, then?"

His question was followed by a sudden curse from the kitchen, followed by the loud clatter of a saucepan bouncing off the wall closest the door. Master Envermet gave it a wide-eyed look and frowned.

"Boy has the ears of a bat," he muttered and headed for the stairs.

The sound of a second pot, this one bouncing off the door, echoed in his wake.

"Well, Deeps and damnation," Per said. "That man has no sense of timing at all."

Marsh had to agree, but Aisha and Tamlin arrived before she could say anything. Both of them stared at the door, and Aisha put her small hands on her hips and glared at the kitchen. Before Marsh had time to stop her, the little girl had shoved the door open and marched right through it.

Tamlin opened his mouth to stop her but closed it again. Marsh exchanged a look with Per and sighed.

"I'll get her," she said, only to stop when she heard Aisha's small voice raised in a piping treble.

"No. Throw. Pots. Is rude!"

The sound of more metal landing punctuated each word, mingling with Daniel's cries of protest.

"Hey! Ouch! Little hoshkat!"

Per laid a hand on Marsh's arm.

"I'd let them sort it out if I were you," he said, and, listening to Aisha's next flurry of words, Marsh had to concur.

"No burn dinner cos you mad either!"

More clatters followed.

"Ow! Fine!"

Silence followed the last clatter, and Daniel spoke again.

"Let me guess. Burning dinner is rude too?"

"Yes." Aisha sounded adamant.

"Fine!"

Marsh heard small steps moving back to the kitchen door and moved to face Per as though they'd been too deep in conversation to hear what had gone on. The footsteps paused, and Aisha's small, clear voice rang out again.

"And is *my* Marsh. *Not* yours!"

Apparently, Daniel hadn't got the good sense to let that go, but he didn't argue.

"Share?"

Well, thought Marsh, at least he's *trying* to negotiate—because for Daniel, that was a first.

There was silence, and Marsh could picture the look on Aisha's face as she thought about it. After a pause and a sigh that said he was pushing his luck, she replied.

"Fine."

Marsh released the breath she hadn't realized she'd been holding, and Per also began breathing again.

"That was close," he murmured as Aisha stepped into the dining room.

She fixed him with a gimlet glare, and Marsh got a good idea of why Daniel might have called the child a "little hoshkat."

"Not nice to spy," the child declared, and Tamlin grabbed her before she could say any more.

"Bath time!" he told her. "Now!"

"I'm not dirty," the girl protested, but she let her brother drag her to the washroom where Brigitte was waiting, his answer floating back to them as the pair disappeared.

"Are so, too. You stink."

"Like hoshkat?"

"Oh, no. Mordan smells a *lot* better than you do!"

Marsh caught the look on Per's face as the two of them disappeared.

"Are they always like that?"

"Pretty much."

Marsh stopped and looked at him.

"I'm going to miss you," she said, and stepped back, with a sigh. "I'd better go…"

She gestured toward the stairs, and Per cleared his throat and nodded, then indicated the bar.

"And I'll have customers soon."

It was the closest they could come to talking about her leaving, and Roeglin arrived in time to interrupt.

"You know, you two could just hug, share dinner with Daniel in the kitchen, and say goodbye in the morning. It's not like we're leaving before the waystation wakes."

Given that her uncle and cousin *were* the waystation, Marsh understood what he was saying, and was grateful he'd interrupted the sudden wave of melancholy that had settled over her. Not trusting her voice, she did as he suggested, hugging Per before hurrying upstairs to pack.

Per and Daniel were waiting to eat with her when she

came down for dinner, and they were waiting again in the morning to say goodbye.

"Be careful," Per told her, and Daniel rolled his eyes as her uncle hugged her.

"Come back soon," Daniel said, and held her tight until a small voice interrupted.

"My turn!"

Marsh almost laughed at how fast Dan let go and stepped back so Aisha could stand in front of her.

"Up," the small child demanded, and Marsh scooped her up so she could wind her small arms around her neck.

It was no surprise when Tamlin hugged her at the same time, and Marsh looped an arm around him in return.

"Don't make us come and rescue you," he told her, letting her go and giving her a stern glare. "Once was enough."

At his words, Aisha leaned back in Marsh's arms and gave her a solemn stare.

"Yes. No trouble," the little girl ordered, and her blue eyes widened with surprise when those standing closest echoed her next two words. "Is rude."

Marsh hugged her again and set her down.

"I'll try," she promised, and added a stern note to her voice. "Be good for Brigitte, and do what Master Envermet tells you."

"Yes," Aisha said, "or he'll get grouchy."

Marsh looked at the shadow captain in time to see him look to the earth and shake his head.

"Deeps preserve us," he said, "and may they give me the First Wanderer's patience."

That brought a round of good-natured laughter, and Gustav signaled they should mount up and move out.

"The sun is rising," he said, gesturing to the sunrise as if that explained it all, "and we want to be under it for the shortest time possible."

We should have left earlier, Marsh thought.

There'd have been no advantage in it, Roeglin interrupted. *It's most of a day's journey to Downslopes, so we'd be out in it regardless.*

He had a point, Marsh thought, and wondered why Gustav had mentioned the sun.

He needed a polite way of telling us to shift our asses.

Yeah, well, that would do it.

Marsh turned back to her mule, noting the two mules tethered, one on either side. Her uncle had asked her to take "a few things" to his oldest son. She snorted as she wove between the mules and clambered into her saddle.

Per's idea of "a few things" had amounted to two mules heavily laden with supplies and gifts. She supposed it only made sense, given he'd had no contact with Gabe since Master Gage's caravan had brought word that her cousin and his family were fine. Gabe and Per hadn't had the chance to visit since Marsh's caravan had been attacked—and the messages between them had been infrequent at best.

"Master Gage was the last," Per had told her the evening before, "and the one before him was at least a month prior. I don't suppose there's any way you could send a message back…"

Marsh had spoken to Roeglin, and Roeglin had made sure he could connect to both Per and Daniel's minds so they could speak with Gabe after the mind mage had reached Downslopes.

"It won't be until the night after we arrive, but we'll try," the shadow mage had said. "I don't know if it will work."

Now, as she guided her mules after Gustav, Marsh hoped that Roeglin's contact would succeed; her uncle needed to speak with his son in the same way he'd needed to know she had survived the ambush. Marsh glanced back once as she hit the gates, and Per and Daniel waved. The sight of them brought a lump to her throat, and she waved in return before turning around to pay attention to the road before her. It was going to be a long journey—and she had no way of knowing where it would end, or when—but there was no point in dwelling on it now.

She was riding with the folk she knew best, the "team" Master Envermet was so reluctant to break up, and part of her was excited to be back on the road. The raiders had been silent since they'd been beaten back from Mika's Outlet just before the wall was complete, and not a single shadow monster had been heard or seen in all the time they'd been in the cavern.

Marsh remembered Master Envermet saying the creatures didn't like being that close to the surface and wondered what other monsters lurked ahead, but Gustav's voice jerked her from her thoughts.

"I want you scanning ahead when we hit the surface."

"Got it."

Marsh looked around and saw Henri and Jakob already coming alongside to take the pack mules. As they dropped back, Roeglin rode up. Marsh handed him the lead rope she'd attached to the mule's bridle for just this occasion, knowing she couldn't both steer the mule and use the shadows and nature to see what might lie ahead.

As they rode through the gates and into the cavern beyond, Marsh realized why Gustav had mentioned the sun. Far ahead of them, a distant gleam was already seeping into the cavern. The team leader kicked his mule into a trot and led the way out between the glows marking the trail.

THE DOWNSLOPES PACK

The journey out of the Kerrenin's Ledge cavern was uneventful. Not even Mordan, pacing them along the edge of the trail, found anything more threatening than the small, furry thing she caught and ate for breakfast. Marsh swore she felt its life fade from her awareness as the big kat's jaws tore through it. Its high-pitched squeal echoed through the cavern and sent shudders up and down her spine.

Ahead of her, Gustav straightened in his saddle.

"Anything?" he asked, when Marsh knew he meant "What was that?"

"Nothing, unless you count Mordan snuffing out the local wildlife."

"Good, and no. Tell her to keep it down. We're approaching the entrance, and we don't know what's out there."

Marsh guessed what he wasn't saying was that they didn't know if there were any more of the crazed wolf-man beasts the wolves' druid had called 'lycanthropes' waiting out under the sun. He drew his mule to a halt several feet from where the path passed from the cavern to sunlight.

"Now's the time to put your bands on," he said, and Marsh knew he wasn't referring to her.

She didn't need the thin, gauzy bands of cloth to protect her eyes. Her vision adjusted perfectly well to seeing under the sun. The same couldn't be said of Gerry, Zeb, or Izmay, and the three shadow guards hastened to pull on the strips of dark cloth they needed to protect their eyes.

As much as she understood their need for it, Marsh couldn't understand how they could stand having something obscuring their vision, even if it *was* to let them see. Her eyes had always shifted focus to enable her to see well wherever she was, but only now was she starting to realize just how great a gift that was.

"Not everyone can see heat," the Master of Shadows had told her, and she hadn't fully understood the implications of his words. Now, watching the three shadow guards hasten to protect their eyes, she did. When they were done, Gustav signaled Marsh forward.

"Do you know the path?" he asked, and Marsh shook her head.

"I've never been," she said, and added, "My uncle said I was too young, and after that, I never went."

She became aware of Roeglin staring at her with wide eyes.

"Never?" he asked, posing the question out loud so the others could hear her answer.

Marsh shook her head, feeling tension coil and knot inside her chest.

"Never," she managed, ashamed when the answer came out harsh with more emotion than she'd imagined she could feel.

She kicked her mule toward the entrance and through into the open ground beyond, not realizing she'd dropped her scans until Mordan's outraged growl of warning split the air. Marsh kicked the mule again and ducked low over its head. The vicious whir of something flying through the space she'd occupied came as a surprise.

"Keep riding!"

Gustav's shout had her spurring her mount forward even as wordless cries and screams rose around her and the sound of people bursting through the underbrush on either side of the trail reached her ears. Marsh rode forward, looking for a piece of the path wide enough for her to turn her mule. Her plans were interrupted when a hand wrapped around her calf and her foot was pulled from the stirrup.

She lashed out with her boot, then Mordan intervened. There was a startled shriek, and the hand let go. Behind them came the clash of metal and more enraged shouts. The sound sent a chill through Marsh. Those voices…

They were close to human but reminded her more of the shadow monsters' mindless howls. She reached a point where the growth on either side of the path thinned and she pulled the mule off the path, slowing it enough to slide from its back before it had come to a complete stop.

Throwing the reins over a nearby bush, Marsh turned and raced back up the path toward the sounds of battle… and of Mordan making yet another kill. The kat made no sound, but her victims certainly did, and Marsh smiled. It was good to know these folks could feel terror.

Without thinking, she reached for the shadows and realized it was bright daylight. The shadows came, but they were nowhere near as thick as she was used to. Still, they came, and they would do. Marsh didn't slow down as she saw the dozen filthy, ragged humans on the path ahead.

She slashed the first across the soft portion of the lower back, her blade biting just as deep as she'd have expected it to. Reversing the blade's movement, she slashed at the next one, the stroke nowhere near as good as her first but enough to distract it from Henri. The blade completed its arc, and she pulled it back so she could thrust it into her opponent.

It slid through muscle, past bone, and deeper, and she jerked it free as he crumpled. His dying scream drew the attention of those closest, and they turned toward her. One went down beneath a flurry of paws and the other grinned, swinging his club in a strike designed to break bone but not kill. Marsh didn't want to think about why he'd want her alive.

His swing left his chest and front exposed and Marsh stepped inside the weapon's arc, calling a buckler so she could block the club as she ducked. The club impacted hard, and she staggered as she drove her blade up into her attacker's mid-section and pushed him so she could twist clear as he fell.

Her maneuvering brought her into range of another of the creatures as her blade caught, jerking her to a momentary halt before she could pull it free. She ducked, and its club whistled over her head. It recovered more quickly than she did, and she was barely able to free her blade to block its next blow, the shadow blade catching in the timber of his weapon.

Marsh released it back to where it had come from and brought her buckler up. Her sword's disappearance had, however, surprised the monster attacking her.

"Magic!" it roared, its cry taken up by its fellows, who sought to disengage.

Their attempt made no difference to the Protectors, who took advantage of those retreating by bringing down as many of them as they could. Mordan did likewise, the big kat pursuing their attackers as they fled until she was sure they would not circle back and try again.

"What in all of the Deeps were they?" Jakob asked once they'd returned to the cave where they'd left their mules while they dealt with the attack.

Gustav's expression darkened.

"Remnant," he said. "They're a kind of human that came about during the Madness. Something back then had driven their ancestors insane, and their minds had never recovered."

He scanned the land around them before continuing.

"The minds of their descendants never recovered either. It's like they lost their humanity, or it was swallowed by the baser instincts of man." He paused, watching as Marsh brought her mule back from the bushes she'd left it in. "Now they follow only their desires to feed and find pleasure."

Marsh wanted to know how he knew all this but Gustav had other priorities.

"We need to reach the waystation. They're bound to

come back in the dark," he said and kicked the mule into a fast trot.

Henri and the others trotted after him, Marsh and Roeglin riding with them as they jolted down the trail. After a few steps, Marsh reached out along her connection with Mordan to see if the big kat was all right. Her inquiry was met with annoyance and a sense of great distaste—the ugly humans did not bathe, and their flesh tasted of sickness.

When she had finished washing her mouth in a nearby stream, the kat informed her, she was going hunting for healthy meat and use it to cleanse the taste of their ambushers from her tongue. Marsh was to be more watchful in the future; the smallest of Mordan's cubs would have smelt those creatures lying in wait. *They* would not have walked into a trap.

Before Marsh could respond to that, the kat had cut the link.

Hunting! was all she would reply when Marsh tried to reestablish it, and it was cut again.

Well, aren't you Miss Popular today? Roeglin said, his laughter echoing through her mind.

Get out! Marsh snapped and bunted him from her head in much the same way as Mordan had just done to her.

Roeglin gave a startled yelp, but when he talked to her next, she could only hear him with her ears.

"You know your eyes flash white when you do that, don't you?"

Marsh hadn't, and she didn't like hearing it.

"Wonderful," she muttered, making it sound anything but.

They rode on, not stopping for the mid-meal but eating dried ration bars in the saddle. To their relief, they didn't see any more remnant and reached the waystation gates as the sun was sinking low on the horizon.

If she'd been in the cavern, Marsh would have enjoyed watching the play of colors across the cavern walls and through the shrooms. Instead, she felt mildly anxious at the approaching dark, searching the nearby hillside and overgrowth for danger. It felt strange to be in the dark and yet so out in the open.

That, and she needed the distraction from the stonewalls rising in front of her...not that watching for danger was helping very much.

"You have to face it sometime."

To her surprise, Roeglin had said that out loud where everyone could hear him, even if they were pretending not to. Gustav rode up to the closed outer gates and reached for his sword. Marsh didn't know who was more startled when the gates started to open before he could draw it, but they didn't stop to wonder why. Instead, they rode right through, reaching the courtyard before Marsh registered that Mordan hadn't come through with them.

She turned her mule around, and kicked it back toward the gates, dismounting when she'd passed through and reached the open space just before them.

"Dan!" she called. "Dan?"

For a long moment, there was no answer, then the kat came padding out of the dark. Judging by her bulging middle, she'd not only found something suitable for taking the taste of remnant out of her mouth, but she'd eaten enough of it that she wasn't going to have to hunt for the next few days. Marsh fondled her ears.

"You *do* know I'd feed you, right?"

The kat rumbled a reply and rubbed her head against Marsh's thigh, her thoughts full of wary contentment and wistful images of a well-lit fireplace. It made Marsh laugh and she tangled her hands in the kat's ruff, walking beside her as she led the mule back through the gates.

They'd been starting to close when she'd ridden through, and now stood partially open in the evening twilight. As soon as she'd stepped back into the waystation courtyard, they began to close again, coming to another grinding halt when a low, mournful howl flowed over the hillside.

Marsh stopped and turned, relieved when a series of soft glows lit up the inside of the courtyard. She kept her hand in Mordan's fur as a large gray shape raced through the gates. It was followed by several more, and Mordan growled. The wolves raced toward her and Marsh stepped forward to meet them pulling shadow blade and buckler from the night.

She heard voices as someone hastily excused themselves from the small knot of shadow guards gathered in front of the waystation's main building.

"Marsh!" Gustav called, but she didn't take her eyes off the wolves.

"Marsh?"

That voice was both familiar and not, and a tall, blond man squeezed her shoulder as he slipped past to kneel before the leader of the pack. It growled at him and tried to slip past, but the man spread his arms and caught it, pulling it toward him even as it growled in furious protest.

"Ironshade," the man said. "Ironshade, they are friends, and she is pack."

The wolf's next growl was angrier than the last, and as full of disagreement as any sound Marsh had ever heard. Marsh's mule snorted, the sound of its hooves on the cobbles telling her it was backing away from the wolf and its pack. Mordan growled in reply.

"Merde!"

Marsh released sword and buckler to the shadows and turned to wrap her arms around the big kat's neck.

"Pride, Dan! He's pride…and his friends are our friends, right?"

The kat stayed tense beneath her hands, seeming to ignore her.

"Dan?"

Marsh got the fleeting impression of being pursued over a darkening slope when all she'd wanted to do was curl up on the warm rocks and sleep off her latest meal. She slapped the kat's shoulder.

"I'd have been worried sick!"

The kat made a sound that suggested she only had herself to blame since she'd been the one to ride out into an ambush of remnant she should have smelt.

"You're not going to let that go, are you?"

The kat made an odd sneezing sound, and Marsh glanced back at the wolves. They were watching her as though she were something particularly interesting.

"You were hunting her?" The man's voice was incredulous. He stared at the wolf. "But why?"

The pack leader gave a whining growl.

"Territory? But you've got the whole damn mountain-side! What's one more to share it? Ow!"

That last comment had obviously been one question too many…or it had been a particularly stupid question because the wolf gave him a hard nip on the shoulder.

"You're just lucky the gate's closed for the night," he grumbled, getting up from in front of it. "Now come and meet the kat and be friends. I don't want to begin the night with an argument."

Marsh thought it was already too late for that, but she didn't say so. Instead, she turned to Mordan.

"And you play nice," she said, giving the kat a brief squeeze.

Mordan huffed out a breath and regarded her with a baleful look. Marsh ignored her and looked at the tall blond man. It took more than a moment for her to recognize him, and amusement played across his face as he let her do it. He broke into a full-blown grin when she said his name.

"Gabe?"

"Marchant!" her oldest cousin said, "It's been a long time."

It *had* been a long time, and he'd gotten taller since she'd last seen him. Marsh took an awkward step toward him. Before she could take another, however, the wolf slipped around Gabe's calves and braced itself between them. Its growl rolled over her and through her, raising the hair on her arms and sending a wave of goosebumps over her flesh. Marsh slapped a hand on Mordan's neck as the kat surged forward.

Curling her hand in Dan's scruff, she brought the kat to a screeching halt and prayed she'd be forgiven. Trying not to think about what the kat might have to say about being grabbed like a cub and held, and *really* trying not to think about what she'd say about her next move, Marsh crouched in front of the wolf. She raised a cautious hand to the side of its face and froze as its jaws closed over it with a sudden snap.

"Iron!"

The wolf growled around Marsh's fingers, a clear warning for the man to back off. Mordan snarled, and the wolf growled again. Marsh stayed perfectly still, leaving her hand in its mouth and resisting the urge to pull away. She was aware of movement among the guards, and glad when none of them came any closer. Instead, she focused on the wolf's bright-green eyes.

"I am Marchant Leclerc," she told it, "Gabrielle's cousin. My parents built this place, but it is Gabe's home, and I have no intention of changing that."

Gabe made a sound of muted protest and started to move, but Ironshade growled at him. Marsh watched as the wolf's eyes flicked from her to her cousin and back. When she had its attention again, she met its eyes and tried to make a connection to its mind, wanting it to see that she meant no harm and had no intention of staying, that Mordan would be leaving with her, that the kat kept her safe, just as the wolf kept Gabe and his territory secure.

She fell, but only a little way, having started to get the knack of stepping between her own conscious and the kat's. Connecting to the wolf wasn't much different, and she regarded it mind to mind, noting how much bigger it seemed than when she stood beside it.

He is my human, it growled, *and his mate is mine to protect.*

"And I am his pack," Marsh assured it. "Not his mate, but his cousin. Among humans our bond is family. I do not want his mate."

Or to take her place?

Marsh snorted.

"That is not the human way."

Why are you here?

"For shelter and for the hunt."

The Hunt?

Now she had its attention. Marsh thought of the raiders, of them attacking the innocent and releasing the shadow monsters into the caverns. The wolf snarled at the thought and Marsh continued, showing Ironshade an image of Kearick.

It snarled louder.

This one was a guest under our roof not three moons ago!

"We hunt him…and there was one more, but I do not know what he looked like," Marsh began, but the wolf interrupted her, showing her the image of another man.

He was tall, taller even than Gabe. As tall as Ardhur but rake-thin and sallow-faced, with hazel eyes and a way of looking at Gabe's mate that she did not like. Marsh snarled as she recognized him, a seeker whose gaze had made her skin crawl on the few occasions she'd encountered him at the Emporium.

"Salazar."

The wolf's ears pricked.

You know this human?

Marsh nodded.

"Only by sight, but I know him. We will hunt him too."

Ironshade let go of her hand, licking the indentations he had made with his teeth and darting forward to nip her at the base of the throat. Marsh recoiled as she felt his teeth bruise skin, but he broke the connection between them, turning to trot over to a stunned Gabe, his bushy tail waving in the air.

Mordan shook Marsh's hand free of her ruff and turned toward the waystation, and Marsh caught the kat's desire for a warm fire and maybe a rug to lie on. She couldn't blame the big beast. If she'd eaten that much shev, she'd be needing to sleep it off as well. She pushed to her feet, wincing as her knees cracked.

The clump of boots alerted her to Gustav's approach before the Protector reached her.

"This hunt we're on," he said. "You want to tell us what it's all about?"

4

ADOPTED SONS

It took Gabe a moment to finish with the pack, and Marsh was surprised when the wolves swept by her to surround Mordan and escort the big kat inside. Why they should bother was made clear by the startled shriek that came shortly after they'd disappeared inside.

"Gabe! Oh, no, you don't. That rug is… *Gabe!*"

Marsh looked at her cousin, and he looked back.

"Ursula's going to have my hide," he said, then closed the distance between them and wrapped his arms around her. "It's good to see you again."

Before he could say any more, there was another frustrated shout from the station house.

"Gabe!"

He sighed.

"Even if you have a knack for getting me into trouble with my wife." He let go of Marsh and headed for the station. "I'll see you all inside. The stables are over there, and there's plenty of room."

It was a clear directive for them to take care of their

own mounts, and Marsh realized she hadn't seen anyone around. Figuring the gates didn't man themselves, Marsh headed for the gatehouse to find out who was there...and maybe to discover what was going on.

Gustav grabbed her by the arm.

"The hunt?"

"In the stables," she told him, and he let her go.

It was no surprise when Roeglin came alongside her.

"There are two of them," he said. "Both a lot younger than I'd expect, and both waiting for the courtyard to clear before they head back to their..."

Marsh pushed the gatehouse door open, startled to see two boys around the ages of ten and twelve. She already knew they were too old to be Gabe's. The Deeps knew Per had nagged him enough for a grandchild, but these would had to have been born before he'd left the Ledge. And they hadn't been.

Both boys had been standing by the mechanism for opening the gates, their attention focused on the door. Now the older one put himself between the younger one and the door, and the younger one was looking around the room as if he could find either find an escape route or a weapon.

It was just too bad for them that the stairs leading up to the wall were next to the door, and Marsh and Roeglin were blocking the way. The kids weren't going anywhere. Marsh kicked the door closed behind her, trying to decide which one to tackle first.

"...master?" Roeglin finished, sounding puzzled.

"You're not our master," the older boy declared, and Marsh stopped.

"What do you mean, 'master?'" she demanded, shocked at the thought Gabe might have bought them.

"Well, he's not our *father!*" the child declared, his tone belligerent. "No matter how often he says to call him that."

Roeglin stopped and backed up a couple of steps to sit on the lower stairs. Marsh caught the look on his face and backed up to lean on the door. Her mind raced to try to work out what was going on.

"So why are you still here then?" she demanded. "He's not forcing you to be here, is he?"

A look of pure scorn crossed the pre-teen's face.

"He wouldn't wanta try."

Marsh decided to let that one slide, but she was relieved to hear the implication that Gabe wasn't keeping them here against their wills. She forced her voice to take a casual tone.

"So why do you stay?"

The kid glared at her, and Marsh had to hide a smile at seeing a nearly identical glare cross the younger one's face.

"None a your business."

Marsh looked at the ceiling and made a show of lounging on the door.

"Sure it is," she told him when she saw she had all of his attention. "Cos where I'm from? There's been a bunch of very bad men taking folk from farms and leaving nothing behind, and I want to know you're not about to open that gate while I'm sleeping."

She dropped her hands onto her hips, following the downward glance of his eyes as he noted the sword strapped to her side. To her surprise, it was the younger one who answered.

"We just closed the gates," he said, "and we won't open them until Uncle Gabe says it's safe."

The "Uncle Gabe" was said with a defiant glance toward the older boy, and Marsh had to admire the resilience of the young. She decided to try a different tack.

"When did they come to your farm?"

She saw the boy's eyes widen, and he scowled.

"Not your business either," he snarled, and started walking toward her.

Since he was clearly intent on leaving, Marsh wondered what he intended to do—throw her out of the way?

Pretty much, Roeglin said, just as the boy reached her.

Marsh didn't move. Instead, when the kid came within reaching distance, she arched an eyebrow.

"Neither of you look like a relative of *mine,*" she said, and Roeglin interrupted.

"Draw that blade, boy, and I'll kick your ass into the middle of next week while shaking you so hard you can't catch up."

The boy's mouth dropped open, and his face turned white. He turned slowly to face Roeglin.

"Where'd you hear that?" He gulped. "And what's wrong with your eyes?"

Marsh followed the boy's gaze and saw that Roeglin was no longer sitting on the stairs. No, the fool mage was standing at the bottom of the stairs and staring at the child, his eyes a glistening sheet of white as he studied the kid's face.

"I took it from your mind," Roeglin told him. "Just like I took your name, Geralt, and your brother's name, Jean."

Fear crossed the boy's face, and he cast an anxious glance in his brother's direction.

"You leave him alone."

But Roeglin was relentless.

"I know you saw your father die and what the raiders said to make your mother go with them, and that they took your sisters." Roeglin blinked, paused, and carried on. "And you are right. If you had not stayed hidden and kept Jean safe, neither of you would be here now."

He stopped, letting silence fill the air before continuing.

"Marsh can find out where they went," he added, indicating where Marsh leaned on the door, "and Marsh can try to get them back."

Oh, Marsh could, could she? Marsh thought, but she watched the wary hope dawning on the boy's face and forced herself to stay still as he turned toward her.

"Will you?"

Marsh shot Roeglin a glare and looked back to the boy.

"Would you really have tried to stab me?"

The boy ducked his head, but the flush of crimson rising up his neck gave her all the answer she needed.

"Had to keep my brother safe," he mumbled.

"You'd have gotten yourself killed," she shot back, glaring at him, and he lifted his head, studying her as though trying to figure out just how much she was bluffing.

Apparently, what he saw in her face was enough to convince him she wasn't, and he paled.

"I'm sorry," he said and gestured at his brother. "I couldn't..."

He couldn't, Marsh thought and followed the gesture. No, of course, he couldn't.

"So," she said. "What *are* you doing here?"

"The wolves found us," Geralt explained. "We wouldn't go near them, so they chased us all the way to the waystation."

"Unc…" He stopped as he caught himself saying the word and his eyes clouded. In the end, he shrugged and went on. "*Uncle* Gabe said we could stay, but we'd have to help out. Earn our keep."

He looked at his brother, who was standing very, very still as he stared at Roeglin and Marsh.

"We all locked down?" he asked, indicating the mechanism beside the boy. Jean nodded, his head moving rapidly up and down as his gaze shifted between the three of them.

"Time to go," Geralt said, holding out his hand. Jean hurried over to take it. "*Aunt* Ursula will be waiting."

Jean nodded again, his brown eyes wide in a pale face. His attention moved swiftly from Marsh's expression to Roeglin, and Marsh glanced at the shadow mage. His eyes had returned to their usual shade of hazel.

"You *could* let them go back to your cousin," he said, and Marsh waited.

Sure enough, Roeglin had more to say.

"Or you could ask them what it is they don't want Gabe to know."

His words drew gasps of surprise from both boys, and Jean shrank closer to his brother's side. Geralt, for his part, shot the mage a filthy look.

"Hasn't anyone ever told you it's rude to look into someone else's mind without permission?"

The sheer exasperation in his tone made Marsh smile, albeit very briefly and with no humor whatsoever.

"Often," she told them drily, "but he never listens. So… what is it you don't want my cousin to know?"

The boys exchanged glances.

"Well?"

Geralt glared at Roeglin.

"Why don't you just take it?" he challenged, but Roeglin shrugged.

"Someone said that was rude," he replied, "and I'm trying to make friends with them."

"By forcing them to tell you what they don't want you to know?"

"It's the only way to establish trust," Roeglin said. "I need to trust you'll tell Gabe what he needs to know, no matter how hard…and you need to trust that he won't harm you when you do."

The boy glared at him and rolled his eyes, taking another step toward the door. He stopped short, though, when Marsh didn't budge. The boy glared at her in turn.

"You know, it's very hard to tell Gabe anything when your big ass is blocking the way."

Marsh shifted.

"Just make sure you do," she said, "or I'll be kicking your ass until you do, Gabe, Ursula, and the wolf pack or no…or didn't you hear the hoshkat that came down the hill with me?"

"That was yours?" the boy asked. "I thought it had just gotten lost."

As a way of dismissing her claim, it would have worked a whole lot better if he hadn't looked so impressed. Marsh figured she'd made her point and stepped out of his way, leaving the path to the door free. At first, neither boy moved, then Geralt led the way to the door and out through it.

She got the impression that Jean wanted to run the instant the pair made it into the courtyard but that Geralt wouldn't permit it. Letting them get a half dozen paces ahead of them, she followed, walking into the waystation commons just after they did and watching them skirt Mordan's sleeping form on the rug in front of the fire as they picked their way between sleeping wolves.

Ironshade's head came up as the boys entered, and the wolf's emerald gaze shifted from the boys to Marsh and Roeglin and back. With a sigh, the wolf stretched and sat up, and as if their leader's movement was a signal, the rest of the pack stirred to wakefulness.

By the time the boys had caught Gabe's attention, the whole pack was sitting up, ears pricked and attention divided between Marsh and Roeglin and the boys. Marsh reached out, seeking to touch the beasts in the room and calm them. She did not expect Ironshade to reach back.

What had his cubs done this time? Why were they afraid of the Hunt Master?

"Hunt Master?" Well, that was a new term for her cousin.

He directs the hunt when we must supply the den.

And by "den," Ironshade meant the waystation. Of course, he did.

Marsh turned her attention to her cousin and the boys.

By now, Gabe had caught the worried looks on the

boys' faces—and connected them to her. He glanced up at her and back at Geralt and Jean.

"What's the matter, boys?"

If Gabe hadn't realized she was the reason for their distress, he did now, because both boys looked over their shoulders at her before turning their attention to him.

"We know when the traders are coming," Gabe said. "We know when they're at the bend above the pools."

Gabe's raised eyebrows told Marsh that this was news to him, and her cousin took a moment to formulate his reply.

"Surely that's not what's got you looking so worried?"

Geralt stared at him, and Gabe stared back.

"It is?" He studied their faces for a moment and shrugged. "Well, I don't know how that sort of gift was looked on where you came from, but here, it is more than welcome."

Silence followed his words as the boys stared at him, and he sighed again.

"What else?"

Geralt nudged his brother. When Jean looked up at him, Geralt did it again, and Jean gazed up at Gabe with frightened eyes. His voice was very small when he replied.

"This…"

He wove his hands through the air and held out his palm, showing the perfectly formed sphere of flame he was holding. With another glance at his brother, he turned and walked back to the door, carefully balancing the ball of fire in one hand and opening the door with the other. When he had it open, he tossed the fireball through and began to close the door.

He froze when a startled shout shook the night.

"Leclerc! What in the Deep's dark ass do you think you're doing?"

Leclerc?

Marsh shot Roeglin a dirty look and marched up to the door, grabbing Jean by the arm as she passed. She made it onto the porch out front and stopped.

"*A la vache*," Jean whispered.

Marsh looked at the six very upset men and women standing in the middle of the courtyard and had to agree, even if she wasn't exactly sure what a *"vache"* might be.

Think of a big, fat shev, Roeglin told her, showing her something like an oversized shev standing under a tree. The creature had curving horns, short mule-like fur, a donkey-like tail, and an outsized udder.

You just made that up, Marsh told him, not at all sure he had.

Nuh-uh. I'll show you one someday.

One day, huh? As if she had any intention of exploring the surface world…or would take him if she did.

Ouch! I'm hurt, he said, and actually sounded it.

"Fine, you can come." She surveyed the Protectors standing outside the station commons. "But only if you help explain this to them."

Jean looked up at her.

"They think *you* did it?"

She glanced down at him, noting the excitement in his upturned face.

"Kid, they blame me for any strange shit that's got something to do with magic."

"That's because she usually *is* the one to blame," Roeglin

told him, leading them past a scorch mark on the cobbles to where Gustav and the others were waiting.

Fortunately, they'd overheard them.

"You mean she's not?"

Roeglin shook his head.

"Not this time."

"Then who..." Gustav let the words go as he caught sight of the boy.

Izmay gave a disparaging snort and looked a Marsh in disbelief.

"You're blaming a *kid*?" she asked. "That is *unbelievable.* I wouldn't have thought you'd stoop that low."

"Hey!"

"Not a good defense, Marsh," Gerry scolded, but his blue eyes were teasing.

"But I didn't..." Marsh began, and Gustav poked her in the chest.

"Then how come I almost lost what little hair I've got?"

He bent his head showing her an angry red patch of scalp surrounded by dark edges. Beside her, Jean gasped.

"Oh! I'm sorry. I didn't know. I should have thought."

Marsh wrapped her arm around his shoulders, pulling him tight against her side. She didn't need to look at his face to know the poor kid was nearly in tears. Giving him a quick squeeze, she pushed him back into her shadow and raised her finger, tapping Gustav firmly on the breastplate.

"Captain Moldrane," she said, more for Jean's benefit than anyone else's, "if I'd wanted to fry your face with a Deeps-be-damned fireball, do you think I'da missed that badly?"

"You mean..." Gustav's eyes tracked to where Jean was

now standing beside Roeglin, holding the shadow mage's hand like his life depended on it.

He looked back to Marsh.

"Are you telling me that that the *waif* really threw the fireball?"

"Hey! Watch who you're calling a waif."

All eyes turned to the waystation porch where Geralt and Gabe were standing. Geralt didn't give them time to reply.

"That's my brother, and if he wants to toss a fireball into the courtyard, then you're just going to let him!"

"The courtyard I don't have a problem with," Gustav snapped back. "It's when the little *merde*-for-brains throws one at my head that I have a problem."

Geralt didn't have an answer for that. By now Gustav had moved into the light of enough glows that the burn from where the fireball had brushed past his head was clearly visible. He turned to Marsh.

"I don't suppose you could…" and Marsh realized what she should have done the moment she'd seen the damage.

"*Merde*! I'm sorry, Gustav. Give me a minute."

Around her, the courtyard stilled, save for the faint movement as Jean and Geralt crept closer to watch, Gabe and Ironshade shadowing their every move. Trying to ignore the fact she had an audience, Marsh carefully placed her fingers around the edges of the burn. Gustav flinched, but he put his hands on her shoulders and held on as though he'd fall over if he didn't.

Marsh didn't want to think of what would happen if he did.

Instead, she pushed all thought of falling from her mind

and focused on the energy around her. As she looked for it, she became aware of its sluggish flow through the cobbles, the life flowing through the air, and the life forces in the people around her.

"I'm going to need to borrow some of your energy," she said, looking at the guards.

Izmay gave a dismissive wave of her hand.

"Sure, kid. Just don't take it all."

The others shrugged.

"Go ahead."

"Sure."

"Okay."

Marsh took a deep breath and focused on the energy around her, taking a little from each of the guards and the boys. She figured it wouldn't hurt them to help fix what they'd broken. Leaving Gabe and the wolf out of the loop, she pulled the energy to her hands and pushed it over Gustav's scalp.

She hadn't realized the boys had gotten so close until Jean gave a soft exclamation of amazement.

"Whoa! Can you show me how to do that?"

"Yeah," Geralt snarked. "It might be good for him to know how to fix what he *breaks*..."

The words disrupted Marsh's concentration, and she hastily checked to see how much more healing Gustav's head might need. None, as it turned out...although a haircut might be in order.

As she thought it, Gustav raised a hand to his head and felt the inch-long hair that now covered the area.

He straightened up abruptly, giving her a look that was torn between outrage and mortification. For a long moment, Marsh thought he was going to shout at her, but then he shook his head, pressed his lips together, and walked past Gabe into the waystation.

No one made a sound until the door had closed behind him, then Gerry dropped to his knees howling with mirth. Izmay turned to Henri and leaned her head against his chest, and Zeb and Jakob just shook with laughter. Marsh didn't see the funny side, but Roeglin was snickering, and Gabe chuckled.

"I'll show him where the razors are," he said.

Marsh nearly asked him not to, since she had to sleep that night and she wasn't sure she wanted to if Gustav could arm himself with a razor. Geralt sputtered at the thought, and she gave the boy a look that brought his amusement to an abrupt halt.

"About that," she said, and they both knew she meant his snooping inside her head. "Didn't *you* have objections to your head being read without your permission?"

The boy scowled at her and Jean looked from one of them to the other, his small face creased with worry. Marsh laid a hand on his shoulder.

"Don't worry, Jean. I'm pretty sure Roeglin can talk to him about that. Looks like those two have plenty in common."

Her tone of voice said Roeglin had *better* talk to Geralt about his abilities, and she had no doubt the mage was far enough inside her head to know it. She decided not to push it but turned herself about instead and went inside, leaving the guards to follow.

5

SURFACE SKIRMISH

"Well, that was interesting," Gabe said when they were all settled around one of the tables and Ursula had joined them from the kitchen. He looked at the two boys. "You should have told us about your abilities."

Ursula's eyes widened, and Marsh guessed there'd be some discussion after the pair went to bed. Gabe caught Geralt's eye and continued.

"We appreciate anything extra you can do, especially if it means we have enough supplies in store for any caravan that arrives. The journey up from the pools or down from the entrance to the Ledge cavern would give us enough time to go hunting with the wolves or dig extra from the garden for the next meal, and we could have the barn prepared ahead of time. The Deeps know we're so short-handed now that any extra notice is appreciated."

He paused and then smiled.

"And I bet you could tell me if any of our guests were planning on doing us harm, couldn't you?"

Geralt blushed, and Jean interrupted.

"He has to close his eyes," the younger brother said, "or everyone can see his eyes change color, and they'll *know* he's in their heads."

Roeglin groaned.

"*Mind-walking*," he said. "It's *called* mind-walking—and yes, you're not supposed to do it without consent."

Coughing and spluttering broke out around the table as the Protectors were caught mid-bite, sip or swallow. Even Marsh found she was smirking at the mage's discomfort.

"And the Deeps thought it was a good idea for a *twelve-year-old* to have it," Gustav muttered and glared at Jean. "At least it's better than giving a ten-year-old the ability to throw fireballs about."

Jean looked mortified, but Gabe reached over and draped his arm around the boy's shoulders.

"If each of us could do *that*, we wouldn't have to worry about the remnant so much," he said. "They don't like fire."

It was the right thing to say, and Jean perked up, looking just a bit pleased with himself. Marsh was glad for him, but worried, too.

"The key phrase there," she said, "is 'if each of us could.' You never thought to try?"

Gustav and Roeglin groaned.

"You know we've got us a raider spy to catch, don't you?" Gustav asked, and Marsh shrugged.

"Yeah, but I've also got family to think about. We can't leave the waystation undefended."

"Master Envermet will be here within the next four days," Gustav said, and Marsh stared at him.

No one had told her that!

"Need to know," Gustav added, catching her look. "We

didn't want to raise people's hopes if the Shadow Master wanted him to stay at the Ledge."

Which meant Roeglin had known too…and hadn't told her. Marsh shot him a glare as well.

"Like the man said, 'Need to know.'"

Marsh wanted to argue that she'd needed to know, but she couldn't think of a single reason why.

"Well, I appreciate it," Gabe said, looking mildly relieved. "My last set of stable hands couldn't handle being under the big blue and complained that the sun hurt their eyes. They waited until Master Gage went through and returned to the Ledge with him."

He sighed.

"I wasn't sure what we were going to do. Between the remnant and the raiders, I was worried. And now the boys…" He gestured vaguely, and Ursula laid a hand on his arm.

"I told you not to worry," she said, snuggling against him. "Silly man."

It made Marsh wonder if the woman didn't have a little magic of her own, but she couldn't for the life of her work out what it might be.

Gustav favored the stationmaster with a broad smile.

"Well, then," he said, "if I give you this, I won't have to worry about the famous Cavallon temper, will I?"

He shuffled back in his chair, digging around in one of the pouches at his belt, pulling out a shroom-paper envelope, and passing it to Gabe. The stationmaster looked at him.

"This has the Council seal on it. Are you sure I can open it here?"

Gustav looked around the table.

"Yep. No one here that won't need to know about it, and at least three folks who you're gonna need to consult with when you make the decision."

Gabe slit the envelope and unfolded the parchment within, reading it swiftly and silently as they all waited to hear what it said.

"Well, shoo?" Ursula pressed when he'd finished reading and sat with the parchment folded in his lap. "What did it say?"

"That idea you had," Gabe began, sounding stunned. "The one you said came in a dream. They're doing it."

A dream? Marsh was curious but couldn't work out any way to ask—and Ursula was far too excited.

"Truly? A dedicated body of Protectors for the Ledge caverns?"

Gabe nodded.

"And for us," he told her. "They want to station two..." He unfolded the paper and looked at it once more. "No. Three or four squads here. Two to train, and two to patrol. Pa's going to be in charge until the trade starts flowing again."

Marsh suspected that Per would be in charge for a lot longer than that but didn't say so, and Gabe hadn't finished.

"And they'll be bringing mages with them," he said. "Shadow guards and rock mages."

He sighed.

"No druids, though." His gaze strayed to the wolves. "We could really do with a druid out here."

Gustav rolled his eyes then looked at Marsh.

"It's your turn to do the honors," he said, and Marsh suppressed a groan.

Instead, she said, "Rock mages *are* druids. They're just called rock mages because of what they do in the caverns."

Gabe's face brightened.

"Truly?"

Marsh sighed.

"Truly," she said, and there was silence around the table as everyone ate their meals and thought about the news.

After a few moments, though, Jean's small voice interrupted their thoughts.

"Will there be anyone who can teach me more magic?"

"More fire magic?" Marsh asked, but the boy shook his head.

"That would be good," he replied, "but I was hoping to learn that thing *you* did where your eyes turned green and you borrowed people's energy to heal."

Before Marsh had a chance to reply, Roeglin spoke.

"Marsh can teach you that," he said. "There's no need to wait for Master Envermet."

Marsh glared at him, and Jean, catching the look on her face, looked shattered.

"You don't have to if you don't want to," he said, and Marsh felt her heart go out to him.

"I can try," she told him. "I just haven't taught anyone that trick before."

"Not a trick," Gustav countered, rubbing the healed side of his newly-shaved head. "See?"

Jean slipped out of his seat and went over to inspect it.

"I'm really sorry," he said, and Gustav patted his shoulder.

"Don't be, boy. You couldn't exactly get rid of it inside, now, could you?"

Before Jean could respond to that, Ironshade leapt to his feet, giving a series of yips that brought the pack to its feet. Next to the fire, Mordanlenoowar growled and rolled upright. Gabe's eyes flashed green, and he ran for the bar at the back of the commons.

"Remnant!" he shouted as wolf pack and hoshkat gathered at the door.

"Where?" Marsh demanded as Gustav and the shadow guards rose from their seats.

Geralt's eyes went white.

"Twenty at the gates. Five or ten trying the postern."

Postern?

"Side gate, Marsh. Like the one you snuck out of at Gravine's."

So much for Roeglin being subtle!

"Let them out, Jean," Gabe ordered. "We're going to need all the help we can get."

As the boy hurried to do as he was told, Gabe looked at the guards.

"Did you bring ranged weapons?"

"We've got crossb—" Gustav stopped as the three shadow guards drew darts from the darkness in the corners of the room. "Or that. We've got that too."

"Anything else?" Gabe asked, and turned to Geralt without waiting for an answer. "How long, Geralt?"

But the boy's eyes were back to their normal dark brown, and he was running for a door at the back of the room.

"Not long! Jean, we need our slingshots."

Jean opened the door, and the wolves and kat raced out into the dark.

"Don't open the postern!" Gabe shouted, but the boy was running after his brother. "And what did I say about slingshots?"

It wasn't really a question, and Gabe hit the door shortly after the beasts. He shouted at Gustav as he passed.

"Get your bows! The rest of you, with me."

Since when had her cousin gotten so bossy? Marsh wondered, but she didn't have time for childhood memories.

She pushed back her chair and hurried after him, only to be stopped when Gustav grabbed her arm.

"Lightning," he told her. "Get on the wall and nail those bastards to the ground."

Marsh nodded and was about to do exactly as he'd said when a soft voice interrupted them.

"Do the postern gate first," Ursula said. "They're almost through."

"Show me."

"We'll come with you," Geralt said as the boys raced back into the room.

Roeglin looked at Gustav.

"We'll join you on the walls as soon as the postern's secured."

"This way," Geralt urged, turning for the kitchens.

"Hurry!" Ursula urged, and Marsh, Roeglin, and the boys headed through the kitchens at a jog.

By the time they got to the postern gate, the remnant were almost through. The gate's wooden panels were cracked, and pieces had started falling off. Marsh caught a glimpse of distorted remnant faces and felt a surge of revulsion, but she didn't stop. She followed Geralt past the wolves gathered in front of the gate and up a narrow set of stairs leading to the top of the wall.

Halfway up, Geralt stopped, blocking the way.

"There are others," he said, but before Marsh could ask him what he meant, an all-too-familiar screech rent the air.

"Shadow monsters," she whispered and grabbed the boy, shaking the white from his eyes. "Get me to the top."

As he scrambled to obey, another gibbering shriek followed the first and Roeglin swore.

"Don't touch those minds," he told the boy. "Find the others. The ones that let them through."

"Okay, but I don't..."

"Just do it," Roeglin told him. "Marsh and I will take care of the rest."

They would?

Of course, we will, Roeglin told her, but he didn't tell her how.

Marsh hit the top of the wall, wondering what in all the Deeps shadow monsters were doing up on the surface. Envermet had said they didn't like the surface. The sight of Mordan leaping off the wall and into the dark brought her up short.

"Dan!"

The kat didn't stop, and she didn't wait. She was hunting, and shadow mages tasted much better than the monsters at the gate. Marsh could deal with *those.*

"Fine."

Marsh turned to the wall, setting her hands on the narrow parapet and trying to see out into the dark. It was almost like being back in the caverns if she ignored the open expanse of sky above her head. Just like being in a cavern…which meant she only had to shift her vision from what she used when the sun shone to what she needed to see through the dark.

That was easily done. What was harder to achieve was actually seeing the remnant she could hear battering their way through the gate.

Since when did you ever need to see what you were destroying?

As annoying as it was, Roeglin had a point. Marsh looked up at the sky, ready to call the shadows from the ceiling. Ready to summon them from the cracks and crevices and around the base of the stalactites…and she froze.

"I-I can't," she murmured, looking up at the clear sky with its array of twinkling stars.

She gestured at them.

"I-I just can't."

Wood splintered and cracked in the gate below, making her jump. Roeglin ignored it.

"Just try."

"But—"

The shadow mage reached over and slapped the back of her head.

"It's all darkness," he said. "It's just on the surface instead of a cave. Now call the damn darkness and do your job!"

"Hey!"

"You really need to hurry," Geralt said, his voice taut with worry. "They're coming."

Oh, "they" were, were they?

Yes, they Deeps well are! Listen.

But Marsh didn't need to listen. She could hear them—hoots and howls and screams that threatened terrible things. She wondered what Mordan was doing and caught a fleeting impression of bushes with the slightly darker outline of a man set against them.

She also caught the overwhelming need for silence and focus, because the night was full of monsters and more were coming through. There was fear, too. The wolf pack wasn't going to be enough. The pride was in danger. Mordan didn't think she could stop them all.

The kat moved, her belly low to the ground as she stalked the rogue mage.

Wood cracked, and there was a sudden growl and a cry of pain. Roeglin reached out and shook her.

"Move your ass," he said. "Hunting with the kat isn't going to save us."

As if to emphasize his words, Marsh heard more wood splinter, and one of the wolves yelped. Geralt stuck his head over the edge of the walkway.

"They're almost through," he yelled, and Marsh knew she had to try.

She knew she could call lightning from the darkness, knew she could summon spears from the cavern shadows. What she had to work out now was whether she could do the same in the clear night air.

"That night air is made of shadow," Roeglin told her. "If you can't use it like you do in the caverns, you have no right to call yourself a shadow mage."

Marsh's mind raced, and she thought about raining

lightning down onto the monsters clustered around the gate. She also registered the hunting cries of the shadow monsters and knew she'd have to deal with them too…and she remembered that Mordan was out there.

"I need to know where the kat is," she said, and Geralt answered before Roeglin could.

"She's over by the trees. There," he said, pointing to show her where a stand of trees formed a dark hollow in the night.

Look though she might, Marsh couldn't see the kat, but she could hear the wolves, and it sounded like several of them had joined the first in attacking whatever part of the remnant they could reach through the broken gate.

"Do something, Marsh."

"The other things are almost here," Geralt added, and Marsh knew what she had to do.

"Show me," she said. "You can see into my mind. Now, show me."

"I…I don't…"

"Just keep looking, boy," Roeglin interrupted, then added, "Here!"

Marsh's world blurred and shook, and she could see what Geralt had been trying to show her. How the boy could handle looking at the world this way, she didn't know, but it helped. Roeglin didn't care.

"Now call the shadows, Marsh."

Call the shadows… Marsh closed her eyes, holding onto the picture of the landscape beyond the waystation's walls. She could do this. There were plenty of shadows. The whole sky was full of them. She could create a storm bigger than any she'd ever brewed in the caverns, one that stretched all around the waystation walls. She could dig a trench with the impact of every bolt, and use the blood of remnant and shadow monster alike to fill it.

This time she smelt the lightning on the air, felt the static brush her skin, and heard the snap and crackle as the bolts formed. The shouts and threats from the remnant by the gate turned into screams of terror. The howls and screeches of the oncoming horde of shadow monsters took on the timbre of fear, and Geralt shouted.

"Stop!" He grabbed her shoulder and shook her. "Stop! Stop! Stop!"

Panic flowed through the link and Marsh stopped, reaching out to soothe the rankled air, aware of the silence descending in storm's wake.

"Stop," Geralt whispered. "The kat needs you."

Mordan needed her?

The kat answered her question with a flood of pain. She'd taken down one mage and changed position to stalk the next. She hadn't seen the storm forming, and her path had taken her beneath its edges. The mage *had* seen the storm, and that had been all that had saved Mordan as she'd chased him up the slope, but even that had not been enough to save her entirely.

The first bolt of darkness had gouged its way across her hip and down her leg, knocking her off her stride. The second had caught her tail and sent a jolt through her hindquarters that had sent her tumbling clear of the rest.

Marsh raced down the steps, relieved to see the postern gate was clear, even if it made it hard to open. She grabbed the locking bar and hefted it, then realized that was all that had been holding the remnant at bay.

The minute she removed it the rest of the boards fell away, landing on the bodies of fallen remnant just beyond the opening. At least, she thought they were bodies. She couldn't be sure.

She wasn't going to look any closer to make sure. Calling a sword from the shadows, Marsh stepped quickly through the dead, ready to defend herself if one should rise. Behind her, she could hear Roeglin following, as well as the boys.

"Dan!" she called as if that would bring the kat to her any faster. "Dan!"

A dark shape flashed past her, and another, and then a third.

The wolves!

Marsh ran harder. The wolves might have been content enough to lie with Mordan beside the fire, but this was still their territory, and she was still new. Who knew how they'd react if they found her outside?

She'll be fine.

How would Roeglin know?

Look.

Marsh looked. Ahead of her, she could see the wolves slowing down, the largest of them lifting his head to howl.

"I'm coming!" she shouted, weaving her way between bushes and pushing her way through tall clumps of grass.

The wolf leaping out of the bushes ahead of her was a surprise, and Marsh barely resisted the impulse to defend herself with the sword. Banishing the blade to the dark, she felt teeth nipping at her hand as the wolf tried to pull her toward her friend.

Marsh yanked her hand free, feeling teeth scrape over

her skin even as the wolf let her go. It skidded to a halt a few feet short of the fallen kat and looked back at her. Marsh came to a halt too and hurried over to where the kat lay.

Roeglin had been right. Mordan was perfectly safe. She was surrounded by the wolf pack, and every single one of its members seemed focused on keeping her safe. Dark lines scored the kat's flank and hip, and her tail was a mess of red and black flesh.

Marsh's breath caught in her throat.

"Oh, Dan," she whispered, dropping to her knees beside the kat. "I'm sorry."

She might have crumbled right then and there, but Roeglin laid his hand on her shoulder.

"You're surrounded by energy," he reminded her. "Just heal her."

Just heal her... He made it sound so easy. The big kat raised her head, catching Marsh's eyes with her own and sending a feeling of trust and reassurance over their link. Mordan's confidence that Marsh could make the pain go away helped steady her.

She stretched out her hand, her fingers reaching for the mottled green and gray hide but hesitating to touch it.

"You don't need contact, do you?" Roeglin asked. "Aren't you just guiding the energy where you need it?"

So the man *had* been listening...and wasn't she just glad he had been. Remembering it was the energy that was important and not the contact was a big help. Taking a deep breath, Marsh reached for the energy in the world around her.

It was there, more than she'd been able to find in the

courtyard with its cloak of cut stone. Much more. She wouldn't need to borrow anything from the wolves or anyone else.

Carefully drawing the energy in, Marsh made herself look at the kat's injuries, inspecting the strength of the life force flowing through each area so that she could direct the energy she'd gathered from the world around them to where it would help the most.

After a few heartbeats, she saw the life force grow stronger in the injured areas, and the kat gave a sigh of relief. Marsh moved her focus from the animal's flanks and hips and out along the tail. The injuries were worse here, but not beyond what she could pull the energy to mend.

"Don't pull too much," Roeglin warned, then added, "She's looking a lot better now."

It was a strange way to tell her to stop, but Marsh paused, inspecting her handiwork before sending one last burst of healing toward the end of Mordan's tail. It wasn't perfect but it would do, and Roeglin actually had a point. She'd used a fair amount of power; maybe it *was* time to stop.

Mordan seemed to agree because the kat rolled to her feet and shook herself. Marsh got to her feet as the kat stretched and looked around. Letting Mordan's attention draw her gaze to their surroundings, Marsh gazed into the dark.

6

POST-BATTLE SHAKEDOWN

Marsh was surprised to see how far they'd run from the waystation, but there it was, a dark square on the slope below them with the trade-route winding past. Beside her Mordan, huffed out a sigh and took a step down the slope. Marsh caught a sense of disgust from the kat as it surveyed the station.

The cave would need cleaning or the stench of carrion would attract scavengers.

From the feeling over the connection, the idea of scavengers so close to the den worried the kat. Marsh studied the slope below them and wondered where the mage Mordan had been chasing had gone. The thought had barely crossed her mind when Roeglin dropped to his knees, dragging at her arm as he did so.

Mordan slunk into the cover of some nearby bushes and the wolves scattered. Geralt and Jean copied Roeglin, and this time Marsh felt the lightest brush of contact as Geralt peered into her mind. She bounced him out again, smirking at his gasp of surprise.

Bet you didn't know I could do that, did you? she thought, then wished she hadn't. It would have been useful to ask him to scan the hillside for the mage in the same way he'd been able to find him before.

Beside her, Roeglin gave a snort.

Make up your mind, he suggested. *The poor kid is still trying to figure out how to tell you.*

Well, it was nice to know that Roeglin still didn't have any boundaries when it came to sticking his mind where it wasn't wanted.

Got to keep my hand in.

And people complain about the examples *I* set.

Point.

But it didn't stop him from linking her to the boy and showing her where the kid thought the mage was hiding.

Mordan, Marsh said, and the kat brushed past her and away.

Well, _she_ seems to be feeling better, Roeglin observed, but he scanned the ground around them.

"Did the portal close?" Marsh asked, then rephrased it in a way they could check. "Geralt, can you sense any more of the other monsters? The ones you hadn't seen before?"

"Who says I hadn't seen them before?" the boy asked, and Marsh stilled

The boy continued, oblivious to her sudden stillness.

"This was the first time I'd seen them *here*, but I saw them attack a caravan after we'd left..." His breath caught, then steadied, "after we left the farm."

There was a roar, then a sudden scream from farther up the slope, and the boy winced.

"She got him."

He sounded shaky, but Roeglin gave him no time to dwell on it.

"Anyone else?"

The boy's eyes gleamed, then dulled.

"Nope. All gone." He gulped and looked at Marsh. "You got them all."

"Pretty sure I wasn't the only one," Marsh said as she started walking back down the hill.

She was trying not to think of what might be waiting for them outside the waystation walls. Picking their way through the dead remnant had been bad enough.

"We'll go back in via the postern," Roeglin said, looking back at her. "Make sure the back trail is clear."

As he spoke, his foot caught on something in the grass and he tripped.

"Are you okay?"

There was a wet, sticky sound as Roeglin regained his feet.

"Su...oh...wow. We might want to find another way back."

He stared at the ground and began delicately picking his way across the slope. Marsh followed his progress and paralleled it, aware of the boys moving in her footsteps and the wolves taking a wide detour around the area Roeglin had been crossing. In the end, they followed the path they'd taken across the hill to get to Mordan.

The big kat joined them at the gate, wrinkling her nose in distaste at the corpses. Marsh counted them. Just in case...

"There's no one," Geralt said. "Just us and Ursula and the others meant to be here."

He led the way around the side of the waystation proper and onto the porch to where Gustav and Gabe were waiting with the rest. Gustav looked at Marsh.

"How are you feeling?"

It was an interesting question, and Marsh stopped to think about it. She *was* tired, she realized. Not collapse-in-the-dirt tired, but pretty close. Until Gustav had mentioned it, she hadn't registered. Now she did, but she wasn't going to admit it to him.

"Fine."

Gustav scowled.

"You shouldn't be."

It made her angry.

"And why the Deeps not?"

"This," Roeglin said, and Marsh found herself looking at a storm that boiled out of nothing and encircled the waystation walls. Cries and screams reached her from the men below, with at least one of them sobbing to be let in and others begging for mercy. These were tempered, however, by those who promised death and vengeance.

When the image and sounds faded, Marsh found herself sitting on the edge of the porch with her head in her hands.

"What was that?"

Gustav gave her a grimace that he'd probably intended to be a smile.

"You."

"No… I… Really?"

"Someone told her she had all the darkness in the night, and she wasn't much of a mage if she couldn't use it," Geralt explained, and all eyes turned to Roeglin.

"You didn't."

Marsh twisted slightly so she could watch as the shadow mage blushed.

"Well, I…" He looked at her, but Jean's quiet voice intervened before he'd worked out what to say.

"She had trouble with the open skies," he said. "If he hadn't said it, they'd have broken through."

He paused, then added, "I need a cookie…and maybe a kaffee."

That got Gabe's attention.

"Since when do you have kaffee?"

But the boy didn't answer, just turned on his heel and went inside. Gabe went to follow, only to be stopped when Geralt grabbed his arm.

"Give him a heartbeat," the boy said, "and let him have the kaffee. It's the only way he'll sleep."

It was the first time Marsh had heard of kaffee having *that* effect, but Gabe didn't argue, just gave the boy a moment before following him inside. Marsh watched them go, hearing Roeglin's plaintive request for a bath and Gustav and Izmay threatening to scrub him down in the yard, but she didn't move.

She just sat, staring at the night and not wanting to close her eyes. Every time she did, she saw bodies and what might have been bits of bodies, and a storm rolling beneath a star-laden sky. She hadn't realized Mordan had come to sit beside her until the kat's warmth threatened to knock her over. Another presence came and leaned on her other side, and the musky scent of wolf blended with the smell of hoshkat.

Another wolf leaned against her back, and two more came to sit against her legs. Marsh let their warmth creep through her, banishing the chill of Gustav's memories even if they couldn't banish the memories themselves. How long she would have just sat there staring into the night, she didn't know, but the sound of boots on the porch behind her made her start.

"You okay, Leclerc?"

Gustav. Well, at least he'd thought to check.

She nodded, not trusting her voice and not wanting to admit to being tired in case he sent her to bed. There was no way she wanted to sleep with *that* nightmare running around in her head. She watched his boots moved past her, bringing the Protector captain into view as he descended the steps to the courtyard.

"Good. Go fetch a wheelbarrow from the stables. There's a mess that needs cleaning up."

Marsh went to stand, and Mordan growled. A second growl rippled out from her other side, and more snarls joined them. Gustav stopped.

"I beg your pardon?" he said, turning around and fixing the creatures around her with a stare.

Looking at the kat and the wolves, Marsh wondered if he might not be biting off more than he could chew, but the man was unfazed. He returned their stares, letting his gaze travel from one to the next, before returning to glare at Mordan.

"I think I've commanded enough men to know what she needs next, so get your furry asses off her before I come over and kick them off her."

At his words, the wolves and hoshkat came to their feet, and Marsh became aware of whispers coming from behind the door.

"Do you think we should..." Gabe began, but one of the soldiers shushed him, and another chuckled.

"Oh, no. *This* I have to see."

Gustav seemed oblivious to all of them. He was eyeing the animals and curled his lip into a snarl of his own.

"Bring it," he said, his voice quiet with challenge, and the pack surged forward, Mordan running neck and neck with the lead wolf.

Gustav extended the arm and hand carrying the shield and ducked under the kat's first leap, catching the wolf across the chest and knocking it to one side as Mordan sailed over his head. Alarmed as the rest of the pack closed in, Marsh got to her feet, surprised to find herself unsteady enough to need the railing for support. She watched as the pack darted around Gustav, nipping at his feet, and saw him use the staff to sweep another two from their feet. A few feet away, the pack leader recovered enough to regain his feet and Mordan circled back, slinking low for another try.

She opened her mouth to call the kat back but Gustav spun, taking two bounding strides before diving for the kat. Mordan gave a snarl of surprise when he caught her off-guard, twisting to meet him even as he hit her side on, wrapping his arms around her shoulders and chest and taking her off her feet.

The kat rolled, letting Gustav's momentum carry them into a rolling tumble where both battled for supremacy.

"Hey..." she tried, taking a couple of steps toward them. She was shocked to discover her voice was nothing more than a thread.

Clearing her throat, Marsh tried again.

"Hey!"

That came out with more strength, but did nothing to cut through the growls and snarls coming from man and beast. Marsh hurried toward them, stopping when she reached them. She stood still for a long moment, staring down at the twisting knot of kat and man, and did the only thing she could think of—she dived onto them.

It occurred to her that she might be making a mistake, but she was mid-leap, and it was too late. Mordan saw her coming, and Gustav must have caught a glimpse because they rolled apart and out of the way, leaving her to hit the cobbles on her own. The force of it jarred through her arms and knocked the wind from her lungs.

"Well, *merde*," she said, and rested her head on her arms.

She heard boots and paws shift.

"Don't make me come up there," she warned, not bothering to lift her head, "or I'll kick both your asses."

Gustav gave a bark of disbelieving laughter.

"I'd like to see you try."

But Mordan had a much better reply. Marsh groaned as the big kat lay down across her, pinning her to the ground. More footsteps moved past her; Izmay and the rest of the guards, if Marsh was to take a guess.

"Don't worry about the wheelbarrow, Marsh," the female shadow guard taunted. "We'll clean your mess up for you."

Henri's comment was almost bitter.

"It's not like we have anything *else* to do."

Marsh tried to move, and Mordan shifted to rest her chin against the top of Marsh's head.

"Thanks a lot, kat."

More footsteps approached and stopped. A boot tapped on the cobbles, and Mordan got up. Marsh lifted her head, recognized Gustav's boots, and pushed up to her feet. When she was halfway there, he reached out to steady her.

"Wheelbarrow," he said, and looked down at the kat. "You, too."

What Mordan was going to do with a wheelbarrow, Marsh couldn't think, but she didn't ask, just followed the direction the other guards had taken. The wolves circled, and Gustav glared at them.

"Go see what the stationmaster wants," he told them. "Playtime's over."

By the time they'd cleared the corpses into one of the deeper craters she'd dug with the shadow lightning and repaired the postern gate, Marsh had to agree—although she was wondering why he'd picked a fight with the kat.

"Someone's got to be in charge," he said, coming to sit beside her, "and she needs to understand it's not her."

The kat hissed softly and stalked into the waystation proper. The lead wolf growled. Gustav caught its eye and growled right back, and the wolf hesitated, then pointedly turned its back on the man.

Marsh laughed.

"Well, *you* sure made yourself popular."

Gustav shrugged.

"Had to be done. You needed to get back on the horse."

An image of the storm flashed through Marsh's mind, and she shivered.

"How about those cookies Geralt was looking for?" she asked, changing the subject. "D'you think the kid left any for the rest of us?"

"If he didn't, Ursula has cake," Gabe told them, having come over without either of them seeing him approach. He gave Gustav a hard look. "And you. Leave my wolves alone."

Marsh caught the look on Gustav's face and relaxed when the captain shrugged.

"Anytime they're not disrupting the discipline in *my* pack, not a problem," he replied, "but when they're working against me like they did tonight, I'll kick their furry tails."

Gabe held Gustav's gaze a moment longer and nodded. "Fair enough."

For a long moment, Marsh thought her cousin would throw a punch or try to throw Gustav into the makeshift pit with the corpses, but he didn't. He just turned and stalked back through the gate…or he tried to. Gustav's next words stopped him cold.

"I need the boy to light the pit."

At first, Marsh thought her cousin would refuse, but Gabe merely sighed.

"I'll speak to his brother. If Geralt says it's okay, I'll send them out."

The boys must have been eavesdropping beside the gate because they appeared as if summoned and walked to the edge of the pit. Geralt looked up at Gabe as he passed.

"It's okay, uncle."

Jean glanced at Gustav.

"Where?" he asked, and Gustav indicated several areas of the pit.

"There, there, and there. As hot as you can make it," he said.

Marsh caught the frown on the boy's face.

"Just think of the heat energy in the air around us," she told him, thinking about how she drew healing energy. "You should be able to feel any you haven't already called, and…" She thought of the way the boy moved his hands to form the fireball. "Just wind it into what you've got."

She had no idea if that would be enough…or even if fire magic worked that way, but it seemed to make sense to Jean.

The boy turned to face the pit, his small face pinched with concentration, his hands moving in the gestures she'd seen them make before. This time the fireball was twice as big as the one he'd tossed through the door, and Marsh caught Gustav pass a nervous hand over the side of his head. She had to sympathize. She wouldn't want to be caught by one that size either.

She watched as Jean threw the ball at the first point Gustav had told him needed to be lit. To her surprise, there was nothing clumsy about his aim. The gleaming sphere flew straight and true, landing to explode in a blazing sheet of flame.

"Stars and fire, boy!" Gustav exclaimed, but Geralt cried out in alarm, and Jean collapsed.

Fortunately, Gustav was standing right beside the boy and was able to grab him before he could fall into the pit. The soldier lifted Jean into his arms and turned to Marsh.

"Do you have enough?"

At first, Marsh was puzzled, but then she realized he was asking if she had enough energy left to make sure the kid was okay. Marsh wondered because she was pretty sure he hadn't been injured. She shrugged.

"Sure."

It was a simple matter to draw the energy from the earth and direct it into Jean's still form. She watched as color returned to his cheeks and saw his breathing deepen into sleep, then lowered the hand she'd raised toward him.

"He'll be fine," she said.

"And you?"

Now he thought to ask? Marsh rolled her eyes.

"I'll be fine too," she told him.

"Good," Izmay snapped, "because I don't want to be carrying you back."

"And I'm not tucking you in," Henri added.

"Well aren't you two just the funniest dark-spawned dirt-eaters in the tunnels," Marsh said and turned away from the flames, only to discover she wasn't as fine as she'd thought.

Her world wavered, the fire growing impossibly bright and blending with the sky. Izmay swore and Henri called on the Deep's dirty britches, but only Roeglin's sudden lunge stopped her from falling into the pit.

"Shag the shadows and shit the shrooms, you're a mess."

Marsh wanted to tell him she was fine, but the world kept spinning. She was just grateful he looped her arm over his shoulders and didn't copy Gustav's example with the kid.

You sure? Because to be honest...

"Just give me a minute," she said, and almost fell over.

"A minute, huh?"

But before Roeglin could reply, Henri gave a short, sharp sigh of exasperation and lifted her from the ground.

"Some of us want supper and maybe some sleep before

the sun comes up," he grumbled, turning abruptly away from Roeglin and stomping through the postern and into the waystation.

Marsh wanted to tell him to put her down, but he wasn't paying her any attention, and she was too tired to find her voice. It was moments like these when she wished she could do what Roeglin did and just say what she needed inside someone's head.

"Where do you want her sleeping?" Henri demanded when Gabe met him halfway across the common room.

Fortunately, Ursula had the answer, because all her cousin could do was gape like a beached fish.

"This way," the woman commanded, "and mind you take her boots off before you put her between the covers."

"It's not like you're not going to have to do the sheets anyway," Henri grumbled and came to a sudden halt as Ursula rounded on him.

"Wrong. *You'll* be doing the sheets. First thing in the morning."

From the look on Henri's face, Marsh thought the man might drop her, and she was very relieved when Ursula spoke again.

"Through here. And if you drop her, you'll be washing floors to boot."

He would? Man, if she wasn't so out of it, she'd try to find a way to make that happen. The bruises would be worth it.

"Don't even think about it," Henri grumbled, showing he knew her far too well, "or you'll be taking a very short trip to the horse trough."

Marsh thought about rolling her eyes, but she couldn't

find the energy,. As she let her eyes close, she wondered if she really heard Roeglin as she drifted off to sleep.

"I'll help you," he said, and Marsh wasn't sure if the mage meant with the sheets or with dropping her into a horse trough.

She fell asleep before she found out.

7

OF FIRE AND MIND

It was late when Marsh woke the next morning. She felt Mordan's familiar weight pinning her under the blankets and pushed on the kat to give her some space. Dan gave a low rumble of complaint, stretched, and hopped slowly off the bed.

Marsh lay there for a moment longer, then swung herself upright.

"I hope someone got the name of that caravan," she muttered as her head started a low-level pounding.

You could always try healing yourself.

And a merry good morning to you too, Ro.

You need a wash and a change of clothes before you go anywhere near Ursula or breakfast. And you need to strip your bed or Henri is going to have a fit.

As tempting as the thought to watch Henri throw a fit was, Marsh decided she'd do as Roeglin suggested. She healed herself first, pulling the energy she needed from the world around her and diminishing her headache to a tolerable level. Mordan was stretched out in front of the fire when she finally made it out to the common room.

She was surprised to find it empty and went to the kitchen looking for Gabe. He wasn't there, but Ursula was kneading dough at the counter.

"Per sent shroom flour," she said, smiling when she saw Marsh, "and Gustav said to give you a ration bar."

She pointed to where the bar sat and added, "He said nothing about you not eating the breakfast roll beside it, though."

Marsh noticed the breakfast roll sitting on a plate beside the ration bar.

"He also said I should send you out to the courtyard for training when I saw you, but nothing about you having to leave that cup of chocolate behind undrunk."

Marsh cast the woman a grateful look and propped herself up against the kitchen bench, eating as Ursula finished with the bread.

"How have things been?" she asked and the woman glanced up from the oven.

She was just as pretty as Marsh remembered her, her copper hair pulled back out of the way and her eyes as blue as they'd ever been.

"Well," she answered, "Gabe worries about the remnant and the wildlife more than he should. I kept telling him he shouldn't worry, but with the caravans coming less often and the boys arriving…"

She shrugged.

"I'm glad the Council finally saw the sense of things."

Boots scraped on the back steps, and the kitchen door opened.

"Thought I told you to report to training," Gustav said, coming inside.

Ursula glared at him.

"How's Henri coming with my washing?"

"All done," Roeglin answered, coming in after the captain.

His eyes fell on the cup in Marsh's hand.

"I don't suppose…"

Ursula gestured toward the door.

"Get out of my kitchen and I'll bring it when it's ready. I suppose the rest of your miscreants will…"

"Yes, please," Henri called from the door to the common room. Someone cleared their throat behind him, and he added, "If it's not too much trouble."

Ursula rolled her eyes and looked at Marsh.

"You, too," she said. "I hear you'll be moving out in the morning."

It was news to her but Marsh went, following in Gustav and Roeglin's path and leaving Ursula in sole command of her kitchen. As soon as they were settled around one of the longer tables in the commons, Gustav turned to Gabe.

"Tell us about the caravans," he said.

"They're coming less often. For instance we had one due the week just past, but it hasn't arrived" Gabe said. "If Master Gage hadn't come through, the hands would have waited for it, but they said they couldn't, and I didn't have the heart to make them. If it wasn't for the attack last night, I wouldn't have been too concerned for another day or so. I'd have asked Master Envermet to check, but…"

"It's been too long," Gustav said, addressing his team,

"and Gabe would like us to see if we can discover what's happened to them."

Marsh wanted to protest that they'd have no way of telling the station master what had happened and that turning back would mean a long delay for their mission to Dimanche, but Gustav already had that covered.

"Master Envermet's force is leaving a day early and will arrive tomorrow night. By then, we should have reached the entrance to the Dimanche complex. The caravan should have arrived yesterday. We think it fell afoul of the raiders close to the surface, so we should be close to discovering what happened by the time Envermet gets here. Roeglin will relay the news."

He turned to Marsh.

"I'm sorry. I was hoping you'd have time to see the children."

If she were honest, Marsh had been hoping for the same, but she swallowed her disappointment and shrugged.

"Can't be helped," she said, and changed the subject. "Ironsides mentioned you had a seeker come through…"

Gabe cast a glance at the pack leader and nodded.

"If he showed you the skinny man with the sallow skin, then yes, that one had the look of a seeker about him. We didn't like him much, and the boys and I made sure he was never left alone. The way he looked at Ursula…"

A low, rumbling growl came from where the pack leader lay, and Marsh had the impression that Gabe and the boys weren't the only ones who'd had their unsavory guest under watch. Gabe gave the wolf a startled look that melted swiftly to surprised gratitude, and Ironsides got up and walked to the door.

Henri got up to let him out, and Gabe shook his head.

"He says he was just doing what any good pack leader would, and that we look hungry enough to need more rabbits."

"Rabbits, hey?" Henri commented, then raised his voice. "He'd be better off hunting us up something bigger. The kat has quite an appetite."

At his words, Mordan shot him a filthy look and rolled to her feet, pawing once at the door in a definite demand. Marsh sputtered with laughter as the kat gave her a clear impression of exactly what she thought, but she waved away Henri's look of curiosity.

"It's not repeatable," she managed as he sat.

"When you've all quite finished," Gustav declared, "we have other matters to attend to."

He turned to Gabe.

"Did he say where he was going?"

The stationmaster nodded.

"He ended up going after Kearick. When he first got here and discovered Kearick had already left, he wasn't sure what he wanted to do. For a while there he was going to head down into the Devastation, but he was torn. His mules were pretty heavily laden, and he had something he wanted Kearick to see. Seemed pretty excited by it too, but he wouldn't say what it was.

"I told him Kearick had said something about setting up a new store in Dimanche, and that decided him. He paid up and headed out the next day."

His face reddened.

"It's a good thing too, or I might have done something I'd have been made to regret. Honestly, it was the way he looked at Ursula that had me worried about keeping Downslopes open without anyone to help us run it. It's more than just me now."

Ursula chose that moment to appear from the kitchen.

"Silly man," she said. "I told you it would be all right now, didn't I?"

She dumped pots of kaffee and chocolate on the table and Marsh started to get up, only to have Roeglin rest his hand on her knee.

It's all under control, he said as Geralt and Jean appeared bringing plates, cups, and cake.

And it was.

They ate in silence, then Gustav turned to Marsh.

"I know Aisha and the mages are coming tomorrow," he said, "but do you think you can teach the boy your version of healing so he's got something to start with?"

He paused.

"Oh, and you might want to explain to Geralt about what happens when a mage uses their magic too much."

"And us," Ursula added, her statement clearly including Gabe. "If we're going to have more of them under our roof, I'm going to need to know what to expect...especially since I'll be the one doing the baking."

Marsh felt her skin heat at the woman's remark and watched as her embarrassment was reflected in Roeglin's face.

It was a long afternoon, particularly as Geralt insisted on joining them.

"You won't be around after tomorrow," the boy told her, his voice gruff with emotion, "and I *am* his brother.

As the morning wore on each boy showed some ability, although both found the nature magic more tiring than the forms they had discovered for themselves. When Marsh saw they were both at their limits, she turned the tables.

"Show me how to do fire magic," she requested when Jean sat back, looking pale but pleased after healing a self-inflicted slice on Izmay's palm.

"Me, too," the shadow guard said and caught Marsh's look. "What? There has to be some compensation for us slicing ourselves open for them to practice healing on."

And Marsh realized the other guards had gathered around to listen. At first, she was going to argue, but she had to admit Izmay had a point. Each of the guards had volunteered some kind of cut or abrasion for her to demonstrate or the boys to practice on. For his part, Jean looked surprised and was at first just a little intimidated.

"I…well…"

Roeglin and Geralt stepped in, getting the boy to go through the steps of crafting a small ball of fire and sharing them with each mind in the room.

Unfortunately, Geralt wasn't quite as skilled as Roeglin and he shared a little too widely, bringing Ursula in from the kitchen.

"Out!" she commanded, her voice as close to the shout she'd leveled at Mordan as Marsh had yet to hear. "Take your balls of fire and get the Deeps out of my common room, you daft, Dark-for-brains, Deeps-addled, misbegotten…"

The stream of invective continued as Henri grabbed

Jean and carried him through the door fireball and all. Gustav was waiting in the courtyard when they arrived and Ursula slammed the door behind them.

"The pack brought back a deer. If all we get is bread and drippings for dinner," he said, leveling a look of disgust at Marsh, "I'm blaming you."

Marsh felt her jaw drop open in surprise, but Gustav turned to Jean.

"Now, boy, if you'd take us through that again but a little more slowly…"

Ursula had other ideas.

"It's lunch time," she told them, and Marsh realized how hungry they'd become.

Once they'd eaten, they spent the afternoon with Jean trying to show them how to pull the heat from the air and form it into fireballs, but only Izmay seemed to have the knack for doing it easily.

"Typical," Zeb said, his face pale from exertion as he crafted a small, perfectly formed sphere and watched as his fellow guard called a second ball of fire, then a third, which she juggled while she waited. Even Henri managed a credible globe, laughing as Zeb cursed him for being able to do so.

"Showoff," Marsh muttered, having been forced to stop after not conjuring anything bigger than a pebble.

"You're thinking of it wrong," Geralt informed her, and she opened her mouth to argue, only to be tapped on the forehead. "I can see in here, remember?"

Marsh rolled her eyes and looked at Roeglin, but the mage just shrugged.

"At least hear what he has to say," the man advised. "You can always practice it on the way to Dimanche."

"Or when we get there," Gustav interrupted. "I want her using her magic for other things once we're on the road."

Gustav had discovered an affinity for fire, but grown tired of creating spheres and worked on calling flames to coat his sword in much the same way as most of the other Protectors called shadow.

"You'll have to teach this trick to Captain Envermet," he told Jean, and looked at Geralt. "Make sure he doesn't forget. It's just the kind of thing they need to know."

The boys had nodded, looking pleased, and Ursula had summoned everyone inside shortly after. That evening, Roeglin made good on his promise to have Gabe and Ursula speak with Per and Daniel. He also pulled Marsh and Geralt into the conversation—Marsh so she could talk to her uncle, and Geralt so he had a chance of learning how it was done.

"I want you to try to connect with me tomorrow night," he told the boy, and pale-faced, Geralt had agreed.

"Tomorrow," the boy had said, clearly exhausted, and Roeglin had patted his shoulder.

"You'll be fine," he said. "It just takes a bit of practice."

There was a swirl of quickly suppressed images showing Roeglin struggling to get his own head around the skill. It was accompanied by such frustration that Marsh wondered how long it had taken the mage to get the hang of it, but she didn't ask. What Geralt needed now more than anything else was belief. He didn't need to know just how hard Roeglin had found it.

And wasn't that just an interesting fact. She started smirking, ignoring Roeglin's scowl as she said goodnight to Gabe and Ursula. The morning with its incumbent goodbyes waited, and she was too tired to avoid sleeping the remaining hours away.

8

THE CARAVAN'S FATE

They were gone in the dawn's gray light, the waystation casting long dark shadows down the hill and onto the ruins below. To their relief and surprise, the trail remained clear to the tunnel mouth leading to Dimanche. Marsh had said goodbye to Gabe and Ursula on the understanding that she would return sometime within the next twelve cycles.

She didn't know how she was going to keep that promise, but Ursula seemed certain she could, and Marsh decided not to question it. Who knew what the future might hold? All she could do was try to keep her promise and hope the Deeps didn't have any other plans for her.

Gustav had her scanning the mountainside before they'd left the waystation gates despite Geralt's assurances that there was no sentient life as far as he could scan, which was almost to the Dimanche complex entrance. Marsh was relieved to find the boy was right, although not reassured to not find the caravan camped somewhere ahead of them.

Gustav called a halt as they reached the tunnel mouth. He looked up at the sky, wincing as the late afternoon sun slashed across his eyes, dazzling him. He blinked, looking around at the rest of them.

"What do you say?" he asked. "Do you want to see one more sunset or bid the sky goodbye?"

It was a hard decision. Marsh had found she missed the colors of the evening, whether they were painted on the walls in the Kerrenin's Ledge cavern or across the sky to the west of Downslopes. In the end, though, they reluctantly pressed on, giving priority to finding the caravan over the pleasure of the evening light.

The entrance to the complex of underground structures leading to Dimanche opened under the sheer cliffs of something that looked like the ruined shell of an ancient structure. Square pillars buttressed the opening, long overgrown by vines and bushes. They continued in semi-orderly rows through a broad, once-square cavern and into more natural tunnels eaten into the stone by a combination of water, landslides, and tunneling.

Staring around her, Marsh couldn't help but shudder at the thought of what it must have been like for people to feel desperate enough to dig their way into the mountain. What had made them do that rather than fight for survival on the surface? The entrance hinted at strength, a building that had surely been a fortress in its own right. Why had they felt the need to flee underground?

She pushed the thought away, forcing herself to pay attention to their surroundings. She scanned the ground ahead, noting the white mesh of rootlike strands coating the walls and wondering what it was. All she could tell was that it was full of life but not sentient. Knowing it posed no danger, she ignored it and focused on scanning the shadows and strange fungi growing horizontally along the walls.

Beyond the usual skitter of insects and small animals, there was nothing. No shadow monsters lurked along the walls. No raiders waited in the shelter of the towering pillars or the shrooms clumped around them. Nothing bigger than the small furry creatures the wolves had termed "rabbits" interrupted their journey until they reached the first cavern.

"Marsh?" Gustav asked as the first whiff of death reached them.

"Nothing," she said, gagging at the foul taste of destruction coating her tongue and pulling her shirt collar up over her nose.

All around her, the others did the same. Together, they kicked their mules into a trot, moving toward the terrible stench. It didn't take them long to reach the source and Marsh coughed, fighting down the urge to throw up. They'd found the caravan Gabe had said was overdue.

Most of it, anyway.

Its mules were lying where they'd fallen, their bodies torn apart, their eyes staring sightlessly into the dark. The caravan's goods were scattered around them, boxes and packages broken apart from their fall—or from the scavengers that had come during the night.

Even as she thought of them, Marsh held her shirt across her mouth and closed her eyes, seeking the life she knew had to be sharing the tunnel with them. It didn't take her long to draw on the shadows and have them reveal the creatures hiding in their depths. She soon found what she was looking for and took a deep breath to report it, but Roeglin was ahead of her, plucking the information from her head and passing it to the rest of the team.

Their mounts didn't need much urging to move quickly between the corpses of the dead pack train or to jolt into a swift canter to put some distance between them and the attack site. Throughout their flight, Marsh tried to keep her eyes open and guide her beast down the corridor while maintaining her hold on both shadow and life scan.

It was difficult, and she knew she was pushing herself past what was wise, but she'd found the hidden scavengers and she needed to make sure they put enough distance between them to ensure they weren't mistaken for prey. As the night-cycle predators began to stir, the pack train's carcasses would draw more than just scavengers—and they needed to be far away before that happened.

"We'll need to keep riding," Gustav said as they passed through the cavern where the caravan had made its last camp, and Marsh felt Mordan's approval.

Perhaps the human captain deserved to lead the pride…

It was not a thought Marsh wanted to share, and she turned her mind to other things.

From the distance the caravan had traveled, the raiders had hit it shortly after it had broken camp and settled into the day's journey. From the carnage on the trail behind them and the complete lack of glows, the raiders had let the shadow monsters loose to take out the mules. It occurred to her that she still didn't know how the raiders prevented the monsters from killing the traders as well.

Not what we need to know right now. Roeglin's voice interrupted her thoughts, and Marsh forced her mind back to the present.

Having lost the threads once, she found it hard to gather them again…and she picked up the dark purple presence of a shadow wraith.

A la putain! Roeglin cursed, but out in the open, his urgent shout bouncing down the tunnel ahead of them. "Wraith! Ride!"

And he reached over and grabbed Marsh's reins.

"Focus!"

Marsh didn't need him to tell her what to focus on. She reached into the shadows, holding tight to the threads that could bring her the information she needed about the predator hovering at the edge of a side tunnel. Mordan's correction sounded as clear as a bell over the link between them.

Not a side tunnel. Lair. Marsh was glad the kat stayed close to the side of her mule, because, as fierce as the kat was, she didn't think even Mordan had a hope of taking the wraith down on her own.

Need more pride or the storm. Mordan sent Marsh an image of the roiling darkness she called when she drew lightning from the shadows.

No! Roeglin's mental shout of alarm was echoed in his voice, and he jerked on the mule's reins to get her attention. "Not unless we can't shake it."

And by "shake it," he meant if the monster didn't follow them.

We don't want to close the tunnel. We're opening *trade, remember?*

Marsh remembered, but that meant Master Envermet's

force would have to deal with it, and Aisha and Tamlin were with him.

They've dealt with things like that before?

It was a good thing he had hold of the mule's reins, or Marsh might have pulled the beast to a halt right then and there.

A shadow wraith? Her children had dealt with a *shadow wraith*? And no one had told her?

I'll show you the memory when we camp, Roeglin told her. *Aisha...*

"Later," Marsh said. She could well imagine what Aisha had done. Daniel hadn't been far off when he'd called the child a "little hoshkat."

The wraith, Roeglin reminded her, and Marsh realized she had lost her grip on the shadow threads *and* her scan of the cavern around her.

Merde.

It was a struggle, but she was able to regain her grip on the shadows and seek the wraith in their depths. She wasn't able to extend her scan to finding its life force, but that was okay because she didn't need to. It looked like the wraith had been content to haunt the edge of its junction and watch them pass. All she could hope for now was that their headlong flight hadn't marked them as easy prey and that the monster preferred the easier meals that would be gathering around the carcasses behind them.

You can hope, Roeglin snarked, *but we'll ride until dawn unless we find shelter sooner.*

Well, at least they could agree on that. There was only one problem with Roeglin's plan, though.

"*Merde,*" the shadow mage swore, lunging out to grab

her as she began to slide. Henri was already coming alongside.

"I've got her."

At a gallop? Marsh wondered. The man must be a better rider than they'd realized.

Yeah, and you can ask him about that when we stop.

Marsh took hold of the pommel and did her best to balance as Henri settled her in front of him. It helped that he kept one arm tucked around her waist as he rode.

"You owe me dinner, shadow mage," he muttered, and Marsh didn't argue.

The man had stopped her from falling on her ass where a shadow wraith could find her. Dinner was a pretty good trade. Of course, that wasn't all Henri had to say about it.

"And you're a pain in the ass."

Marsh wanted to argue that, but when she thought about it from his perspective, he had a point. Not that he didn't owe her for warning them of the shadow wraith's presence… In the end, it was easier to focus on staying on the mule and not say anything. She didn't expect to be half asleep by the time Gustav called a halt, but she was.

"Do you think we've gone far enough?"

"Marsh?" Roeglin's voice was tentative, but Marsh nodded and held up two fingers.

Taking a breath, she put aside her desire to get off the mule and out of Henri's lap and closed her eyes. The shadows shook beneath her touch, and she asked them to show her what lay in the cavern around them. It was no surprise to find life, but a relief that there was no trace of a shadow wraith or anything else that would be a threat.

Marsh breathed a sigh of relief and felt Henri lift her sideways.

It took her a heartbeat to realize what he intended, and even then she wasn't ready. Her feet hit the cavern floor and her knees folded.

"You misbegotten son of the Deep!" she managed, adding, "No dinner for you."

"No deal. I coulda left you for the wraith."

"I'da picked her up," Izmay told him, riding alongside to give him a swift slap upside the head. "You're not the only one knows how to ride. You were only the closest."

Henri turned and stared at the shadow guard and she arched an eyebrow, daring him to dispute it. Marsh left them to it, glad when none of them moved to help her regain her feet. It didn't take her long to use the little power she had to draw on the natural energy running through the floor of the cavern. Stone it might be, but it was still in its natural form and connected to the natural world, unlike the cut cobbles she'd encountered at Kerrenin's Ledge and Downslopes.

The energy moved slowly but it was there, and she pulled enough of it to her to soothe away some of the fatigue. She decided it would take more energy than she had to get rid of the aches and pains resulting from her ride, besides which, Gustav was waiting.

"No wraith," she told him. "No joffra, shroom walkers, or centipedes."

He glanced around the cavern and looked at Roeglin.

"What minds do you sense?"

It was a good question, and one Marsh was glad the captain had added to his repertoire. Roeglin's eyes turned white, and she waited with the rest until they returned to their normal shade of hazel.

"Just beasts. No remnant or shadow monsters, and nothing human."

Some of the tension went out of Gustav's body, and he looked around.

"We'll camp here," he said. "The mules need a rest."

The mules aren't the only ones, Marsh thought and looked around for hers. She was glad when Roeglin dismounted and handed her the reins for her mount.

"Thank you," she managed, and he gave her a roguish grin, indicating Henri with one hand.

"That's okay. You can cook me dinner when you cook for him."

Marsh rolled her eyes, and Izmay sputtered.

"Men. Always with the food."

"Not always," Henri protested and blushed crimson when they turned to stare at him.

Gustav broke the tension by handing him a shovel.

"You can dig 'em, seeing as your mind's already there."

Henri groaned but took the shovel, handing Izmay his reins. To Marsh's surprise, the shadow guard handed her the reins of both their mules and pulled a second shovel from her packsaddle, moving to help Henri.

"Thought you'd need a hand," she said, and Zeb snickered.

Izmay blushed and turned her back on him. Gustav tapped him on the knee.

"Kindling," he ordered. "Looks to be plenty of shrooms around here."

He looked at Gerry, but the guard was ahead of him.

"I got it," he said before Gustav could say anything. "Jakob and I are clearing the campsite, while Roeglin and Marsh keep watch on the cavern."

None of them asked what Gustav was doing, but he hadn't handed out all the duties there were, and set about caring for the mules. It took them a turn of the hourglass before the camp was finished, and Marsh was wishing they'd added one of the rock mages to their number by the time they were done. Even though Jakob and Gerry had cleared a good space and bordered it with a low pile of rocks, she still didn't feel safe.

Zeb had lit the fire and placed a small blaze at each of the four corners of the campsite, surprising Marsh when he lit each one by conjuring a small globe of fire and settling it inside the hollow of dry fuel he'd created.

Izmay and Henri returned, each bringing an armful of fuel for the fires. Izmay watched Zeb light the last one and gave an appreciative whistle.

"Nice work, Zeb," she told him, and he smiled.

Marsh scanned the dark, again, this time drawing a little extra energy from the shrooms around them so she could sense the life forces in the cavern. It was almost enough, but the world still wavered, and she knew she'd have to stop soon.

"Soon?" Roeglin asked, deliberately letting his voice be heard. "You need to stop now, Leclerc, or you'll be no use to us tomorrow."

At his words, Gustav looked up from where he was setting up his bed.

"Enough, Leclerc. You, too, Leger. I'll need you both on your feet when we move out."

Marsh noticed he didn't say "in the morning" and hoped that meant he was letting them all sleep a little longer.

That's because it already is morning, Roeglin told her, handing her a ration bar.

"We might have a fire, but none of us are in any shape to cook…unless you want to settle your debts early?"

Marsh took the ration bar and registered Mordan lying alongside her. She looked for her mule, thinking she should find the kat something to eat, and realized the kat was already tearing at a hunk of something.

"Kat's fine. Go get some sleep."

And wasn't Gustav just super-alert right now? At least he'd taken care of *all* the animals.

"He's thinking if you don't go to sleep on your own, he's going to find a rock and rock you to sleep," Roeglin murmured, pitching his voice low to keep the comment between them.

"You tucking me in?" was out before she had the sense to censor it, and she felt her face go red.

The other guards laughed. They laughed harder when Roeglin replied.

"I'm sleeping right beside you," he told her, his words carrying the suggestion of more mischief than either of them was capable of.

9

THE GROTTO

Suggestions and predators aside, Marsh slept well that night, glad when the shadow captain said they'd be camping for a second night. The reason for that became clear when he had Roeglin make contact with Gabe to let the station master know what had happened to the caravan. He also asked to speak with Master Envermet, and Roeglin dragged Marsh into the conversation as they discussed how the captain was going to tackle the tunnel section. Master Envermet reported encountering another group of remnant.

"They remind me of shadow monsters," he said, "but they're not. The stationmaster is of the opinion that this group is new to the area, and not related to the raiders. He says they come and go."

"He's been there long enough to know," Marsh assured him. "How are they?"

"Your cousin and his family are doing well, and the boys are proving apt teachers as well as students. This fire magic has potential."

Well, that was one way to put it.

When the two Protector captains had decided on how they were going to tackle the lack of glows and the scavengers and predators on the trail, Roeglin released Marsh and settled into a conversation with Geralt. From what she could tell, the conversation turned rapidly into a training session, which left the mind mage slightly worn. Gustav wasn't happy.

"No more training until we reach Dimanche," he instructed. "It's a good thing we're not moving out until morning."

By "morning," he meant an hour before the day cycle began.

"We've got ground to make up," he said when Henri noted the hour, "and I want to spend tonight at the waystation that's supposed to be ahead of us."

He didn't add "if it's still there," but Marsh was sure she caught it at the edge of his thoughts.

You sure you don't want to see what kind of mind magic you can tap? Roeglin suggested when he noticed that impression, but Marsh shook her head.

"Ask me after we get to Dimanche."

He might have asked more, but the trail ahead of them was lit. The sight of the living glows lining each side of the trail was enough to make Gustav signal a halt. He turned in the saddle and fixed his gaze on Marsh.

"Anything?" he asked, and Marsh had to wonder why such a welcome sight would bring such immediate suspicion.

Trust me, he has good reason.

Marsh scowled. Roeglin's commentary was sometimes

a lot less useful than he thought, and right now she needed to be focused on the world around them. She took a deep breath, half expecting him to interrupt her concentration once again, but he remained silent, allowing her to search the shadows ahead and try to find what lived in the groves and rocks around them…or who might be responsible.

Once again, she found nothing outside the creatures she'd come to expect in the Dimanche tunnels. There was certainly nothing that would be capable of lighting the glows, and she relayed that to Gustav.

"Nothing?"

From the tone of disbelief in his voice, he wanted proof. Marsh rolled her eyes and slid from the saddle, passing the mule's reins to Roeglin.

"Come on, Dan," she said and stepped sideways into the deeper shadow beneath a clump of calla shrooms.

Before Gustav could protest, Marsh had slid into the shadows, becoming one with them, yet not. She felt the hoshkat's surprise when she kept her hand on Mordan's ruff and caused her to become the same.

Stay with me, she told the kat, and chose a patch of darkness beside a cluster of rocks farther down the trail. The kat tensed but didn't try to break her grip, and Marsh took them through the darkness from one patch of shadow to another. When they arrived, she let go of the kat and again scanned the cavern. Again she found nothing, and she wondered if a rock wizard would have noticed something she was missing.

Back down the trail, Gustav had signaled the advance, no doubt getting Roeglin to keep him updated on her progress. To her relief, they didn't move too fast, and the guards kept watch on the trail on all sides. Izmay even remembered to glance toward the tunnel ceiling. Marsh shifted her attention away from them and paid attention to the new areas she could scan.

Again, she came up with nothing.

Yet the glows still shone. They were a mix of lemon and lime to the usual white, but they shone… and by all rights, they shouldn't have.

When the trail widened into a junction, Marsh stopped, releasing the kat to explore for herself.

"Thanks, Mordan," she told her, and the kat rubbed her chin along Marsh's arm and shoulder in a single quick swipe.

Marsh sighed. One of the beast masters had explained the significance of that gesture.

"You know I'm not your property, right?"

Her only reply was a derogatory flick from the hoshkat's tail, then Mordan vanished into the tumble of rocks and the fungi that grew between them. Watching the kat's coat change color with the purple bioluminescence of the calla shrooms overhead, Marsh noticed a soft, greeny-yellow gleam coming from next to one of the rocks.

She crossed over to take a closer look and saw a cluster of low-growing fungi, each shedding greenish-yellow light from beneath a pure-white cap. It reminded her of the glows on this section of the trail, none of which shone in the shades she was used to. Marsh glanced back to the trail, studying the glows—and then she looked at the fungi.

"Oh."

Hearing the mules approaching, she returned to the

trail, looking for a cluster of shrooms growing closer to the glows. Surely…

She found several clusters and inspected the glows to see if their light was a result of some kind of luminescent paint. It wasn't, and she was crouched beside one, examining it to see if it showed any signs of being alive, when Gustav and Roeglin drew their mules to a halt beside her.

"It's shroom-light," she said, gesturing from the glow to one of the gleaming clusters. "Someone's drawn the light from the shrooms and charged the glows with it."

Gustav's eyes sharpened with interest, and he looked at Roeglin.

"Have you heard of this?"

The shadow mage shook his head, but Gustav had to be sure.

"Not even in the time you spent with the rock mages… or on the surface?"

Again Roeglin shook his head.

"No, this is something entirely new."

Gustav looked down at the fungi, his gaze shifting between them and the glows.

"If this is the work of druids," he said, "the shadow mages might have help keeping the glows charged on the trail. Perhaps we'll meet those who did the recharging and ask them."

He turned his mule's face back to the trail and kicked it back into a walk.

"Mount up, Leclerc. It's getting late, and I want to make the waystation tonight."

Marsh took the reins to her mule from Roeglin and swung into the saddle, reaching out into the dark to see what had become of Mordan. The big kat surprised her by emerging from a cluster of brown noses beside the trail and sending her mule snorting sideways.

"Thanks a lot, kat."

Mordan's tail quivered, and the kat looked up at the mule. Unbidden, the mule dipped its muzzle to snuff at the kat's shoulder, and then it snorted and followed after Gustav.

What was that all about? Roeglin wanted to know, but Marsh couldn't help him.

Instead, she took her place just back from Gustav and stretched her magic into the caverns, seeking the secrets of the shadows and trying to find what lives might be lurking in the dark. The first stirrings of things that hunted during the night cycle disturbed Marsh's scans, but nothing that truly promised trouble until the first joffra made their appearance out of a side tunnel.

"We need to be in that station before those things decide we're the best that's on offer," Roeglin said, and Gustav glanced back.

"Joffra," Marsh supplied, and the Protector captain kicked his mule into a trot.

The waystation lay only a small way ahead, but the path leading off the main trail looked disused, with scattered rock and clusters of brown noses and blue buttons already crowding over it. Drifts of ghost moss hung over sections that would normally be kept clear by the waystation owners. Marsh felt a sudden sense of foreboding as Gustav used a shadow blade to clear enough room for them to pass.

Marsh noticed the bright sparks of life lighting the

rock-dark shapes of spiders scuttling away from falling webs of moss. She hadn't encountered this in her last three years of travel, and she was glad. If the rest of the cavern wildlife was anything to go by, the spiders were probably venomous as well.

You'd better believe it, but they're also not very aggressive, so short of swatting them, most people find they usually run away.

It wasn't very comforting.

Neither was the first glimpse of the waystation.

Its stone walls looked like they had been carved from some a dark and distant rock that had been carried into the tunnels from somewhere else.

Almost, Roeglin told her, but he didn't elaborate. Glancing back at him, Marsh could see that the forbidding cast to the waystation's façade had caught his attention as much as her own. *I don't think there's anyone home...*

Marsh was about to suggest he try finding someone when his eyes shimmered white, and she knew was already searching for any kind of intelligent thought.

"Nothing," he said. "You?"

"Nothing," Marsh agreed a few heartbeats later, although the shadows hadn't been able to show her what lay behind closed doors or areas blocked by rock falls.

Her ability to sense the bright shades of life showed nothing, even if there were at least two areas where the walls were too thick for her to penetrate.

I saw no minds in there, Roeglin told her, *neither beast nor man.*

It was something to be aware of as Gustav took them through the waystation's broken gates and into the small, deserted courtyard beyond. The soldier pointed to Henri and Izmay and indicated the building to the right.

"Check the stables."

He nodded to Jakob and Gerry.

"Take the commons and kitchens."

Looking at Zeb and Roeglin, he gestured at the walls.

"Perimeter. Leclerc, you and the kat are with me."

They ground-tethered the mules, and the others spread out around them. Once they were safely on their way, Gustav turned to Marsh.

"We're checking the grotto. Stay sharp and keep the big beast close."

The grotto. Marsh searched her memory but didn't find any mention of it, and she recalled that Kearick hadn't sent her to Dimanche via the surface route.

"What am I looking for?" she asked.

Gustav's answer sent chills to her toes. "Serpents and scorpions."

Hear that, Dan? Marsh sent the kat an image of a scorpion and a serpent. *We need to be careful of those.*

The kat gave a snort and stalked ahead of them, her disdain echoing clearly in Marsh's head.

Even her cubs knew to be careful of *those*.

"I thought I told you to keep her close," Gustav protested as the kat reached a small arched entrance into the back wall of the station.

Marsh didn't answer but eyed the entrance to the grotto that supplied the waystation's water supply. She wasn't sure if she should be happy or worried that the station got its water from a natural pool located in a small cave at the rear of the cavern. Even though it was enclosed by the station's walls, there were no guarantees something couldn't dig its way through.

"Kat's got her own mind," Marsh replied. "Besides, I think she'll smell them before she runs into them. Any particular reason why we need to go in here?"

Even though neither she nor Roeglin had been able to sense anything, it didn't seem like a smart move for Gustav to split the group.

"Water," the Protector told her. "We're low, and I don't want to get their hopes up. Besides, you said there were joffra in the cavern, and that means we need to find a secure place to hole up. We can't defend the entire station. The best we can do is find the most secure position and wait for the day cycle to begin. Joffra are nocturnal, right?"

Marsh nodded.

As far as she knew joffra were nocturnal, coming only during the night cycle. The lizards were voracious hunters, able to camouflage themselves, climb, and run fast enough to bring down a galloping mule—and they hunted in packs, but they were careful what they attacked.

"The pack I sensed has around a half dozen members," Marsh told him. "They'd be unlikely to take us on unless they had more…or were starving."

"And what are the chances of that?"

"No idea. It's not the sort of trouble we'd know about unless we lived here." She looked around at the deserted station. "And it doesn't look like anyone's lived here for quite some time."

"No bodies, though," Gustav observed. "Raiders?"

Marsh nodded. Raiders seemed the most likely cause. She followed him toward the grotto entrance, scanning the station as she went. As far as she could tell, there was no one hiding in the station and nothing lairing in its depths, and they reached the grotto entrance without any trouble.

To Marsh's surprise, it led to a winding set of stairs descending through the rock. After walking the equivalent of two flights, they reached the bottom and followed a short length of tunnel to a small cave. The hoshkat was standing at the entrance, staring out into the small space, and she turned her head to as Marsh approached.

At first, Marsh wondered what was wrong, but then she felt the hoshkat's awe at the beauty before them. Marsh and Gustav stopped beside her, taking in the view. The rocks at the bottom of the pool glowed, their light painting the walls and towering purple calla shrooms in rippling blue light. Golden gleams as big as barstools shone like suns, and ferns clustered around their feet.

"Why didn't they turn this place into a base?" Marsh asked, but Gustav didn't answer.

Instead, he stepped out into the grotto and cautiously made his way to the water's edge. Marsh followed, surveying the surrounding shrooms for anything that might harm them. She remembered Gustav's warning and wondered where the scorpions and serpents were, but Mordan curled her lip.

She could scent no threat in the small cave before them.

As if to prove the point, the kat padded over to the pool and dipped her nose to its surface, snuffing at the water. Gustav showed the same caution, kneeling beside the kat as he tentatively dipped a hand into it. Nothing. He glanced at the kat.

"You going to drink this?" he asked, and Mordan turned her head and blinked at him.

He sighed and scooped a palmful of water to his mouth. Marsh tensed, but the guard swallowed and took another scoop before unhooking his canteen and looking at her.

"We're on water duty."

Marsh let go of her scans. It had been a long day, and she was beginning to feel the strain of using her magic so often and for so long, even if it *was* easier than before. Refilling her canteen, she cast her gaze around the grotto once more, and again saw nothing.

The return journey seemed to take longer, and her legs were burning by the time she reached the top.

"Water duty, huh?" she asked, eyeing Gustav where he was standing, his hands on his knees, puffing and blowing like a race mule.

Instead of answering immediately, he straightened and started moving toward the stables.

"We'll do the mules first," he said.

10

THE DRUID'S DEFENSE

In the end, they discovered another secret of the waystation—piped water and hand pumps.

"You are shitting me," Gustav exclaimed when he arrived at the stables and found the water troughs filled.

Izmay grinned.

"Nope."

Henri eyed the captain and added, "Not a hope in all the Deeps."

Gustav glanced at Marsh.

"Well, looks like you're off the hook, then."

He looked around the stables.

"How secure is this place?"

"Secure enough to have a tunnel to the commons," Roeglin announced, coming through a door at the end closest the waystation's main building.

He looked at Marsh.

"It's the same as the others."

Which meant there'd be meals on the table and

personal possessions in any occupied rooms. She looked at Izmay and Henri.

"Were there any other mules in here when you arrived?"

Henri frowned and shook his head.

"No."

"But there were fresh droppings," Izmay added. "Looked to be no more than a day old."

"Not the other caravan?"

"Nah. That was three days' old at least. These were from someone passing through after."

Marsh thought of Salazar and wondered if the man had managed to avoid the shadow wraith and other scavengers, only to fall victim to his own side...or maybe he'd just spent the night there in peace, the bastard.

"How many?"

"About a half dozen. From the tack, I'd say it was a small trader desperate enough to try to make it to the Ledge on his own."

"The tack?"

"Sure. It's over here. Whoever took the mules left it behind."

Izmay gestured toward some stalls at the other end of the stables. Set on the low barriers between each one were pack saddles, with bridles and lead ropes hanging from the posts at the end. Marsh headed over and took a look. The packs were loaded with shroom fiber and leather, ready to be processed into goods.

There was only one riding saddle, which indicated that Izmay might be right. Before Marsh could make any comment, however, they heard the whisper of claws and a series of short coughing barks.

"Joffra," Henri shouted and raced for the open stable doors.

Izmay beat him to them, slamming the doors closed and helping him lift the locking bar into place.

"Where are Gerry, Zeb, and Jakob?" Gustav demanded, and they stared in horror at the doors.

"In the kitchen," Roeglin replied, "making sure dinner doesn't burn. Whenever the raiders hit, it wasn't too long ago—and they left the supplies intact."

"Maybe they were going to do what they did at Midpoint," Marsh suggested.

"In which case, they'll be back," Gustav said. Something sniffed along the bottom edge of the stable doors, and the joffra's chuffing call was heard again.

One of the mules shifted restlessly in its stall, snorting nervously, and Roeglin went to soothe it. Mordan moved over to the door and rumbled a threatening growl. It was answered by a startled screech, followed by the skitter of retreating claws, but the kat continued staring at the narrow gap beneath the door, her ears cocked and her tail flicking slowly from side to side.

When the next joffra call sounded from farther away, Mordan raised her head, gave the gathered humans a scornful stare, and padded away through the door Roeglin said led to the commons.

"Well," Gustav said. "Talk about being shown how it's done…"

The mule closest him snorted, and they left the beasts to their dried shrooms and water.

"It's not normal for the raiders to take the mules," Marsh murmured.

"Maybe they needed the extra mounts," Roeglin suggested.

"But why leave the tack?"

"That I can't tell you," Roeglin replied.

It was a puzzle Marsh chewed over until she went to sleep, ignoring the banter of those around her to explore the deserted waystation and promise its vanished inhabitants that she *would* find them.

And if she could, she'd bring them back.

Sleep came slowly, and when it did, it was haunted by dreams, nightmares that exploded from shadow and crawled out of rocks, and the hoots and screams of dark abominations. She woke to the weight of a paw draped over her shoulder and the musty smell of the hoshkat curled around her. She also woke to find she wasn't alone in the room.

"We ride inside a turn," said Gustav, staring down at her and giving orders.

Seriously? Marsh thought but didn't say aloud. Before she could think of a decent response, Roeglin's voice sounded in her head.

Henri's trying to steal your breakfast.

It was just the incentive she needed and Marsh was on her feet in a heartbeat, pushing Mordan's paw off her and shoving back the covers. As her feet hit the floor, Gustav nudged her pack.

"Bring it down with you."

Marsh snatched the pack from the floor and beat him to the door, glad she'd slept in a bed and not her sleeping roll. Less to pack. She ran down the stairs and into the kitchen in time to snatch a shroom roll from under Henri's fingers.

"Not nice to steal a lady's breakfast," she said, biting into it before he could take it back.

"Who said that was *your* breakfast?" he demanded as Roeglin sputtered with laughter.

Marsh froze mid-chew and stared at him, but Henri figured it out.

"You told her I'd eat her breakfast?" he asked, glaring at the mage.

Roeglin gave way to laughter.

"Your face!"

Marsh finished her mouthful, swallowed, and looked at Henri.

"Sorry."

She set the rest of the roll back on the plate and turned to the shadow mage, aware of Henri turning with her.

"Horse trough?" she asked, and the big guard nodded.

"Horse trough."

Gustav ruined their plans.

"No time. We have a lot of distance to cover."

Marsh and Henri exchanged looks and turned back to the table. Marsh noticed another plate of rolls next to the oven Zeb and Gerry were standing beside.

"Didn't know either of you could cook," she said, taking a fresh one and handing it to Henri.

"Pa was a baker," Zeb said. "We *did* have other lives before becoming mages."

Gustav didn't give a toss for their other lives.

"Jakob, Izmay. You're with me."

He took two rolls from the plate and headed for the door to the commons.

Marsh followed them, taking another roll for herself, and Roeglin fell in step beside her.

"Not speaking to you," Marsh told him as Mordan came to join them.

"That's okay," Roeglin said. "I have the kat."

"The kat" gave him a disdainful look and pushed past him out into the courtyard.

"She's not speaking to you either," Marsh said.

He didn't try to change their minds, just helped get the mules saddled and ready for the road. By the time they were done, Zeb, Gerry, and Henri had joined them.

"Kitchen's clear," Jakob reported as they moved out. "New owners shouldn't have any complaints."

"Except for a few unmade beds," Gustav grumbled, but he didn't order them back to make them, and Marsh wasn't the only one who blushed.

The first part of the ride was back through the ghost moss and brown noses, some of which were already showing signs of recovering from their passage the day before. Marsh scanned the way ahead, noticing how the small life forces of insects and spiders flared and scurried through the vegetation around them.

They made it to the main trail without encountering any trouble, and Marsh was glad to see the glows were still alight. Roeglin and Gustav followed her gaze and relaxed just a little. Gustav had just turned back to say something when Mordan let out a sudden growl and bounded into the undergrowth by the side of the path.

As she disappeared from the trail, a grove of calla

shroom started to sway, long white tendrils spreading from beneath their caps to wrap around the hooves of the passing mules. The animals panicked, stumbling as they tried to pull their legs free—and Henri gave a startled shout.

Turning toward him, Marsh watched in horror as a thick many-stranded tentacle of white reached up from the morass around his mount's hooves and wound around his waist. Henri tried to draw his sword, but the strand trapped his arm to his side and yanked him clear of the saddle. His mule plunged away from it and fell.

By then Marsh was struggling to keep her own panicked mount under control.

Easy, she thought, seeking to connect to its mind and calm it. *You are safe. I will protect you.*

The animal snorted and stilled and Marsh breathed a sigh of relief, only to be thrown from the saddle when three thick strands rose from under its muzzle and startled it into an abortive plunge. The white mass that had spread under and around them caught her, a wall of white thread rising from it to cling to her clothing and begin to drag her under.

From the side of the path, Mordan roared, and alarm flooded the connection between them. Marsh caught the impression of brown tendrils blending with the white, and fear flashed through her.

She might have only seen one brown slime in her travels, but she remembered it. She'd seen a snake carcass thrown into one, and similar threads of brown had risen around it, pulling it into the slime's body where it had been dissolved. Glancing wildly around her, she saw no sign of what had alarmed the kat, but she didn't doubt the danger was real.

She looked at the glows and wished that for once they weren't so bright. They made the nearest shadows seem so much farther from reach.

"Distance…doesn't matter," Roeglin wheezed. "Step. You can…step."

Pinned flat to the ground right next to a glow?

"Yes. Step. Just. Believe."

He sounded like he was having trouble breathing and Marsh wished she could see him, but the mules and the rising morass of white stopped her. Marsh tried to get her feet under her, but the multitude of threads held her fast.

Shadow. Step.

Roeglin's insistence brought a scowl to her face, but it also annoyed her enough to drive the rising panic away.

He wanted her to shadow-step? She grabbed hold of her annoyance and looked for a suitable patch of shadow, pushing away the thought that she wasn't shaded. He laughed, a terrible wheezing thing that didn't bode well.

The mule.

And she realized he was right. Her feet were shaded by the mule, which now stood exhausted over them. Fixing where she wanted to be in her mind, Marsh thought about becoming one with the shadow, about her body taking on the substance of the dark, and of how she should be crouching under the mule. She had to shove the image of the mule kicking her in the head out of the way, but she managed, going from prone to crouched in seconds.

Another moment of concentration, and she was free of the sticky white shroom stuff and crouched in the sheltering darkness she'd desired. The only problem was that she wasn't alone. Someone else crouched there too, but he hadn't noticed her arrival. His attention was focused solely on the mired mules.

"Come feed," he murmured, his eyes blazing green as he swept his hands in a complex motion. "Leave the hard-toed ones, for they are innocent, but the raiders you can have."

"We're not raiders," Marsh said and was surprised when he turned and thrust one hand toward her.

In hindsight, she thought it might have been better if she'd said "*they're* not raiders," but it was too late for that. Shards of stone ripped themselves out of the floor, thrusting toward her with deadly intent. She had barely enough time to sight on a nearby patch of shadow and will herself into it before the shards tore through where she'd been.

"We're trying to restore the trail...and defeat the raiders."

She'd added that last as an afterthought, but as the shroom behind her got suddenly brighter and stretched to absorb her, she hoped it was enough. The sudden press of shroom flesh over her face made it difficult to breathe, and panic drove the picture of her next patch of shade from her mind.

Marsh flailed against the rubbery skin surrounding her, finding her mouth and nose covered. Her lungs burned as the shroom tightened around her and she found herself trapped. She was trying to think of what to do next when it pulled back from her face, and she filled her starving lungs.

"Not raiders, eh?"

The voice startled her, but not as much as the craggy

face that came into view. Its eyes still burned a faint green, but Marsh was sure she could see gray peering through it.

"Not raiders," she gasped. "Fighting raiders. Trying to reach Dimanche. Catch raider spy."

The eyes showed surprise, and iron-gray eyebrows rose.

"And why should I believe that?"

"Kat," Marsh said, still trying to catch her breath. "Ask kat."

She tried to connect to Mordan and saw the flare of emerald reflected in his eyes.

"Dan?" she called, her voice cracking. "Please tell him."

She waited for a dozen heartbeats and had almost given up hope that Mordan had heard her when the kat arrived. Mordan wasn't happy to see Marsh trapped inside the skin of a calla shroom and swatted the man to one side.

"Dan! Don't—"

She reached along their link, trying to impress on the kat with how important it was she didn't kill the man beneath her claws, and Dan froze, keeping her prey pinned beneath a very large forepaw as she turned her gaze to Marsh.

"He needs to know we are friends."

The kat snarled, clearly disputing that the stranger was any friend of hers.

"Not raiders," Marsh corrected. "Please, Dan. He fights the raiders too."

The kat looked down at the man, letting herself be caught in his gaze. Their eyes flashed green, and Marsh caught herself holding her breath.

"Please, Dan. Just show him what we've fought to get

here. Show…" She stopped whispering as the mushroom released her.

And she ran for the mules and the men trapped in the white mass on the trail. She had to make sure the brown slime didn't catch a single one of them. She stumbled over rocks and slid on patches of a tarry substance she didn't want to investigate more closely. She hadn't realized she'd stepped so far from the path, or that the druid had been able to attack them from so far away.

Druid? It was a relief to hear Roeglin's voice back inside her head. *Well, that explains a lot.*

He sounded tired, but he was upright and leaning against his mule when she arrived. Seeing that the sticky white threads had retreated from the path and now spread away from it, she hurried over to inspect the rest of her friends. They were all there, but they all looked exhausted, and their mules were dark with sweat. Gustav looked up as she approached and gestured to the rest of them.

"This *druid*," he growled. "I don't suppose he's got enough healing to fix all of *this?*"

Marsh was about to respond to that when the druid spoke from behind her.

"I'm sorry, but no. I can take you to a safe place to rest and give you a boost to reach it, but heal *all* of that? Not a hope in all the Deeps."

Gustav shifted his gaze past Marsh and scowled at the man following her. Watching his face, Marsh noticed that for once he seemed at a loss as to what to say. The druid saved him the trouble.

"It's this way," he said, coming into view as he passed Marsh. "Let me redirect the slime. There is some carrion toward the back of the cave—a straggler, or a scout, I can't be sure. He died too quickly to tell me."

"They took the waystation," Marsh told him as she walked slowly over to her mule.

It snorted uncertainly and she went to stand to one side of its head, letting it get a good look at her before rubbing its muzzle with her palm and stroking its face. She didn't move until it rested its head against her chest and heaved a long sigh, and then it was only to take its reins and prepare to lead it wherever the druid chose to take them.

She noticed that none of the others got back onto their mounts, but all looked at the druid for guidance.

"When you're ready," Gustav said after they'd stood still for too long.

At first, the druid looked puzzled that they weren't going to ride, but Marsh thought she caught approval too.

"This way."

11

A STRANGE WELCOME

At the druid's first stop, Marsh had to wonder if it wouldn't have been better to just keep walking. The man had secured the entrance to a cavern behind a screen of calla and brevilar shrooms, seeding the area with the usual brown noses and blue buttons as well as emerald fern and scarlet darters.

"*Don't,*" he said when Izmay moved to inspect one of the pretty red toadstools. "They have a range of three feet, and you'd be sick for weeks…if you survived."

Marsh stared at him, wanting to know more but not daring to ask. The druid ignored her, scanning the cavern around them before turning back to the callas and brevilars. He laid one hand on the broad white trunk of a calla and the other on the blue-skinned flesh of a brevilar and bowed his head.

If Marsh hadn't known any better, she would have thought he was praying to the lords of the Deep, but the man seemed more concerned with nature than any long-forgotten gods. She watched as the shrooms changed beneath his touch, their trunks curving away from each other to form a portal.

The rest of the shrooms in the cluster followed suit until a hollow pathway formed, and the druid lifted his hands away, green light fading from his eyes.

"Come," he said, leading them through and into a narrow rocky passage.

Marsh saw the green return to his eyes before they'd exited the shroom and heard a faint chirping whistle. The druid made the sound again, and then again. He paused long enough to speak as he led them through the rocky slit.

"Don't stop until you reach the white rocks, then wait."

He didn't explain what he meant or why but threaded his way back through them to the rocky tunnel. Marsh exchanged puzzled glances with Gustav and Roeglin as they heard the whistling chirp sound behind them, but they did as the druid had told them. It was almost a mistake.

"Stop right there!" called a voice as they reached an outcrop of glistening white stone.

Gustav slid Roeglin a sideways glance.

"Do you think we've come far enough?" and it was clear he meant Izmay and Henri, who were walking in the rear.

Whoever owned the voice had no doubts, though.

"I said stop!" The order was followed by the snap of a bowstring and the whirr of an arrow.

Another whirr followed, and then a third.

The first arrow hit Gustav just below the shoulder, and he dropped his reins with a startled cry. The second arrow took Roeglin in the thigh. The third hit Marsh in the upper arm. The direction of the shots making it clear their attacker had walked his fire across their line of advance and hadn't been aiming to kill.

Roeglin hit the ground with a wordless cry of pain, and Gustav folded slowly to his knees. Marsh looked down at her arm and sat beside the nearest rock. With muttered curses, the other guards moved forward, Izmay and Jakob pulling bandages from their saddlebags.

Henri and Gerry moved forward to guard the path, taking up positions just in front of Roeglin. Two arrows bit into the earth at their feet.

"No farther."

Gerry said nothing, but Henri held his blade at the ready with one hand and made a single-fingered gesture at the dark. Marsh waited for another arrow to come flying out and pierce his hand, but all that came was a soft chuckle.

"I understand your sentiment, but that won't save you if Alois doesn't appear soon."

Marsh lifted her head. Alois?

"The druid? He went back in the tunnel, you string-happy asshole."

The voice tutted.

"That's not very nice language for a lady."

"Go shag yourself; the shrooms have better things to do with their time."

Roeglin groaned, and Marsh wasn't sure it had anything to do with the pain he was in. The owner of the voice was not impressed.

"You're lucky Alois would be upset if I shot you again."

"Marsh..." Gustav sounded like he was trying to give an order through gritted teeth, but Marsh understood.

She sighed as Izmay and Jakob quickly inspected Gustav and Roeglin and gave a quick glance in her direction. It was disappointing when they didn't come over for a closer look, but she guessed they'd already found which of them needed the most attention.

"Great," Roeglin muttered when they settled down beside him. "You had to pick me."

"We could always let you bleed out," Izmay retorted, probing the entry point.

"Would it hurt as much?"

"It could be arranged."

She poked him, and he yelped.

Marsh snickered, and Izmay looked at her.

"Your turn is coming."

"I can hardly wait," Marsh retorted, but under her breath, where she hoped Izmay couldn't hear her.

Roeglin started laughing, right up until Izmay snarled at him.

"Hold still. I need to see what sort of head it has."

"Lanceolate, and the kind you can pull out without making the wound worse...unless you'd rather *push* it through."

"Do I get a vote?"

"Shut up, Roeglin. And hold still."

Marsh leaned her head back against the rock, feeling mildly light-headed and nauseated. She looked down at her arm, then focused on the cavern ceiling, wishing she hadn't. She flinched as a figure stepped out from behind the nearest shrooms, tilting her head to take a closer look.

"Asshole," she managed, noting the bow slung over his

shoulder and the long blond braid tucked into his shirt front.

"And very pleased I am to meet you too," he said, before kneeling beside her to inspect the wound.

It hurt, and Marsh gritted her teeth as sweat sheened her skin.

"Just…had to…get…your arrow back, huh?" she managed as he worked carefully to remove it.

He frowned, laying the shaft to one side as he pinched the edges of the wound together.

"Hush."

Marsh felt a soft rush of energy from his fingertips and breathed a sigh of relief.

"You're a healer too?"

There was a moment's pause as more energy flowed into her and she felt less fatigued, and the archer replied.

"Alo says I should be prepared to repair what I damage."

"He also says you should try not to damage it in the first place!"

Alois had returned, and he was obviously displeased by what he'd found. The archer got to his feet and slowly dusted off his knees.

"There were too many of them, and I couldn't see you."

"I told you to let them reach the rocks."

"I didn't think they were going to stop."

"Do you mind?" Gustav's voice stopped them cold, as faint as it was.

"You shot *three* of them?"

"Only the ones in the front."

Marsh watched them move away and tucked her knees under her. At least they were blocking the view of everyone else. This way, if she fell over, she could do it without an audience.

Don't bet on it, Roeglin said, and she looked up.

Henri and Gerry were heading in her direction.

Marsh sighed, but she didn't try to get up before they reached her. She still wasn't sure she could.

"You could have yelled," Henri told her, and it was obvious he meant the arrival of the archer.

"Sure I could," Marsh said, "because you'da got here before I got skewered by something else."

"Girl has a point," Gerry noted, reaching down to offer Marsh a hand. "Here."

Marsh let Gerry help her up, and they crossed over to where the archer had retrieved his arrow from Roeglin. Izmay observed as he pulled healing energy into the shadow mage. Alo had moved on to tend Gustav.

"I am sorry," the druid murmured. "He is more cautious than I'd like."

"I understand," Gustav replied, although Marsh wasn't sure he did.

He said no more though, just watched as Alois healed his chest and shoulder, then let the druid help him to his feet.

"How much farther?" he asked, earning a sharp look from the archer.

Alois must have caught it as well because he frowned.

"They're staying the night, Nellee. We need allies."

Henri snorted, then uttered a soft "oof" as someone elbowed him in the midriff. Roeglin leaned toward the druid.

"He's easily bought," he said, *sotto voce*. "How well can you cook?"

"You'd be surprised," Alois replied, and again he told the exact truth.

The trail wound around the outcrop of white rocks before opening out into the broad flat base of a wide, low, cavern. From the ceiling and the regular arrangement of pillars as well as several carefully blocked tunnels mirroring each other at opposite ends of the complex, it looked like Alois had set up home in some form of ancient building.

He caught the direction of her gaze and shrugged.

"I don't know what it used to be, but it's home now, and I have made it as safe as I could so that it could be a refuge for the others."

"Others?"

Marsh realized she'd been so caught up in the cavern's architecture that she hadn't taken notice of the porches and porticoes dug into the wall opposite her. She'd also missed the orderly plantings of shrooms and the other people working in the fields or gradually emerging to stand and watch them arrive.

As she studied them, she realized one more thing.

"They're not druids…"

Alois gave a short laugh.

"No, mage," he agreed. "They're not druids, although some of them have proven to have the aptitude."

There was a note of hope in his voice that was close to longing.

"We need more druids."

"And what of other forms of magic?"

Although Roeglin tried to keep his voice neutral, he couldn't quite stop a slight tone of reproach. Alois shot him a curious look.

"Why, mage? Are you recruiting?"

Roeglin's face flushed.

"No…" and here, he slid a glance toward Marsh, "but a good friend once told me that everyone had the ability to do magic, even if the types varied."

This earned him a sharp look from Nellee.

"Anyone?" he said, and Roeglin nodded, but he was not alone.

The other four shadow guards answered as one.

"Yes."

"Anyone."

"Even me."

Alois paused, and Nellee looked stunned.

"Can you stay long enough to help us test this theory?" Alois asked, but Gustav shook his head.

He stayed the druid's obvious protest with an upraised hand.

"I *can*, however, arrange for a training contingent of shadow guards and Protectors if we can find them a suitable base nearby."

Nellee answered before Alois.

"The waystation's free."

They walked the mules across the cavern toward the settlement, the trail becoming broader as it followed the cavern wall along to where a large hall had been built by filling in the spaces between pillars. A field fenced by a low stone wall was attached to the back, and it was here Alois had them release the mules before leading them inside.

"You can stay here the night. Longer, if you change your minds about training."

"We can help folk explore their potential this afternoon," Gustav told him, "but we must reach Dimanche and organize an alliance between them, Ruins Hall, and the monastery. If we succeed, you will have help maintaining the trail."

Alois regarded him for a long moment and nodded.

"Very well. I'll send word around and see who is interested. When did you say you could be ready?"

Given it was just coming to the middle of the day cycle, it would have been ungracious to put things off too long.

"We need to wash and change, but after that, we'll be fine."

"And eat," Alois told him. "As promised, I'll cook and send the food over. If folk are ready after lunch, we'll send them to you."

He glanced at Nellee.

"The fields are able to withstand an afternoon of light attention."

"Will you be here?" Gustav asked. "I mean, we can help people find their affinity for shadow and flame and perhaps healing, or calling light for the glows, but an aptitude for plants or rock is something you'd probably do better."

"You can help with discovering potential mind mages too, I gather," Alois added, giving Roeglin a sly grin.

Roeglin turned red and Alois continued, "I *do* know what white eyes mean, boy, and I can tell when you're trying to poke your nose where it doesn't belong."

Roeglin's blush deepened

"I…" He looked at Gustav for help, but the Protector captain only shook his head. "If you do find someone with mind-walking, you might want to remind them that peeking into other people's heads is rude."

He chuckled but hearing him mimic Aisha's precise tones caused an unexpected wave of sadness to crash over Marsh and she turned away, hiding her face until she had the surging emotion under control. Nellee came to her rescue.

"Washrooms are over there," he said. "I'm sure you can find the way."

She looked at Gustav and he nodded, even if his face said he was worried. Whatever it was, he didn't let it distract him from his conversation with Alois, and Marsh slipped away to get clean. By the time she was done, she was not alone. Other cubicles echoed with the sound of happy sighs and scrubbing as water piped through the cavern walls and through cooking fires filled the tubs.

It was a good thing Marsh emerged when she did. Dinner arrived as she chose a place for her sleeping roll and got ready to check on the mules. Mordan had silently followed them into the cavern, drawing raised eyebrows and a part-raised bow from Nellee. Alois had pushed the bow down with his hand.

"Be thankful she didn't take your head when you shot her mistress."

Her mistress? It had been a new one for Marsh, but she hadn't argued. She'd just been happy for Mordan to walk with them unmolested. The kat had refused to go into the washroom, though. She'd sat herself down by shroom burner at one end of the hall and refused to budge. She sat up as the door to the hall opened, a warning growl filling the space between them.

The door paused, and Marsh looked up.

"Dan! Do you want to be fed or not?"

Her words seemed to give whoever was there the courage they needed to enter.

"Hello?"

"Hello," Marsh replied. "How can I help you?"

At the sound of her voice, the door was pushed all the way open and a young woman entered. Her curly dark hair was cut short, and her brown eyes were wary.

"Just make sure it doesn't eat us," she instructed when her gaze found Mordan.

Marsh followed the direction of her look.

"The hoshkat? I've got some jerky for her. She'll be fine."

The woman was horrified by the idea.

"Oh, no. We brought her some rabbits, and there'll be mouton later for her to have in the morning."

Marsh didn't have the heart to tell her that the kat shouldn't eat before traveling. Mordan would eat if she was hungry and carry the meat with her if she wasn't. Either way, there'd be no refusal to insult the people feeding her. Judging from the response she felt from Mordan, rabbits would do just fine.

"Are you staying to see what magic you have?" Marsh asked, and the woman's eyes widened.

"I… Oh, no. I'm a farmer, not a mage. What would I need magic for?"

Marsh frowned.

"You don't need to be a warrior to have magic," she told her. "Everyone has magic."

The woman shook her head.

"I've never shown any sign," she said, unpacking the basket. She turned to her assistant, who seemed to be hanging onto Marsh's every word, "and Lucille has no need."

Her assistant scowled, and Marsh wondered what the matter was between them.

"What brought you to the cavern?"

"Alois warned us there was going to be an attack on our farm. We'd heard of folk disappearing up and down the trade trail, so we decided to trust him, no matter that he was a mage."

Lucille scowled at her mother.

"If we'd known how to use magic, we wouldn't have had to leave at all," she snapped. "I *miss* the farm...and the animals..."

"Alois will fetch them as soon as he can."

"But it's been three days," the girl wailed. "They'll be running short of food."

"We don't know if it's safe," the woman insisted. "Don't be foolish, child."

Where the argument might have gone from there, Marsh didn't know, but she intervened.

"We can help with that," she said, gesturing to the food. "It's the least we can do in return for your hospitality."

Her words were interrupted by a sigh from the washroom door. Gustav stood there, having paused in the middle of toweling the stubble on his head.

"What's she hiring us out for this time?" he demanded

as he resumed rubbing the water from his short-cropped hair and dried his ears.

"To check on the farms," the woman told him as he arrived, "and maybe bring our livestock to safety?"

He slung the towel over one arm and stuck out his hand in greeting.

"Pleased to meet you, Mrs...."

"Vara. Call me Vara," she said, blushing, and Lucille rolled her eyes.

"Mama!"

Gustav pretended not to notice.

"We can do that," he agreed to Marsh's surprise, and he surprised her further by adding, "but only if you come and see what your magic is."

Marsh's eyes grew as wide as saucers and Vara gaped in surprise.

Close your mouth, Marsh, Roeglin said, appearing in the door behind the captain. *You look as surprised as she does.*

Marsh closed her mouth and managed a non-committal look and shrug when Vara turned to her for confirmation.

"He's the captain," she said as if that explained it all.

It pretty much does, Roeglin muttered, advancing across the hall and tucking his pack beside hers.

She noticed he had changed into a fresh uniform, even if it was a bit crumpled from being in the bottom of his pack—and she was glad she'd done the same. Looked like they were going official on this one. Vara looked from one of them to another as though trying to find a second opinion, but in the end, she sighed.

"Very well." She glanced toward the door. "Only, will

this take very long? I promised to spend some time in the fields this afternoon."

"She's afraid the others will arrive and see her," Lucille mocked, and Marsh saw the truth in her mother's rapidly heating face.

To take the pressure off, Marsh turned to the girl.

"Let's start with you, then," she said. "Your mama can watch and try it if she thinks she's ready."

The girl's face lit up, then dimmed with anxiety.

"May I, Mama?"

"Yes, child. If you want to see your chickens again, you'd better."

"Well, *you'd* better do it so that we can get the canards and moutons."

That settled it for Vara, and she came to stand before Marsh, making it clear she was going first and didn't need coddling.

"What do I need to do?"

Caught off-guard, Marsh at a loss, then she had an idea. She caught Roeglin's eye.

"Ever wanted to know exactly what your daughter was thinking?" she asked, and Lucille gasped with horror.

12

FINDING THE MAGIC

In the end, Vara didn't leave before the others arrived, and she took great delight in teasing her daughter.

"Master Leger says I have to practice this every morning and every night," she said, and Lucille groaned.

"Did you *have* to?" she whined, slightly put out that she hadn't been able to see into her mother's mind in return.

"It seemed only fair at the time," the mage answered, "given the amount of teasing you were doing."

The girl pouted, then her face brightened.

"Well, let's see if I can do a fireball, then."

Vara looked momentarily alarmed, then she snickered.

"It would be *one* way to clean your room…" she said as she came to stand beside the girl.

"What are you doing?"

"Well, I've found I can do *one* kind of magic, but I have *two* kinds of animals to test for. It *was* your idea, you know."

"Maamaaa!"

"What's Lucy wailing about now?" asked a voice at the

door, and they turned to discover quite a few of the druid's rescues waiting.

Many of them eyed the kat with uncertainty until she flopped down in front of the fire and closed her eyes. Marsh sent a feeling of appreciation over their link, and the kat huffed out a sigh. Knowing the big beast would stay there until their students had relaxed around her, Marsh bent to the task of helping folk discover what they could and couldn't do.

The afternoon passed quickly, but the results were better than Alois had dared hope. Although most of the farmers and prospectors had come when it became known that Gustav's team would help retrieve any animals from their steadings if people tested their ability, there was not a single person left in the fields. The Protector looked at Marsh.

"This is all your fault," he murmured as the students moved between instructors.

She blushed, torn between apology and defiance. Fortunately, he saved her from having to choose.

"Good work."

By then, their respective students had gathered before them, and they had to focus on helping them see if they had an affinity for healing, shadow, or fire. By the time they had to break for the evening meal, it was time to stop —regardless of whether their students wanted to.

"We need to eat," Gustav had told them, "and you do too, which brings me to another important part of being a mage..."

While Gustav had explained about the dangers of using their magic too much, Marsh, Zeb, Gerry, and Izmay had helped prepare the evening meal, laughing when the kat got up to pointedly sniff at the haunch of mouton that had been brought.

"Now?" Marsh asked her. "You know the rabbits were supposed to be enough, don't you?"

From the look on the kat's face, she did not. Marsh sighed.

"You'd better not be hungry in the morning. We've got a long day ahead of us."

Longer than they'd wanted and Master Envermet was not pleased when they took a second night's sojourn in the druid's cavern.

"He says he's only two days behind us," Gustav told them when he and Roeglin returned.

"And he wants our tails on the trail first thing in the morning," Roeglin added.

Alois looked disappointed.

"I was hoping…" he began, and Roeglin's eyes flashed white.

He followed it with a look of apology.

"I'm sorry," he said. "I cannot take them. We don't know when we will return to the monastery or what dangers we will encounter on the road from Dimanche."

"Take who?" Gustav asked, and Roeglin explained.

"Alois was hoping we'd take those with shadow ability back to the monastery with us." He stilled Gustav's refusal with a slightly upraised hand. "It's okay. I will consult with Master Envermet and the Master of Shadows. I believe they will want the waystation as an outpost."

He turned to the druid.

"If they do that, our people could patrol the trade routes together."

"What do you mean?"

And Roeglin told him about the plan to set up a group of soldiers to guard the trade routes and the communities of the Four Caverns.

"Five," the druid declared, indicating the cavern above the hall. "This one makes five."

"Soon to be six," Marsh reminded them. "Once we have defeated the raiders, the folk of Leon's Deep will want to go home."

"How will they do that?" Alois wanted to know. "Weren't they all taken?"

Marsh gave him a look of pure determination.

"I will be getting them back."

"All of them?" he pressed, and her heart sank.

There was no way that all of them would be alive to *be* retrieved, but that wasn't going to stop her from trying.

"As many of them as I can," she told him. "It is one of the reasons we are uniting the caverns. Once they are able to defend themselves, I'll be able to hunt the raiders down to the source."

Roeglin laid a hand on her shoulder.

"*We'll* be able to hunt them down," he corrected, and from around them came five more confirmations.

Marsh lifted her head in surprise and met Izmay's determined gaze.

"What? You didn't think we'd let you finish the job on your own, did you?" she said. "Not when you've dragged us this far."

"*Especially* not when you've dragged us this far," Henri

added, looking torn between anger, resentment, and utter determination not to be left behind.

Marsh opened her mouth to say something, but couldn't find the words and ended up imitating a beached fish. Roeglin reached over and placed his finger beneath her jaw, closing it.

"That's decided," he said, "and we'll talk more about how we're going to go about it when we're back at the monastery."

There was a finality to his tone that defied anyone to argue with him and silence fell. Fortunately, Alois had obviously been thinking over their plans for the Protectors.

"We've found a way of recharging the glows," he said, reminding Marsh of a topic Gustav had meant to pursue earlier, "and we've been training more of our people how to fight, although getting the weapons was going to be difficult."

He cast a look at the shadow guards.

"That's a lot easier now that so many can call on the shadows to protect them."

"And the rocks," Gustav reminded him.

"And fire," Izmay added, looking far too pleased with herself.

They'd been surprised to find a half dozen who'd taken to creating fireballs, and pleasantly surprised to discover many of those could also draw life energy from their surroundings to heal—even if the latter did not necessarily parallel their ability with flame.

"You'll be welcome to train with the Protectors too," Gustav told them. "I'll arrange a meeting with Master

Envermet, and the two of you can discuss what that might look like.

Alois turned to Roeglin with a look of concern.

"I'm truly sorry for training those who came to me," he said. "They had no one else, and I did not know when your people might come around again…and then there were the raiders, pressuring people to give up their children. It's why I took them in. I knew your people would be coming and would never use such tactics. I should have told you before…"

Roeglin shrugged. He'd been caught off-guard when he'd discovered the druid had been helping some of those with shadow abilities, but not upset—and he'd already guessed why.

"You have nothing to apologize for. If you hadn't helped them, there would have been no one else. And you saved them, and didn't treat them as cursed or outcasts." He paused. "Did *you* take the mules from the waystation?"

The druid nodded.

"Oh, yes. Couldn't have the poor beasts starving. They've been a big help here."

Marsh could only imagine they had, and she was glad, which left only one thing more.

"If you knew the raiders were on the trail, why didn't you warn the caravan?"

The druid looked shocked.

"Oh, but I did. I told them there was something on their trail, but they were sure they could make it to the surface, and when I warned the waystation, they said their walls and gates would be enough. They didn't count on someone impersonating a trader and opening the gate from the inside. I couldn't save a single one."

He looked so sad that Marsh laid her hand on his knee.

"You did your best," she said and looked at Roeglin. "Someone told me once that I couldn't save them all, and he was right."

"It doesn't make it any easier to live with," the druid told her, but Marsh shook her head.

"It will. You just have to accept the truth of it—and acknowledge that you did all you could do short of drugging them and stuffing them in a sack...which I'm told is not allowed."

Alois managed a smile at that.

"Yes," he admitted. "There is that."

"Were there any other travelers beyond the lone merchant, the raiders, and the wagon train?"

"No. Wait." Alois's brow furrowed. "Yes, there *was* one, and I couldn't understand why the raiders didn't attack him as well. They'd heard him coming and hidden on either side of the trail, and I was sure they'd take him just like they'd taken the others, but they didn't lift a finger. Just watched him pass. It was very strange."

"Can you describe him?"

"Oh, yes. Narrow-faced fellow with long, dark hair. Build as thin as a cane, with an expression that would have curdled milk. I didn't like the look of him. No. Not at all."

"Salazar," Marsh growled, and Mordan echoed her from her place beside the fire.

Roeglin laid an arm across her shoulders and squeezed her.

"We'll get him," he said. "We'll even manage it before he vanishes back into the Desolation or the Deeps."

"Promise?" she asked, but he shook his head.

"No promises save that we'll try."

"I'll take it."

"And speaking of taking things," Alois said. "What shall I tell my people with shadow ability?"

"Tell them they will have perhaps three choices: they can stay with you and train with the shadow guard when the Protectors set up in the waystation, they can join the Protectors, or they can wait for a changeover of personnel from the monastery and go with them to apprentice there."

Alois looked relieved.

"I…thank you," he said. "Now, is there anything else you want to know?"

"The glows…" Roeglin began. "How do you charge them? I mean, we take the light energy from the shadow and charge the crystals with it, but you… How do you manage it?"

For a moment the druid looked anxious, and Gustav sought to soothe him.

"We're not worried about who does what. We just want to know how. Perhaps it is something we can share with the rock mages so that more glows can be charged and the trails returned to life more swiftly."

Alois relaxed.

"It is simple," he said. "I had not thought there might be light in the shadows but I know that there is light in the shrooms, because they have lit the caverns since before I was born—and I know the shadow monsters do not like it because they always stick to the darker parts of the caverns or find ways to destroy the shrooms before they enter. I just asked the shrooms to share their light energy, then put the energy into the glows. It doesn't harm them since it's like healing energy, something they can replenish."

Marsh stared at him, and Roeglin nudged her in the ribs.

"You know you have to try this, right?"

"Already there," Marsh said and looked around the cavern.

"Does it matter what kind of shrooms you ask?" she wanted to know, and Alois shook his head. "I don't think so. I just prefer the lumins, since their light is closest to the color of the light the shadow mages use. Do you want me to help you?"

"Oh, Deeps yes!"

The druid's smile was almost a reward in itself, but discovering that Roeglin had brought a dead glow was almost her undoing.

"You knew!" she accused, but he shook his head.

"I hoped," he corrected. "Now, are you going to stand there waving that thing in my face, or are you going to go with Alois and see if you can learn something new?"

For a moment Marsh was tempted to swat him with the glow stick, but she didn't want to break it on his armor, so she hurried to where Alois was waiting beside a cluster of several different types of light-producing shrooms.

"Right," she said, examining them. "How do we do this?"

"You mean how do *you* do this?" Alois corrected but continued before Marsh could answer, "It's like healing or scanning for life energy. You just reach out with the part of you that's connected to your magic, and you can feel the energy that is shroom light. After that, it's like healing: you take some from the shroom and guide it into the glow."

He made it sound easy, but Marsh couldn't quite grasp it. She stared at the dead glow in her hand and looked up at the shrooms. What made it harder was the fact the others had gathered a short distance away to see how it worked… at least, that was what she kept telling herself.

They weren't there to judge. They were just there to see how it was done. She could do this. What had Geralt said? She was thinking about it the wrong way. She was…Marsh closed her eyes. It was hard to process what Geralt had tried to show her.

Like the poison, Marsh, Roeglin murmured, breaking through some of the confusion. *Remember?*

"The poison…" Marsh echoed, and the druid's voice was sharp in query.

"What poison?"

Marsh opened her eyes.

"Shadow-monster poison," she replied. "I draw it out of the wound and catch it in a cloth or something that can absorb it. Roeglin was just reminding me."

She tilted her head and scowled at the mage.

"But I can't work out what that has to do with recharging the glows. I—"

"The poison is a natural substance, and you call it like you would call healing energy," Alois interrupted. "It's the same way you can call the shadows, and even summon a little fire."

Marsh blushed as his voice took on a teasing note. He'd watched them call fire and seen her used as an example to soothe recruits disappointed by their apparent lack of ability. He knew she struggled with fire. Alois didn't give her time to dwell on it for long.

"And yet healing energy comes easily when you ask." He looked up at the purple glow of the calla shrooms. "Their light is more like that than fire. Find the part of you connected to your magic and reach out with that."

With a sigh, Marsh knelt.

"I don't want to fall over," she explained. "It wrecks the concentration."

"Fair enough."

Alois knelt beside her.

"Now try to feel the light."

Marsh closed her eyes and did what she did when she was focusing on finding the life forces of those around her or when she was sensing the natural energy flowing through the environment. First, she found the calla shroom and concentrated on its energy. As she did, she felt its life— its energy—beating strong in its trunk.

She followed it as it flowed from earth to stem and up into the caps. At first, she didn't notice any difference, but as she approached the calla's gills, she felt the change. Some of the energy flowed back through the underside of the cap and back into the shroom stem, returning to the earth. The rest...

"Oh..." The word came out on a breath.

Keeping the energy fixed firmly in her mind, Marsh drove the glow into the earth so that it stood just as it would beside a trail. Stepping away from it, she wove her hands through the air, gathering the calla's light into a glowing ball. When she had it balanced on one palm, she used the fingers of her other hand to draw it down toward the glow.

The motion was similar to what the spinners of mouton wool used to draw the fleece into a thread, only this time she poured the thread of light into the glow. From the gasps she heard from the slowly gathering crowd, it was working more effectively than anyone had expected...Including Alois.

"Remember to leave some for the shroom."

His soft voice interrupted her, and she realized she'd been so fascinated by the way the light moved through her hands that she'd taken most of what the calla had to offer.

"Oh."

Thinking about it, she lofted the ball back to the underside of the calla's cap, feeling the warmth of its energy bathing her as its soft light lit the air around her. Near her feet, the glow blazed like a captive sun. Marsh made sure she separated the thread between the calla and the glow and looked down at what she'd done.

The glow was bright enough to make her eyes water, and she felt her jaw drop. A slow clapping rose from the shadow guards, and they came closer to admire her handiwork.

I knew you could do it, Roeglin said, and she heard enough pride in his voice to wonder how lighting a glow could have earned it.

He didn't answer that, but wrapped his arm around her shoulders and gave her a quick hug.

Even Gustav was impressed.

"Nicely done."

Even though she'd done something she hadn't done

before, Marsh felt strangely energized instead of exhausted. When they'd returned to the hall, she turned to Alois.

"There's so much I don't know…"

"Where would you like to start?"

"I…don't know. Where *should* I start?"

"You don't have a lot of time," Gustav reminded her, stopping by their table. "We leave early."

Marsh sighed, but Gustav had already turned away. Roeglin slipped into a seat beside her.

"He didn't say you *couldn't* start…"

The man had a point and Marsh was glad he'd made it, even if she couldn't work out why he stayed as she turned back to the druid. Alois took that as a signal to begin.

"You could start with the names of the living things you see," Alois told her. "*That* is something you can do on the road. You can also ask those around you what they know about each one, and perhaps get one of the rock mages to guide you when you return."

He glanced at Roeglin.

"That *is* possible, isn't it?"

The mage smiled and laid a hand over Marsh's.

"Yes," he said, and the discussion continued until the fire had burned low, and Marsh gave a jaw-cracking yawn.

Alois stood and brushed aside her apology.

"One of the lessons you must learn is to listen to your body. It is easier to learn what others need for healing when you are in tune with what you need for yourself."

He was right. She knew that, but it didn't make saying goodbye any easier.

"I will see you in the morning," he assured her. "How else are you going to be able to leave the cavern?"

Marsh hadn't thought of that, and she went to sleep more easily because of it, frowning as Roeglin laid his bedroll next to hers.

"What?" he asked. "I'm just sleeping, is all."

Marsh said nothing, but when she stood there for more than a few heartbeats, he bent to pick it up.

"I can always go sleep near Henri…"

The thought made her laugh, and she discovered that she did *not* want him sleeping near the other caravan guard.

"No. You can stay," she told him. "That way, if anything attacks, it's got a good chance of eating you first."

She turned away before Roeglin could think of a suitable response, sliding into her bedroll and turning her back on where he'd chosen to sleep. It was hard not to smile when Mordan settled her great bulk between the two rolls.

13

SHROOM FIRE

Gustav was true to his word.

They left early the next morning, eating a quick breakfast before collecting their mules and following Alois out onto the trail. To Marsh's surprise, Vara and Lucille were there to bid them goodbye.

"I just wanted to thank you," Vara said, coming alongside Marsh. "I'd have never learned of my gifts if you hadn't insisted."

"You're welcome," Marsh said. "You never know when you'll need them."

Vara cast a sly look at her daughter, followed by an evil smile.

"No, you never do."

The girl blushed as red as a beet and glowered at Marsh.

"*Oui*," she said. "Thanks a lot."

They left the cavern the same way they'd entered and were soon back on the trail, Marsh riding beside Gustav and using her nature and shadow magic to scan the tunnel ahead. It didn't leave her any time to ask about the fungi and insects she saw along the way, but she got the impression that none of the guards knew much more than she did. It was something she planned to ask when they set up camp.

A good idea, Roeglin told her. *Now focus.*

Marsh wanted to tell him that she wasn't the only one that should be focusing, but she didn't need to. He'd already turned to the front, his eyes flashing white before he closed them, trusting the mule to follow the trail without his guidance.

They'd traveled a half-day when she sensed the first ambush.

"We have—"

Raiders.

Roeglin's voice inside her head reminded her that she didn't need to speak aloud. His next communication confirmed it.

Ten each side. First cluster of four will let us pass and block the trail behind us when the six ahead of them spring the trap.

There was a pause before he spoke again, and Marsh knew he was speaking for Gustav.

We ride on. Marsh, have Mordan deal with the four at the back. Engage those closest as soon as you see them.

His words gave Marsh an idea and she scanned the trail ahead, pinpointing the location of each of the ten men and women waiting in the shadows at the base of the calla and rock formations.

See them, huh? She might actually be able to do something about that.

Deciding that if she could see the callas' glow and sense the life forces of the raiders crouching beneath them, she should be able to sense the energy of the shroom's light, Marsh focused on the six who would spring the trap.

First, she needed some light…

It was difficult to draw the shrooms' light energy while she rode but not impossible. Behind her, Marsh heard a sharp intake of breath and a muffled hushing, but she refused to let it distract her. When she was sure she'd gathered enough, she draped her reins over the pommel of her saddle and held up one hand as though she held the ball of light in its palm, then began drawing down a thread of light, connecting it to the first man's head.

Once she'd gotten it flowing, she drew a second thread of light, tweaking the first to keep it flowing while she directed the second thread to wind itself around the second raider's head. She started directing the third thread onto the third man as they passed the first pair of raiders.

It was as they passed the second set that the raiders opposite those she was wrapping in light noticed what was happening.

Get ready, Roeglin warned. *Ours are unlit. Speak to Mordan.*

It was good of him to realize she'd forgotten and remind her while she still had time to do it. Marsh separated the threads from the ball of light and sent what remained back to the underside of the calla shrooms from which she'd taken it.

Ahead of them, someone gave a sharp exclamation of surprise, but that wasn't what caught Marsh's eye. The raiders hadn't let their suddenly highly visible companions distract them for long.

"Bows!" she shouted as the flaming outline of life showed those on her side preparing to fire into them.

Without waiting for Gustav's instruction, she slid from her mule's back, drawing a buckler and sword from the dark and sliding into shadow before her feet had touched the ground. Roeglin followed in more tangible form as she headed for the closest raider.

His aim wavered between the two of them, and Marsh caught his crossbow bolt on her buckler.

"Yours," she said, stepping past him to attack the next one along, knowing Roeglin could see what she saw because he had the cheek to be looking through her eyes to catch the outline of their life forces and pin their location in his mind.

"Got him," she said as Gustav drove his mule past the two raiders closest him to allow Henri and Izmay to engage them.

Mordan roared from behind them, and the mules bolted. Zeb cursed as the kat shouldered him out of her path, knocking him into a patch of brown noses as she passed. Mordan roared again, and Jakob shouted in reply as a raider screamed.

"Again!"

But the kat didn't oblige. Judging from the next scream, Mordan had taken down her first victim and left Jakob to kill his own prey. She didn't have time to concentrate any further because the raider she'd attacked had blocked her first strike and was pushing back. She blocked a vicious strike to her gut and used the buckler to push his blade up and away.

He wasn't fast enough to block her counter-thrust with the dagger he wielded in his off hand, and he went down with a wound in his chest. He didn't stay down though, and Marsh had to finish him as he tried to rise. It made her sick to the stomach, but she didn't have time for regrets.

The third raider moved to take advantage of her distraction, and she barely got her shield up in time. The force of the raider's attack pushed her back, and she almost tripped over the one she'd just killed. As she struggled to regain her balance, Roeglin proved he was no gentleman, slashing her opponent across the lower back and making a second cut before they could turn to parry.

Together, they scanned the surrounding shrooms for more before turning to see where they were most needed. Gustav was already walking down the trail after the mules. He was making chirruping noises as he went, but Marsh doubted they'd come. She figured they'd have at least an hourglass of walking before they caught up with their escaping mounts.

Zeb, Izmay, Jakob, Gerry, and Henri had gathered in a cluster around one of the raiders and Marsh went to see why.

When she got there, she saw the man was as dead as the rest of their opponents but that his corpse still glowed with the purple luminescence she'd borrowed from the calla shrooms.

"Not a bad idea," Henri said as she came up. "Made him a lot easier to hit."

Marsh didn't know whether to be glad or not. Now she

could light up her enemies for her friends. It should have been a comfort, but she could hear the raider who had attacked her at Midpoint: "At least they get to live."

He'd been talking about his wife and children. He'd refused to surrender or to change sides because he'd wanted to keep his family safe. Looking at the glowing corpse before her, she could only wonder if this man had been fighting for the same reason. It took her a moment before she realized the guards were all staring at her.

"What?" Henri demanded. "You did good."

As if that was supposed to be *any* comfort.

"I'd better give the calla back its energy," she said to change the subject, and she closed her eyes.

She had to open them moments later so she could direct the energy, but the need to focus saved her from the swirl of sadness that had threatened to overwhelm her. Envermet's words clung.

It is never wrong to mourn the loss of a life, or the lost potential for that life to have been used for other, better things.

With a twirl of her fingers, she had the light disentangle itself from the fallen raider and directed it to the shroom. Try as she might, the sadness swirled back, and she ducked her head to hide the tears that threatened to fall. She didn't know whether to be grateful or angry when Roeglin settled his arm around her shoulders and turned her away from the others.

Instead of turning her into his chest, he merely moved her so she was facing the next glow-lit raider and let her return the light energy she had borrowed for him too.

"Best we don't highlight our presence," he said, and

Marsh felt a smile quiver along her lips even as she sent the luminescence back to the shrooms.

"If we lit them on fire, would the energy dissipate or keep burning?" he mused, and Marsh knew the thought would haunt her until she tried it.

The opportunity to do so came far sooner than any of them would have liked.

They'd resigned themselves to walking, and Marsh was wondering just how far a frightened mule would run when the first unearthly screech echoed out of a side tunnel.

"You have got to be shitting me," Henri grumbled, drawing his sword. He glared at Marsh. "Why didn't you see *this* coming?"

Marsh didn't bother answering him. She couldn't be everywhere at once, and he knew it. Instead, she reached out and curled her fingers through the scruff of Mordan's neck.

"Stay," she murmured and the kat tilted her head to look at her, sending a protest over the link between them.

Roeglin caught it and looked at Marsh.

"Hunt them together," he said, and Gustav gave a sharp nod of agreement.

"Close the gate."

It was all the permission they needed. Marsh shifted to take on the substance of shadow, her hand allowing her to transfer the shift to Mordan. She wasn't ready for the kat to shake herself free of Marsh's grip and step into the closest patch of shadow with the same practiced ease Marsh did.

What the... The rest of Roeglin's question was left behind as Marsh followed the kat.

Just when and how the kat had managed it would have to wait until after the shadow monsters had been defeated...and she'd killed the shadow raider mages who'd summoned them. It was strange, but she didn't feel the same pang of sorrow for their deaths as she did for the soldiers. It was as though she thought they were somehow more responsible.

But that didn't matter now. What mattered was that she killed the mages and broke their connection with the portal they'd opened between the shadow monsters and the trail. She strode through the shadows, stepping from one patch of darkness to another and moving more swiftly than would have been possible in her solid human form.

They reached the entrance to the side cavern and Mordan led the way through, the kat picking a path even faster than Marsh could.

This way, the kat directed, showing her the trail to take. *There.*

Marsh felt a moment of disconnection as she saw something that wasn't anywhere in view. It took her a few seconds to realize she was seeing through Mordan's eyes, then she saw the mages. There were four, not two.

How big a gate did they intend to open, anyway?

It was a question that didn't have an easy answer, save that the portal they'd created was already larger than any she'd yet seen—and it was growing larger by the heartbeat. Again her vision shifted, but this time two of the mages were highlighted.

Mine. Mordan laid her claim with clear precision and followed it by highlighting the second two. *Yours.*

Marsh found herself alone as the kat cut the link,

leaving Marsh with the distinct impression that "mommy was busy."

"Not your cub," she muttered, but the kat didn't respond. She focused instead on the two mages Mordan had said were hers to take.

She noticed how they'd gathered in the bright glow of a cluster of calla shrooms and golden gleams and remembered Alois telling her that the shadow monsters tended to shun the light. It was curious, since the mages were clearly visible, and yet the monsters racing out of the portal paid them hardly any attention. It was as though the maddened creatures already had a target in mind, and the mages were nothing beside it.

Perhaps they planned to come back and kill them later. Marsh wouldn't put it past them. Right now that wasn't her problem. Her problem was taking the mages out and trying to kill as many of the monsters as she could because there was no way Gustav and the others could stop them if she didn't.

Roeglin.

I've got it. We'll discuss you talking to me when you get back.

They would, and the realization of what she'd just done almost broke her concentration to the point she dropped out of shadow form right then and there. She'd just spoken mind to mind!

Don't let it go to your head.

Like she ever could. She had to live to do that.

Mordan's hunting yowl screeched across the cavern, and Marsh chose the next point to step to. If she didn't hurry, the kat would start the party without her. She stepped out into the shadow behind the calla grove where the two mages were sheltering.

Mordan must have seen her because she sent a growl rolling out toward her and one of her mages screamed. Marsh didn't wait any longer. Instead of pulling sword and buckler from the shadows, she pulled a dart and flung it at the closest mage before charging across the open ground between her and the next mage.

He'd raised his hand as though to summon a weapon, but Marsh gave him no time. She plucked a second dart from the darkness and hurled it through his chest, and had the momentary taste of blood as teeth rent flesh and Mordan took down the second of her targets. As the taste faded, the portal snapped shut, shredding the monsters that were only part-way through as it winked out of existence.

The kat let out another roar, this one full of belligerence and challenge. Marsh saw the last of the shadow monsters falter, then continue to run in the direction they'd been going. She thought about calling the lightning, then realized that the opening to the cavern had been flanked with brown noses, but that groves of calla and brevilar had grown a little farther back on either side.

Their luminescence had mingled in almost separate streams, but it had been there. Marsh looked for it and saw how the monsters squeezed together to avoid passing through any but the very edges of the shroom light, then remembered what Roeglin had said about setting them alight. It would be *one* way to thin their numbers.

Wait, she ordered the kat, and reached for the energy running through the cavern.

It was easy to find now that she knew what she was looking for, and the calla-brevilar groves were thick with it. She drew on the light energy, but didn't try to gather it into a ball. Instead she lifted it in a rolling cloud above the shadow monsters...

And called the heat.

Just like she'd called it when she'd first been trying to light a glow.

She drew the heat into the light and directed the entire sheet to drop down onto the rearmost monsters, winding tendrils of burning light around and through them as they ran. Roeglin's cry of alarm reached her just as she realized what she'd done.

You're going to set the cavern alight.

His voice was accompanied by a growl of alarm from Mordan and the kat bounded over to where she was standing, seizing her by the hand and trying to drag her away. When that didn't work and Marsh stood there staring at the inferno building in the midst of the shadow monsters, the kat switched tactics.

She knocked Marsh off her feet with a swipe of her paw and seized her by the shirt, bounding into one patch of shadow and out of another as she tried to put some distance between them and the fireball. When they'd gone as far as the cavern would allow, she dumped Marsh behind an outcrop of rocks and crouched over her.

Marsh, you need to do something about that.

Marsh wondered what Roeglin was shouting about, but she had to fight Mordan to get the kat to let her up enough to look.

"Oh, the Deep's dirty-assed britches and shag-ended shrooms!"

Nice...

Shut it, Ro.

Marsh took another look out from behind the rock and felt heat lick at her face. The man was right for a change. She really *did* have to do something about that. But what?

It wasn't like she could return the light to the shrooms. She had to... She needed... She peered out from behind the outcrop again. What did she do with the shadows and the lightning? She sent them back, sent the energy to the form it used to have. She calmed them.

She looked at the fire and knew she didn't have much time. The shadow monsters had spread it through the cavern in their panicked attempts to evade it and now the light was everywhere, clinging to the bodies of the dead monsters and slowly shriveling the shrooms closest. She had to send the light back, dissipate the heat...

Taking a deep breath, Marsh focused on the center of the fire. She had no time to nibble at the edges. If she didn't take care of the core of the firestorm she'd made, there'd be no time to deal with the rest. She thought about the light, thanking the shrooms for lending their energy and light and sending it back to them. She thanked the heat also, treating it the same way she treated the shadows, dispersing it back to where it had come from...and she discovered she had another problem.

The fire she had created had spawned more fire. Parts of the cavern were burning that hadn't burned before, and she had more heat to deal with than she'd had when she started. She had to find somewhere for the extra heat to go…or something for it to burn itself out on. Her sight fell on a shadow monster corpse. Now that it wasn't coated in shroom light, it was rapidly cooling, and would soon become just another carcass rotting in a cavern.

It would attract scavengers, and they would attract… The memory of the shadow wraith came unbidden and she shivered. Better if there were no corpses to draw that kind of attention. It took a little bit of effort to guide the extra heat and flame to the bodies left behind by the shroom light but she managed it, even if it was Izmay who saw what she was doing and finished the task with only a fraction of the energy Marsh was using.

"You're an idiot," Roeglin told her when he'd picked his way across the cavern and found her propped against the outcrop.

"Quit your bitching. They're dead, aren't they?"

"It's going to stink of burnt shadow monster for weeks," he told her as he helped her across the cavern.

Izmay and the others joined them as they got to the other side. It wasn't until Marsh stepped into the tunnel through which the trail ran that she had any idea of how far the fires had spread. Roeglin caught the look on her face.

"We were lucky we had Izmay…and Henri and Zeb…" He indicated the ex-caravan guard and the dark-haired shadow guard, who sat propped against each other.

Gustav turned away from them as they approached.

"You'd better have some healing left in you," he growled. "We can't camp here."

He had a point, and Marsh headed across to crouch beside the pair. Henri scowled.

"This does not get you out of dinner."

Marsh ignored him as the shadow guard gave her a weak smile.

"Any excuse to get your hands on me."

Marsh tried to scowl at him but she couldn't. That smile was too infectious.

"Just keep telling yourself that."

"He'd better not."

She might have asked Roeglin where he'd gotten the idea he had any say who she put her hands on, but she didn't. Instead, she focused on finding the energy to draw on to help Zeb and Henri. She should have realized the fires would have had a greater impact than she'd planned. The damage had left the surroundings low on life.

Mordan surprised her by pushing her head under the hand Marsh had placed on the ground.

Pride, the kat sent, emphasizing the thought with an anxious rumble and the idea that she had the energy to spare.

Marsh wound her arm around the kat's neck and leaned into her, taking just a little of what the big beast was offering and pushing enough of it into Zeb and Henri for the guards to regain their feet.

"It's enough," Zeb told her. "We just have to catch up with the mules."

At his words, Henri gave an exaggerated sniff.

"We're never getting the mules back," he muttered morosely. "Not with the stink you've created."

"*A putain a vous*," Marsh snapped and turned away, taking her place beside Gustav and not protesting when Roeglin came to walk beside her.

Mordan pushed her way in between them, casting the mage a defiant look as she did so.

"You'd better protect her from Henri then," he told the kat, and Mordan flicked her tail in a way that said Henri could try.

"As if I would," Henri muttered. "She still owes me dinner."

14

DIMANCHE AT LAST

They didn't catch up with the mules until they'd reached the outskirts of Dimanche. The creatures had found themselves a quiet patch of shrooms to browse in and were standing together beneath the golden glow of a cluster of brevilar.

"You sodding ungrateful beasts," Henri shouted as they turned their heads to watch them approach and then slowly moved away.

Mordan, Marsh thought and the kat slunk swiftly and silently off the trail, appearing in front of the mules shortly thereafter. Gustav's mount ducked its head and pawed the air in front of her but the kat stood her ground, flattening her ears and curling her lips in a silent snarl. When the mule repeated its actions, she hissed at it and it backed away, glancing back at the advancing humans.

"Easy there," Gustav murmured, and indicated the kat. "You know I'm a better option."

He chirruped at it, unbuckling the flap of his belt pouch. The mule caught the movement of his hand and its ears came forward. When he pulled his hand out, it snuffed the air.

"Wait here," Gustav told the others and walked forward, his hand closed around whatever he'd taken out of the pouch.

The mule watched him come, snorting as he got closer but stretching out its neck so it could investigate what he held in his hand. Gustav let it snuffle at his closed knuckles, resisting the questing nibbles of its lips until it had stepped close enough for him to grasp its bridle.

"Easy there. See? It's not so bad. Here you go…" And he uncurled his fingers so that it could take the shroom ball from his palm.

While it crunched happily, he took its reins and began inspecting it for any injuries. When he was done with that, he checked its tack, making sure everything was in order and that no sensitivity lurked when he ran his hands under the edges. When he was sure it was okay, he checked the girth and swung into the saddle.

The mule danced a little under him but it didn't protest, and Gustav signaled them to come collect their mounts.

"You'll need these," he added and tossed each of them one of the shroom balls out of his pouch.

Marsh sniffed the one she caught and understood why the mule had stayed. The sticky sweet smell of candy cap caught her nostrils, tempting her to eat the thing herself, but she caught the interested lift of her mount's head and decided it deserved something for the fright they'd caused it.

She tried to catch its eye as she walked toward it, seeking to connect with it and reassure that it was safe. It bobbed its head, snorting for a few strides as it resisted her call.

"I have candy cap..." she called, holding the shroom ball where it could see it, and it stopped.

Marsh watched the flare of its nostrils as it sought the scent of what it could see in her hand, and it met her gaze and accepted her contact. It was happy to see her, Marsh realized as the connection between them flared to life... even if she was the reason the kat was always so close.

Marsh reminded it that the kat was the reason they had been able to keep it safe, and watched as its ears drooped to either side. It had forgotten the kat was there to protect it, and its next burst of curiosity felt a little sheepish.

Did she really intend to give it the sweet shroom?

The unspoken desire made Marsh laugh.

"Of course, I do, you silly beast. Come here."

Once it had arrived, Marsh followed Gustav's example, feeding it the shroom ball and taking its reins as she inspected it for injury and adjusted the girth before mounting. All around her, the other mules were slowly letting the shadow guards mount, and they were soon riding past the first stone structures that told them they'd arrived in Dimanche.

The anger in the raised voices coming from the town square was unexpected, and Gustav signaled a stop before they reached it.

"We'll tether the mules here," he said. "Scatter through the back and try to blend in."

"Blend in, huh?" The voice came from a sheltered doorway ahead of them. "And why would you want to do that?"

They all turned to look, Gustav freezing half in and half out of the saddle before dismounting entirely. The woman who stepped out of the doorway was of the same slight build as Marsh and the rest, but her long straight dark hair, dark eyes, and well-defined features gave her a slightly exotic look.

"We're new in town," Gustav explained, keeping a firm grip on the mule's reins. "We blend in, we might be able ta learn somethin' to keep ourselves outta trouble."

He'd dropped into the way of speaking he'd used when he was with Greta, Marsh noted, and she wondered why.

"Not doing a very good job of that, are ya?" the woman replied, and Marsh heard the shift of accent in her tones as well.

"Never did," Gustav said, turning to look over his shoulder.

Marsh turned to follow his gaze and realized Mordan was nowhere to be seen.

Dan? she asked, seeking the kat via the connection between them.

She felt a faint reassurance in response, and the urgent need for silence.

"Where are you, girl?" Marsh asked, turning her mule and preparing to ride back the way she'd come.

She should have thought to keep the kat close, but she'd been so distracted by the stone buildings that made up the town that she'd forgotten her—again.

You're not the only one, Roeglin told her as if he had any responsibility for Mordan's welfare. *You'd be surprised.*

Oh, she would, would she? Well, that was just another

topic they could add to that talk they hadn't had yet. How many were they up to, now?

Mind-speaking, Mordan... What else was there?

For the life of her, Marsh couldn't remember, but she was sure there was something. Roeglin shrugged, turning his mule to follow her.

We'll think of it.

"And just where do you think the pair of you are going?" Gustav wanted to know.

"Dan," Marsh replied, and he sighed.

"Yes. Fetch her."

"We can find your companion," the woman said, but Gustav shook his head.

"You don't know what to look for."

"And since when has that ever stopped us?" The woman sounded amused.

Gustav's reply wiped the smile from her face.

"Since this companion..." He stopped and shrugged. "Let's just say it would be better if the mages go and find her. Safer all round."

"Ooh, safer. Now you *do* have me intrigued. Very well, they can go fetch your companion."

Marsh tapped the mule in the ribs and turned it, then realized why the woman had sounded like she'd thought she could stop them from going anywhere. An archer had appeared at each of the second-floor windows across the street. There were six in all, and six crossbowmen in the floor above that—all with their bows drawn or cocked.

She froze, staring up at them, and glanced at the captain.

"Go along, Marsh. I'll still be here when you get back."

The expression on his face was much less reassuring than his tone of voice. His tone said it was okay for her to go. The look on his face said he didn't have a choice, and he needed them to return. Roeglin nudged her.

He'll be okay.

Hiding her misgivings from her face, Marsh kicked the mule into a trot.

Where are you? she wanted to know, and the kat gave her the impression of a flat stone roof with a low wall surrounding the lip so the children wouldn't fall off.

Children?

There were three, all more enamored by the big kat's presence and the softness of her fur than their mother.

"Uta, Simel, Tanith, you leave the kitty alone and come over here right now!"

The urgent call reached Marsh's ears as she pulled the mule to a halt in front of one of the first houses they'd passed on their way in.

"Can't get me," one small voice cried.

"No, can't get *me*," sang out another.

"Me! Me! Me!"

"Children!"

Marsh arrived just as the woman took a tentative step toward where Mordan was sitting, three small forms crawling over her shoulders and back, with the kat pretending to try and swat them with a very lazy paw. The fact the kat had no intention of swatting anyone was clear, but the fact she appeared to be trying was enough to have the woman nervous. Marsh stepped around the woman, ignoring her startled glance and Roeglin's very formal "Pardon me, ma'am."

"Dan," she began, "those are not your cubs. You can't keep them."

The kat gave her an obliging growl of protest.

"No. I'm serious. You need to give them back to their mother and get your tail back to me, or there's..." She thought fast. "There'll be no mouton for you tonight."

No mouton? The kat was laughing at her inside her head, but the look on her face was one of mortification. She carefully stood, keeping one child on her back and picking the nearest up by the back of its shirt. With a long-suffering sigh, she looked at Marsh.

"Give. Them. Back," Marsh repeated, pointing an authoritative finger at the mother as though she thought the kat was having second thoughts. "Honestly, Dan. It's the same in every single town. I can't take you anywhere."

"Every town?" the woman asked.

"Oh, yes," Roeglin answered as Mordan brought the child back to its mother. "Every town. Raiders took her cubs, so she tries to adopt nearly every place we go. We're trying to catch up to them, but so far no luck."

He gave a very eloquent shrug and sighed.

"I don't suppose..."

From the way the woman's eyes widened with fear and the very hasty shake of her head, she knew more about raiders than she was willing to tell. Marsh and Roeglin didn't press her, but watched as she pulled the little boy from Mordan's back and picked up the girl the kat had deposited at her feet. The third child stood at the edge of the roof scowling.

"No," she said. "Not going."

Mordan walked over to her and licked her face.

"No..." the little girl giggled and squealed with delight when the kat picked her up and took her back to her mother.

"I'm really very sorry about this," Marsh said, burying her hand in Mordan's scruff. "We'll go now."

"I...it's fine..." the woman replied and closed her mouth as though she didn't know what to say next.

15

AN OLD FLAME

Marsh left her and descended back to the ground floor and out into the street, wondering what the kat had thought she was doing.

Hiding, the kat told her, and gave her the impression of an empty roof and surprised mortification on being pounced on by three small children when their mother brought them up to play.

Marsh had to laugh, and Mordan shot her a wounded look. Roeglin started to sputter, but he swallowed his laughter when the kat hissed at him.

"Come on," Marsh said, taking the reins of her mule in her hand and leading it back the way they'd come.

She figured it was safer to be seen walking beside the hoshkat than having her pace the mules—and she'd be more able to react to anyone who might object. Gustav and the other guards were nowhere to be seen when they got back to where they'd left him, but an archer stepped out of the same doorway the woman had been standing in.

"This way," he said.

He was not alone. Two crossbowmen stepped out behind him, their weapons trained on Marsh and Roeglin, although one shifted quickly to cover the kat. Mordan hissed, and Marsh stepped in front of her.

"The kat comes," she said.

Their escort opened his mouth to protest, so she cut him off.

"Or you can shoot me now."

He closed his mouth and gently pushed the crossbow down when one of his guards moved to oblige.

"No. The kat can come."

Mordan gave a soft rumble and lashed her tail from side to side.

If Marsh didn't know any better, she'd think the kat wasn't happy with their situation and laid the blame for it squarely at her feet.

"Give it a rest, kat."

She tethered the mule and followed the first man inside. He was tall for their kind, with ash-blond hair, gray eyes, and the same sharp-edged features the woman had. Same family or clan, Marsh thought, and let her eyes rove over the two crossbowmen.

Their brown hair was netted in short ponytails, and their eyes were dark. Neither looked like they knew how to smile, and one was scarred up the left cheek as though he'd been caught by a fireball sometime in the past. None of them spoke as they passed through a corridor and into a large common room. Gustav looked up from a table at the far end as they entered.

"You took your Deeps-damned time," he grumbled and gestured for them to join him.

"And you," he added, looking at the kat. "Stay with me."

As if the kat could understand him—except Mordan tilted her head to catch Marsh's eye and gave her the impression she'd do as the man asked. She let go of the kat's scruff and watched as the big beast padded ahead of them to sit beside Gustav's chair. It was hard to keep her surprise from her face, but seeing the expression the woman wore was worth it.

Stop laughing, Roeglin said, and Marsh had trouble keeping a straight face. *It would be really unwise to crack up now.*

You're not helping.

And you're doing it again. Tell me, did you close your eyes?

Crap.

She'd kept her eyes on Gustav and seen his eyes widen as he watched her face. Her only hope was that the woman didn't know the significance of what she'd just seen happen. It was a hope that was short-lived because their host turned to the Protector captain, drawing her sword and extending it so that the tip reached his throat.

"Really, Gus? You consort with mind-walkers now?"

Marsh watched him tense and flick his eyes anxiously toward her and back to the woman.

"That's new for her," he said, swallowing nervously. "This is the first time she's shown any sign..."

"And the other?"

So *Roeglin* hadn't had his eyes closed! Marsh looked up at the mage.

"My bad," he murmured, and they came to a halt before the table.

"Sit," the woman commanded, pointing to the empty chairs between Gerry and Izmay, and they obeyed.

"Gus?" Marsh asked, taking her place.

"Long story," the woman told her, withdrawing her sword, "but I swore I'd kill the next mind-walker I saw."

Marsh tensed, getting ready to move, but the woman continued.

"So it's a good thing I can see you're shadow mages, isn't it?"

Marsh nodded, aware of Roeglin mirroring the action beside her.

The woman sheathed her sword and propped herself against the wall near the head of the table.

"My name is Valerie. Gustav knows me from some time past." She shifted, studying them as they sat. "And you are mostly shadow guards from the monastery, regardless of your uniforms."

Her eyes shifted to Henri and Jakob.

"Except for the ex-caravan guards in your midst."

She fell silent, studying each of them in turn and looking at the kat.

"Tell me, why has she joined you?"

Marsh caught Gustav's look as the Protector captain directed Valerie's attention toward her. The woman's eyes narrowed.

"You again? So, the kat is under your control?"

Marsh couldn't help it. She gave a startled bark of laughter and followed it with a short-lived chuckle.

"I wish," she replied, "but the kat is her own creature. She chooses to stay with me because I made her a promise."

"Oh?"

"To find her cubs and retrieve them from the raiders."

Mordan gave a soft growl, and some of the men nearest them dropped their hands to their sword hilts. The smarter ones backed up, reaching for their bows or crossbows. Marsh was out of her seat and moving around the table before any of them could be raised to fire.

"Call your dogs to heel," she snarled, reaching for the shadows and pulling her own sword and shield into being.

"Marsh…" Gustav spoke quietly as though he struggled to keep his voice calm. "Stand down. They will not harm us."

"They might not harm *you*, captain, but Mordan has no such guarantee."

Marsh didn't take her eyes from the men nearest as she took a stand between them and the kat. All around the table, the shadow guards pushed their chairs back and slowly moved to join her.

Valerie didn't say a word. She only watched as they positioned themselves, and glanced past them to her own people.

"Stand down," she ordered. "These are our guests. You will treat them as such."

"Unless they try to leave," came a voice from the doorway, and Valerie dipped her chin.

"*Oui*. Of course, unless they try to leave."

"Our beasts need tending," Henri said. "They've had a long ride."

Again Valerie seemed to agree.

"See to it. Stable them with our own."

Gustav cleared his throat.

"You *do* have mounts, don't you?"

Valerie shot him a startled look and then laughed.

"Yes, of course, we do. I only ever played that trick once. Your mounts will be returned to you when you leave."

From her tone, Marsh thought that might be "if" they left, and she looked at Henri.

"Go with them," she said. "Take Izmay with you."

The two guards sheathed their blades and made to step away from the table. They were immediately stopped by Valerie's own. Henri looked down at the blade making a slight indentation in his armored gut and he stared into the man's face, placed a gloved finger against the sword blade, and gently pushed it to one side. Beside him, Izmay did the same.

The swordsmen dipped their blades under the offending digits and put them right back where they'd started. Henri and Izmay exchanged glances and put their fingers against the blades once more. This time they clenched their other fists, and flame covered their gloves.

Before they were forced to put their plan into play, Valerie spoke.

"Let them through," she said, "and if the rest of you could take your seats?"

Her men took the hint and sheathed their swords, letting Henri and Izmay through with a polite gesture to those already at the door. It made Marsh smile to see the pair make a show of blowing out the flames on their gauntlets as they left.

She was still smiling when she returned to her seat, but Roeglin's quiet mind contact soon wiped the smile from her face.

Gustav is going to have your head, he said.

And putain *to him.* Marsh retorted, looking up to see the Protector captain observing them closely.

As soon as he'd caught her eye, he sat back in his seat.

"I might not be able to hear you," he told them, his eyes boring into her face, "but I sure as shit can read your faces —and you, Master Leclerc, are on latrine duty for the next week."

Marsh stared at him, and Valerie laughed. She stopped laughing as Gustav shifted in his chair.

"I'm going to assume you didn't take us off the street for your own entertainment," he said, "but I don't have time for games, so maybe you can tell us what *you're* doing here, and what you need us for."

All traces of amusement vanished as Valerie pulled out the chair in front of her. Turning it so its back was to the table, she straddled it and sat.

"You first."

Gustav sighed.

"We're here to offer Dimanche an alliance of mutual protection between Ruins Hall, Kerrenin's Ledge, Downslopes, and the Deeps Monastery. After we've heard your reply, we're moving on to Ariella's Grotto. Along the way, we're restoring the trade routes and setting patrols to guard them. Once we're done, Master Leclerc is going to try to find where the raiders are coming from and put an end to their depredations. Your turn."

It sounded very rehearsed to Marsh, but Valerie just nodded.

"It's more than I was hoping for. As for me and mine,

we are hires for Gaebler's Gems, protection for the mine and its caravans."

Her face clouded

"Although there hasn't been one of the latter for some time."

She swept a hand to include the men in the room.

"We are the off-shift, but there's not usually this many of us when the caravans are moving." She paused. "While your proposal is good, do you have any idea of how the town is run?"

"It's not a council?"

"No. More like a conglomerate of traders. The founders each had different areas of interest and decided they were better served by having a central location for administration and trade. It helped that there was already a small community in place when they arrived and the founders thought it would make it easier for caravans and traders if they built their offices around the central square and allowed inns and waystations to grow up around them. My company was one of the first, but Gaebler holds primacy when our contracts compete."

She sat back, her gaze shifting from face to face. For a moment it seemed as if she was waiting for one of them to speak, but then she leaned forward.

"You came from the surface, did you not?"

"Yes." Gustav's reply was wary.

"Do you have news of Aimery's caravan? It left five days ago. You should have met it near Downslopes."

Gustav sighed, and his expression told her the news before he'd opened his mouth. Her face fell.

"Tell me," she said, anticipated sadness roughening her words.

"We found the mules," he told her. "They'd been dead at least a day, maybe two, but there was no sign of any human, dead or alive."

He glanced at Marsh and continued.

"We think the raiders took them…like all those previous."

Valerie followed his gaze.

"What has *she* got to do with them?"

Marsh opened her mouth to refute the idea but Gustav held up his hand. Roeglin laid a hand on her knee, and she subsided. They had one chance to get it right.

"Marsh is going to pursue the raiders. She will be the one responsible for bringing back those they've taken."

Valerie fixed Marsh with a stern stare.

"When?"

Well, at least that was an easy question to answer.

"As soon as the caverns are secure."

Valerie froze, then sat straighter.

"Then you need to understand how decisions are made in this town."

From outside came angry shouts, and the sound of people chanting.

"Or at least how they *were* made."

"What do you mean *were*?" Gustav asked.

Valerie gestured toward the closed windows.

"I mean that the folks outside are about to simplify the governance at the same time as they complicate the Deeps out of it."

"What do you mean?"

"It's simple. Those people are going to lynch Monsieur Laberge because they think he's responsible for the disappearance of the Iselins from their farm."

"Let me guess," Marsh cut in. "No people and no bodies, but animals, items, and wealth all intact?"

"Yes," Valerie admitted. "How did you know?"

Marsh pushed back her seat, her movement mirrored by Gustav and the rest of the team.

"Because that's how the raiders leave every property they empty," Gustav told her, moving toward the door, Mordan by his side. "We have to stop this."

"But the merchant said he was sure he'd heard Laberge threaten them. That Laberge had spoken to soldiers…"

"Merchant?" Marsh demanded, halting after starting to follow. "Kearick?"

"I believe that was his name, yes. Said he'd come from Kerrenin's Ledge to set up a store here…"

"That Deep-spawned demon," Marsh spat. "He was probably lying."

"Leclerc."

Gustav's quiet voice reached her across the room, her name as good as a command. She turned and followed him, the other guards moving alongside her. Across the room, a door opened and Henri muttered a startled oath. Marsh glanced up in time to see him and Izmay hurrying to join them.

"We'll go with you," Valerie said, and her tone left no room for argument. All around them, her men moved toward the door. "Aymeric. Show them the way."

The blond man who had met them stepped away from his post by the door and walked through it ahead of

Gustav. Valerie joined them, walking a little behind Gerry and Zeb, who were bringing up the rear. They hurried into the street, and Aymeric broke into a jog.

To their puzzlement, he led them away from the square and across two major cross streets before turning a corner.

"This way," he shouted, breaking into a run.

16

CROWD CONTROL

They were arrayed in front of Monsieur Laberge's house by the time the mob arrived. Gustav and Valerie had knocked, then forced their way past the steward who came to answer the door, calling to the merchant as they'd hurried through the house. Gustav had left Marsh and Roeglin in charge, and Valerie's second Aymeric stood alongside them, casting doubtful glances at the kat who had come to sit by his feet.

Mordan rose to her feet as the mob rushed into the street in front of them, her movement causing those at the lead to slow their pace. Aymeric raised a hand, and the archers arrayed on either side of them raised their bows and drew their strings taut. Roeglin and Marsh drew their swords, aware of their fellow Protectors doing the same beside them.

The crowd came to a halt, but the men leading it stepped forward.

"We've come for Laberge."

"Wrong," Aymeric told them.

"He is guilty."

"Wrong," Marsh added.

"He's killed the Iselins."

"Wrong," Roeglin retorted.

One of the leader's stepped forward.

"We don't think so."

Marsh stepped forward to confront him, reaching for the voice she used to call time in training.

"Shadow raiders took the Iselins. We will retrieve them."

The leader turned and looked out over the mob. When he turned back, there was mockery in his eyes.

"*You* will retrieve them?" he asked, poking her in the center of the chest with his long narrow forefinger.

Marsh returned the favor.

"*I* will retrieve them." She backed up a step so she could have a clearer view of the crowd as she continued, gesturing toward the house. "He is not guilty."

"How do you know?" roared someone in the crowd, and they surged forward.

They stopped abruptly when Mordan roared, darting forward a couple of paces to swat at the air before them. Marsh shouted into the silence that followed.

"We will investigate this man's guilt or innocence, but murdering him will not catch those responsible." She paused to let that message sink in and added, "Or stop them from striking again."

Mordan gave a long, low growl, finishing it with a screeching yowl—the hunting call of her kind. Several of those in the front rank backed away. The kat growled again, pacing in front of them before returning to Marsh.

They are all prey.

Marsh hoped that the kat meant all those in the front rank were townsfolk and not raiders and felt the push of confirmation.

"Promise it," the crowd's leader challenged and Marsh raised her head, but Aymeric was ahead of her.

"We so swear!" he shouted, and raised his hand.

All around him, his men echoed his promise.

"We so swear."

But the crowd wouldn't let him off so easily.

"You're not unbiased."

He swept his hand to direct their attention to Marsh, Roeglin, and the others.

"They are."

"And who *are* they?"

Marsh resisted the urge to respond, letting Gustav step forward.

"We are emissaries. I am here on behalf of the Founder of Ruin's Deep to deliver an offer from Kerrenin's Ledge."

He signaled for Marsh and Roeglin to join him.

"And these are the emissaries for the Deeps Monastery."

A low murmur ran through the crowd, but Gustav quickly quelled it.

"They are not here to recruit."

The crowd stilled. Gustav waited, looking out over them, and the crowd stared back. Finally, the crowd's leader broke the silence.

"What *are* they here for?"

Gustav gestured to Roeglin.

"We are here to show our support for the Four Caverns and to confirm our alliance to both Ruins Deep and

Kerrenin's Ledge. We are also here to offer the same alliance to the people of Dimanche."

"What if we don't *want* your alliance?" someone shouted.

"Yeah! Our kids stay here!"

"You're not taking anyone away!"

Roeglin waited, and Gustav interrupted the growing discontent.

"Have you had mages trying to convince you to give up your children?"

Rumbled assent answered him.

"Those mages were not from the Deeps."

Sounds of disbelief greeted him, but the crowd's leader held up his hand.

"What are you saying?"

"I'm saying that folk in both Ruins Deep and Kerrenin's Ledge reported dark mages trying to recruit their children or to convince parents to send their children away to some kind of school."

Surprise murmurs replaced the disbelief. Gustav waited until they died down.

"Those mages did not come from the Deeps Monastery."

Cries of "How do you know?," "How can you be sure?," and "Of course they'd say that" met his answer, but Gustav let the argument die down.

"We checked, and the monastery was able to account for its people. There were also no new recruits when we visited, and no signs of any."

He stopped and looked at Roeglin, who took the cue.

"We *were* planning a recruitment drive," he began, and

waited for the crowd to settle before continuing, "but at the founder's request and in agreement with the Kerrenin's Ledge Council, there will not be one."

The faces before them mirrored surprise.

"But why not?"

Roeglin surveyed them, his face showing surprise and curiosity.

"We know of the other mages," he said. "We are not them, but you have no way of telling the difference between us."

While that was not entirely true, Marsh knew it was safer for the crowd to believe that. She stayed silent as Roeglin continued.

"As such, until this cavern has its own group of defenders to accompany us, we will not be recruiting here."

"Defenders?" someone called out.

Someone else laughed.

"Good luck with that," came the call from another.

"Yeah, not a hope any of the Five will agree to that."

"I'll put up a fifth of the funds for them."

Marsh heard a door close in the house behind her, and then boots echoed over stone before crunching on the gravel path leading down from the porch. The crowd's leader looked past her as she, Roeglin, and Gustav half-turned to see who had arrived.

"You?" the crowd's leader clearly didn't believe the claim.

The new arrival stopped when he reached Gustav.

"I am Monsieur Laberge. My consortium produces shroom paper and leather, which is why people believed I might harm the Iselins."

"Are you saying you didn't?"

"I am."

This was met with open disbelief and mutters, and Gustav held up his hand.

"We will investigate."

"Not if he's paying you a fifth of your startup, you won't…"

And Gustav turned.

"He's not paying *me*. I'm only seeking an alliance for Ruins Hall and Kerrenin's Ledge. They have their own Protectors."

"Protectors? I thought you said we needed defenders?"

Gustav shrugged.

"You can call them what you like. Ruins Hall calls their defenders Protectors, as does Kerrenin's Ledge. Each cavern controls its own defensive force."

"Why can't there be just one?"

"Because we don't have time to set up one. We want to do that once our caverns are secure. Until then, each cavern is responsible for its own defense and the defense of the trade routes. We'll provide consultants to assist with set up and training, but only if asked. Beyond that, it's up to you."

The crowd's leader looked at the people on either side of him. It was almost as if he was looking for a direction to take them in next, but they seemed just as lost as he was. Around him, people stirred uneasily, some shrugging and others frowning. Finally, a stocky man with wild dark hair streaked with silver shouldered his way forward.

"Hugh Travers," he announced. "I'll put up Shameless for an HQ if you'll keep me on."

Monsieur Laberge looked worried.

"But I'm not the one hiring. I will help with expenses, but it needs to be run independently of any of the Five."

"That's why I'm putting Shameless up," Hugh said. "It's not aligned with any of the Five."

He caught Laberge's eye.

"No disrespect."

Laberge shrugged.

"None taken, but you raise a good point. How are we going to build a force?"

Valerie stepped forward.

"We will," she announced, and they were almost deafened by shouts of protest.

Instead of trying to fight the tide of noise, she waited.

"We will cancel all standing contracts by the end of the day and pay the penalty fees."

Around them, her men shifted to give her looks of surprise and astonishment. Valerie ignored them and turned to Laberge.

"The Five know our terms for wages and upkeep, do they not?"

Laberge nodded, his expression giving nothing away.

"You're expensive..." he muttered, and the crowd laughed.

"But we know the cavern better than most, and we have the skills needed to defend it."

"Yeah, but not the numbers!"

That call came from the crowd, and Valerie snapped a glance toward it.

"We'll be recruiting."

"When?"

"First thing in the morning."

She turned to Hugh.

"With your permission."

"If you want to be Dimanche's defenders and these folks agree, you don't need my permission."

Valerie smiled.

"But we do," she said, "since you're going to be our recordkeeper and coordinate the feeding and housing of our people."

Hugh looked astonished, so Valerie kept going.

"Or weren't you serious when you said Shameless was available?"

"I…I wasn't going to kick you out…"

"Uh huh? What *were* you going to do with us, given we take up half your rooms?"

"I…uh…" Hugh stuttered to a halt. "Oh."

"Good. You're our recruiting officer and recordkeeper, and you'll be working with Quartermaster Owain."

"D-does he know?" Hugh's eyes were wide.

Valerie gave him a hard look and an even harder smile.

"He will."

She turned to the crowd, sweeping a hand toward Hugh.

"This man will be on the recruitment desk tomorrow. You know where to find him."

"Behind the bar?" one smart ass called, and Valerie surveyed the crowd, looking for them.

Marsh saw when she found them.

"No one gets to the bar until they pass rookies," she said. "You think you're good enough?"

"I don't know about Kels," came a voice from one side of the crowd, "but we are. You need us to sign?"

From the way Valerie's people tensed and half-raised their weapons, the newcomers were both unexpected and a potential threat. Following the mercenary leader's gaze, she saw the crowd ripple as people moved aside to let a wedge of soldiers pass through them. The man at its head had the build of a surface dweller and a well-defined face.

The nearest members of the crowd looked apprehensive, and those nearest the edge of the road began moving quietly toward a side street. Marsh got the impression the man noticed and did not care.

"Well, Val? What do you say?"

"Don't you have contracts?"

He shrugged and looked back at his men.

"You're canceling yours. We'll do the same. You need men. We want to help."

Valerie crossed her arms, her face taking on a hard expression as she studied him.

"No, Luka."

His jaw dropped in disbelief, but Valerie hadn't finished.

"You don't get to be recruits."

"But…"

"You get to be equal partners. We'll merge."

Marsh watched Luka's mouth move as though he wanted to say something but the words escaped him. Valerie stared at him.

"What do you say?"

It took the man beside him giving him a shove for Luka to gather himself enough to speak.

"I…" He glanced at the man at his side and back at Valerie. "I…accept. And thank you."

"We have a long fight ahead and a lot to organize. Will you come and stand with us?"

The man known as Luka led his men forward.

"Join them," he ordered, and his troops dispersed themselves among the mercenaries facing the crowd while he went to stand beside Valerie.

Marsh was close enough to hear what he said when he stooped to murmur in Valerie's ear.

"Thank you."

Valerie dipped her chin in acknowledgment and looked out at the crowd.

"Are you satisfied?"

The crowd continued to disperse, but its leaders came closer.

"You'll protect us?"

"We will do our best."

"And the mages?"

Valerie looked at Gustav, Roeglin, and Marsh.

"They'll stay to assist us until we can stand on our own."

Gustav opened his mouth as though he'd argue and closed it again.

"We also need to meet with those authorized to make alliances."

"We'll see to it."

The crowd leader turned to him.

"And Monsieur Laberge?"

"We'll investigate," Gustav assured him.

"And he is under our protection," Valerie added. "An

attack on him is an attack on the cavern. Make sure that is understood."

The man paled and backed away.

"Understood."

The other leaders repeated him, then they broke and went in several different directions.

When they had gone, Monsieur Laberge turned to them.

"Thank you for your assistance," he said and began to walk back to the house.

He stopped just as quickly, surprised when they moved with him.

"Can I help you?"

"When we're back inside," Valerie told him.

He looked a little worried but hurried inside. Marsh, Gustav, and Roeglin followed, standing to one side of the man's office while the troops lined the corridor outside the door.

17

SECRETS & SHADOW MAGES

"What can I do for you?" Monsieur Laberge asked when they were settled in his office.

Marsh and Roeglin leaned against the wall on opposite sides of the door, letting Gustav, Valerie, and the leader of the other mercenary group, Luka, take the seats in front of the desk. It was Gustav who replied.

"We need to know your activities for the last five days."

Surprise flashed across Laberge's face, and he frowned.

"I… Let me see…"

He glanced around the desk and picked up a large leather-bound book. It took him a few heartbeats to leaf through its shroom-paper pages, but finally, he passed the book over, holding it open as he did.

"Here," he said. "It's all here."

Gustav took it and glanced down at the page, then passed it to Valerie and Luka.

"Roeglin."

The dark-haired mage closed his eyes, and Marsh did the same. Maybe she could…

Not this time. Later.

As if that made a difference.

Marsh kept her eyes closed, figuring Roeglin was about to be too busy to notice what she did or didn't do. How *did* he look into someone's head, anyway?

Maybe it was like finding the natural energy of the world around her...Maybe thoughts had energy...Maybe she just had to want to know what someone was thinking and the magic would take her into their heads. Maybe...

I'm going to kick your ass when we're done. Now focus on being quiet and just watching.

If it was possible for anyone to sound impressed and thoroughly annoyed at the same time, Roeglin managed it. Marsh tried to do as he said, although it was strange to feel his presence in someone else's head and stranger to *be* in someone else's head, and yet she knew she was.

She stayed at the edges of Monsieur Laberge's mind, just getting used to knowing what someone else was thinking and feeling. The man was worried. He knew he'd done nothing wrong and knew without a doubt that he'd had nothing to do with the Iselin disappearance and had no idea how to prove it.

He had no idea how to prove it?

That thought made Marsh want to know more. She followed the thread of thought, looking for the reason connected to it.

Why could he not prove it? What had he done that he couldn't...

Oh.

Marsh couldn't help it. She burst out laughing, losing her connection to Monsieur Laberge as she doubled over with mirth. Across the desk from her, the merchant looked mortified, his face turning crimson with embarrassment.

Roeglin sighed and opened his eyes, not seeming to care that the white hadn't quite faded from them. Monsieur Laberge looked up at the ceiling and closed his eyes.

"You could have warned me," he murmured as Luka and Valerie looked on in puzzlement.

"Would you have allowed it?" Gustav asked, and Laberge shook his head.

"At least we know you're not guilty." Roeglin sounded tired, and he glared at Marsh. "Although I was hoping to be more subtle."

Marsh straightened up, swallowed her laughter, and cleared her throat.

"Sorry."

Valerie shifted in her chair.

"Care to share?"

Marsh looked at Roeglin, trying to work out how to respond.

So now you want advice?

Please!

I'll take it from here...and I'm busting you back to apprentice.

Before Marsh could work out what to say to that, Roeglin had turned back to the merchant.

"Please accept my apologies for the apprentice. She has a lot to learn."

Gustav said nothing, but his face said they'd both be hearing from him later. Roeglin continued as though they had nothing to worry about.

"I think, Monsieur, that your alibi might be better

coming from you. You are going to have to tell us where to find your witnesses."

If the merchant's face had been crimson before, it was the color of a fire-glow now, and burning with the same intensity. Marsh no longer felt amused, and as funny as it had been to walk in on his secret, so to speak, it wasn't funny now.

"Perhaps you should start by telling us where Madame Iselin is hiding," she suggested, keeping her eyes on the merchant when everyone else turned toward her.

We are way beyond ass-kicking, was not something she wanted to hear from Roeglin.

Fortunately, whatever else he might have wanted to say was cut off as Monsieur Laberge began to speak.

"She's safe. Devastated by her family's disappearance, but safe. My wife…" He moved his hands in a helpless gesture. "She doesn't know. We didn't mean…"

He sighed again.

"I sound like a teenager making excuses, but at least you know why I would never have moved against them."

"And why there are a few people who think you've shown enough interest in their property that you might have been planning a takeover," Valerie finished for him.

"It would have come out eventually," Luka added. "Nothing stays secret for long in this cavern."

Marsh wanted to argue that the raiders had managed it, but she decided she was in enough trouble as it was.

You have no idea.

She wanted to tell Roeglin to shut it but thought better of it. Like the man said, she was in enough trouble as it was…apprentice-busting trouble, even.

"You mentioned 'witness-*es*,'" Gustav prodded, looking at Roeglin, before turning his attention to Monsieur Laberge. "What did he mean by that?"

Monsieur Laberge's face had almost returned to its normal color. Now he blushed again.

"He means that Madame Iselin was not the only person I was entertaining," he admitted, "but I want your word that you will not tell anyone who was with her."

"I don't see how…"

"It's either that or you don't get to speak to her," Laberge insisted. "They are old friends, but…"

Luka guessed what the man was desperately trying not to say and cut across him.

"Which of the wives is involved?" he demanded.

All eyes turned to him, then returned to the merchant.

Laberge kept a close eye on Valerie when he replied.

"Madame Gaebler."

The mercenary's jaw dropped, then she closed her mouth with an almost audible snap. For a moment nobody moved, then Gustav shrugged.

"I don't see what was so funny," he muttered, "and we have more important things to discuss."

He didn't see what I did, Marsh thought, but she kept her eyes on the floor and stifled the smile that threatened to appear.

No, but no one needs the detail, Roeglin told her, *as entertaining as it is.*

He had a point, but Valerie was speaking.

"I had people protecting her."

It was as much a question as a statement of fact, and Monsieur Laberge knew the answer she was looking for.

"They refused to leave her."

"A short-lived secret, indeed," Luka observed to no one in particular, but the merchant ignored him and continued.

"So she swore them to secrecy and made it clear their lives wouldn't be worth living if anything about us ever came to light."

"It wouldn't have been worth living if they'd left her," Valerie muttered. "As to whether *I'll* let them live after this…"

Monsieur Laberge looked alarmed.

"Please don't say anything. They refused to leave their posts and they've kept her secret, which is just another part of keeping her safe. If Monsieur Gaebler ever found out…"

"He won't!" Valerie snapped. "My people know their jobs. I'll still need to speak to them. You and she will have to give them the freedom to do that."

Monsieur Laberge relaxed, but only slightly.

"Only to the five of you here," he agreed, even if he cast a dubious glance at Marsh as he did so.

"Agreed," came as a single murmur from everyone present, and most of the tension left Monsieur Laberge's face.

"Thank you," he said. "Now, what else can I do?"

"What do you know about the last caravan to head to the surface?" Gustav asked, and the merchant blinked.

"I…why? Is it okay? Did it arrive at Downslopes okay?"

He stopped, catching the looks on their faces.

"That's why you're asking…because it didn't make it to Downslopes."

He gave a heavy sigh and bowed his head, rubbing a hand over his eyes. Marsh watched him, wondering at the grief she saw in his eyes when he lifted his face to look at them. He didn't leave her to wonder for long.

"My son…" He paused, looking as if he'd aged a century in seconds. After a pause, he tried once more. "Were there any survivors? Did you retrieve the bodies?"

Gustav shook his head.

"There were no bodies…unless you count the bodies of the mules. That section of the trail is closed until the clearing force goes through. There's at least one shadow wraith hunting the scavengers."

Laberge's next words revealed a father's hope rather than a businessman's concern.

"So they might still be alive?"

It was clear who he meant: the merchants, the guards, and the people taking their goods to the surface, his son included. Gustav nodded.

"It's possible. We know the raiders take prisoners."

"Do you know where they take them?"

"No. That is something we will pursue once the caverns are secure."

"And you'll try to get them back?"

There was no doubt who he meant by "them."

"Oui. Shadow Mage Leclerc is tasked with that responsibility."

Laberge regarded Marsh with an uncertain expression.

"Are you sure?"

And Marsh rolled her eyes.

"I've already tracked one group to a blank wall." Roeglin snorted but she ignored him, hoping he wouldn't reveal that she'd been the raiders' prisoner at the time. "I can track them again. Right now, though, I need to find my boss...the merchant who came through town recently."

Laberge's gaze sharpened.

"Kearick?"

"*Oui.*"

"Why?"

Marsh's expression hardened, and Laberge flinched. His reaction didn't stop her from answering.

"Because he's helping the raiders and I'm going to stop him."

Laberge looked at Gustav.

"You might have mentioned this sooner."

Gustav's face was bland as he replied, but Marsh noticed the slight flicker of his eyes as he tried not to look at Valerie.

"We had other concerns."

Marsh remembered how Valerie and her people had ambushed them and thought that was an understatement. Apparently, Valerie thought so too.

"We detained them," she said, and Laberge stared at her.

"Why?"

Valerie gave him a small and secretive smile, darting a quick glance at Gustav before she replied.

"Let's just say I'm used to Gustav *bringing* trouble, not solving it."

Marsh saw the color rise to the Protector captain's cheeks and wondered why.

You'd be surprised.

Care to share? she demanded, mimicking the mercenary leader's earlier question.

Roeglin's reply was as abrupt as it was short.

No.

Marsh changed the subject, addressing Monsieur Laberge directly.

"Do you know where Kearick is?"

Laberge's brow furrowed.

"He asked directions to where the shadow mages meet."

From his tone of voice, that location was common knowledge to the locals. Marsh waited for him to continue, but he remained silent. In the end, she had to make it obvious.

"We're not from the cavern. Perhaps you could direct us?"

"Yes. You take the road to the mines at the north end of the cavern, past the Iselins, and…" He stopped, as a sudden realization struck him. "But those shadow mages have been among us for years. They have no connection to the raiders. Why would he want to see them?"

It was a good question, but Gustav had the answer.

"Are they the only known magic users in the cavern?"

"They are now that the Iselins are gone," Luka replied.

"What?" he added when they all turned to him. "It was one of our assignments: Let them know where they could find 'magical resources.'"

"Who?" Valerie demanded, then added, "Who set it?"

"The Piermonts. Oh. The Shadow-deviled Deeps! We have to hurry."

Luka was out of his seat and moving for the door even as Roeglin cursed the shrooms and called the shadows. Marsh followed the shadow mage out the door, both of them preceding Luka as they ran for the first floor and front door. Gustav was hard on their heels, and Valerie started calling names as she assigned Laberge's protection.

"Don't let him out of your sight. Make sure he lives."

"*Mais oui.*"

"Finn, you're in charge."

Finn?

Marsh couldn't put a face to the name and made a note to find out who he was. They hit the front door and crossed the porch, slowing their pace to let Luka and the other mercenaries catch up.

"This way," he called, and Gustav dropped back to give him the lead, glancing back just as Valerie raced through the door.

"There's no time for the mules," she said, falling in alongside Luka as they settled into a jog that would carry them for miles.

"Not heading for the mules," he replied.

Marsh pushed aside the thought that they'd already walked most of the day and stretched her senses into the cavern. Even if she didn't know exactly where they were going, she could at least try to look ahead. The cavern was full of life, mostly insects, but also other creatures around the size of the "bunnies" she'd seen around Kerrenin's Ledge.

It was a relief to both see and not see any sign of human life.

Mordan paced beside her until they reached the edge of town, then the kat slid into the rocks and shrooms lining the path, vanishing into the background of pale stems and stone. She hoped none of the mercenaries would forget the big beast was on their side when she re-emerged.

The path was deserted, and Marsh made a note to ask what was normal for the cavern. Had the raiders been there long enough that folks didn't venture outside the town without the mercenaries? She hoped not. That would mean the raiders would be harder to remove from the cavern...unless they took out the mages who opened the gates.

The mages!

Dan?

The kat caught her concern and sped off into the cavern, the sound of her movements causing several of the guards to reach for their swords.

"Stand down!" Gustav snapped. "It's only the kat."

"Only..." muttered one of the men, and several others snorted in agreement.

None of them argued, though, and Luka and Valerie didn't falter, keeping the pace as they ran along the trail.

At first, Marsh wondered just how far they were going to have to run and when they'd know they'd gotten there, but then she focused on her magic. It was hard maintaining her contact with the shadows and lives around them while she ran. She was getting to the point where she'd have to stop when she'd realized they'd arrived.

Roeglin caught the images before she could speak, sending a silent mental alert to all in range. Marsh caught his projection of what she'd seen ahead and felt a moment of unreality—and she dropped the scans.

Calling sword and buckler from the darkness, she raced forward with the rest.

The local shadow mages were barely holding their own, but they weren't giving up. Outnumbered, they fought back, sliding in and out of patches of darkness to avoid being struck, then coming at their attackers from another angle. The only problem was that the raiders had brought mages of their own.

Marsh watched as one of the locals stepped into the dark beside a rocky outcrop, only to be bounced back into the light of a stand of callas. Two raiders moved to attack but the mage scrambled back, lashing out with tendrils of shadow to take them off their feet.

Marsh changed course to help. Her battle cry drew the raiders' attention, but only one of them faced her when they got back up. The other acknowledged her with a glance and moved to deal with the shadow mage.

The mage lashed out with more dark tendrils, her face lighting up with an evil grin.

"How'd'you like *these* odds, you Deeps-forsaken shroom beetle?"

Marsh blocked her opponent's first strike, thrusting beneath it to gut him in a single move, but her eyes were drawn by the black flame that sprang up along the tendrils as they wrapped around the raider's body.

"Burn!" The shadow mage pulled the tendrils tight and the flame burned from black to blue, engulfing her opponent.

He screamed even as the mage released the tendrils back to the darkness, pulling the flame into two glowing balls that she threw onto the next-closest raider. Her eyes met Marsh's, and they turned toward the closest raiders.

All around the clearing, the battle raged, but the raiders hadn't planned for a larger force and were soon over-whelmed. When the last of them fell, the shadow mages looked at the mercenaries, and one of them stepped forward.

"Valerie," he said, barely-reined hostility lacing his tones. "Why are you here?"

Marsh thought he might have at least tried to sound grateful, but the mercenary leader wasn't surprised.

"Devin. You're welcome. We're here to save your asses."

One of the raiders groaned and was promptly impaled from several directions by shadow spears that disappeared as soon as they'd torn their way through him.

"Why?"

"Because we need your help."

Marsh noted she didn't add that the mages clearly needed her help, too. She let that fact hang unspoken in the air between them.

"And why would I help the likes of you?"

"Because these raiders threaten more than just this cavern. Because you've lost people to them, just as the town has, and because you want your people back."

Until she'd said those last few words, the look on Devin's face said he was going to disagree. Instead, he gestured toward a fire that had burned throughout the melee.

"Come and talk." His gaze swept the mercenaries and registered curiosity when it came to the shadow guard Protectors. "Bring your people...and your friends."

Without waiting for a reply, he turned away, catching sight of the mage Marsh had helped. She saw him relax just a fraction and a very brief smile crossed his lips.

"Es, you made it."

The mage laid a hand on Marsh's arm.

"I had some help from a new friend."

Devin looked at Marsh and his eyes flared white.

Welcome...friend.

Marsh stared at him, too surprised to react, but his mind touch was light and gone as swiftly as it had come.

"See to the cleanup," he ordered, turning back to Es. "Take who you need."

He gave Marsh one more assessing look and moved over to the fire, gesturing for the mercenaries and Protectors to join him.

"I'll help," Marsh said when Es looked around.

"And me."

It was no surprise when Roeglin came over. Henri's arrival was another matter.

"What?" the big guard asked when Marsh stared. "I can help too, can't I?"

"I'm not making you dinner in exchange," Marsh told him, and Roeglin laughed.

"Caught," he said, nudging the guard, and he asked Es, "What would you like us to do?"

"I need the dead in one pile," the female shadow mage instructed, "and the wounded through there."

She gestured toward an arch formed from a single large fungus. Golden light bathed the area beyond in a warm glow.

"Infirmary. We grow our own gleams and moss," she added by way of explanation. "It's handy to have a supply close by."

Roeglin arched his eyebrows.

"Get hurt a lot, do you?"

Es scowled at him, her reply short and hard.

"Not as often as the miners that we have to rescue."

Marsh was sure there was a story behind that but just as sure that now was not the time to ask for it. Instead, she followed Es's orders and helped Henri move the wounded into the infirmary while Roeglin and two of the local shadow mages set the dead to one side.

18

KEARICK THE SLIPPERY

As soon as the wounded were settled, Marsh returned to where Roeglin and Es were standing by the pile of dead.

"Where do you want us to dig?" Roeglin asked as Marsh arrived, but Es shook her head.

"No digging necessary," she told him. "Not yet, anyway. The shrooms over there could do with the ash."

Ash? Marsh thought, but Es hadn't finished.

"Stand back," the mage commanded, and Roeglin, Marsh, and Henri followed the locals in moving away several paces.

"Now watch," the female mage ordered.

They did as they were told, watching as Es moved her hands, drawing long lines of darkness from the ground and wrapping them over the small pile of bodies. Once they were covered, the mage made a scooping motion with her palms as though she was throwing dust into the air and the woven shadows burst into blue-tinged flame.

On either side of them, the other local shadow mages

made a gesture that made Marsh think of they were gathering air into an invisible bundle before them. The flames glowed brighter, going from dark blue to light blue to a brilliant white. When Marsh thought the light couldn't get any brighter, the mages clapped their hands once and the flames went out, leaving her blinking as her eyes tried to adjust to the cavern's normal levels of light.

When she could see again, the pile of bodies was gone, replaced by a pile of ash.

"We'll take that to where it's needed later," Es told them and walked over to where the mages, mercenaries, and Protectors were gathered around the fire.

Marsh was just about to follow her when she heard Mordan roar and a man shriek. Everyone turned toward the sound, and Gustav looked at her.

"Go see if the kat needs help," he ordered and Marsh took off through the shrooms, aware of Roeglin and Henri running beside her.

Behind her, she heard Devin's voice raised in puzzled query.

"You brought a hoshkat?"

It was rapidly followed by outrage.

"To *my* cavern?"

Marsh figured that was something she could deal with later. Right now the most important thing was to make sure Mordan hadn't bitten off more than she could chew. Once again, Marsh called on the shadows and sought the life in the cavern around her. She was surprised to find Mordan was much closer than she'd realized, but not surprised to see the figures running from the kat.

Or rather, *three* figures running from the kat, while four more turned to face her.

"Oh no, you don't," Marsh muttered, calling a spear from the darkness and hurling it at the nearest raider.

She had drawn her sword and was running for the next one when Roeglin interrupted.

Henri and I have them. You go after Kearick.

Kearick? Marsh scanned the shadows again, this time looking for a thread connected to the rogue merchant.

There were many.

She traced them, veering away from the raiders facing Mordan and pursuing the ones that were strongest.

"Kearick!" she shouted, and one of the human life-signs she was pursuing hesitated.

"Kearick!" Marsh screamed again, focusing on that life-sign while noting that the other two had also turned toward her voice.

As she closed the distance, one of the raiders moved to intercept her while the other ran a few paces more, then stopped. Marsh couldn't see what he was doing until she pushed through a stand of calla shroom and brown noses, and by then the first raider was on her.

She blocked his first wild slash and he blocked her counter-thrust, sweeping it out to one side. Marsh turned with him, deflecting the blows that followed with her buckler as she prepared her second strike. Beyond him, she could see Kearick, but the merchant seemed more concerned with what the other raider was doing than the fact that she was so close.

We're going to lose him, she thought and parried another attack from the raider blocking her path. She followed that with a series of broad strokes that pushed her opponent back even as he parried them. One got through, and he snarled a curse as he broke away and put a few strides distance between them. He remained between her and the other two though, so Marsh followed him, trying to put him down as fast as she could.

The mage with Kearick was opening a portal on his own, which she hadn't known they could do. If he let shadow monsters into the cavern, they'd have more on their plates than anyone wanted to deal with. Her momentary distraction cost her—the raider took advantage by darting forward and lashing out.

Marsh caught the movement from the corner of her eye and barely brought her blade up in time to block it. The impact jarred its way through her blade and down her arm, and it was Marsh's turn to be pushed back by the flurry of blows that followed.

"Move, Lemos!"

The order came from the mage, and Marsh's opponent glanced back. Marsh did likewise in time to see Kearick step through a tear in the shadow. She caught a glimpse of wooden panels, bookcases, and half a dozen soldiers dressed in raider black. Behind them stood several mages, balls of swirling darkness in their hands. This time she didn't see the raider's attack coming.

He didn't use his blade but swept one hand toward her, pushing a block of shadow into her. It hit hard, crushing the arm holding her buckler into her chest and knocking her off her feet. Marsh gave a yelp of surprise and ended up on her backside in a cluster of blue buttons and golden gleam, watching as the raider ran for the opening.

Mordan got to him before he reached it. The kat sprang from beneath a clump of calla, slamming into the raider's side and knocking him from his feet as Marsh scrambled up. The raider's mage took one look at them and leapt through the portal. Marsh leapt after him, but she was too far away and the rift closed before she could reach it.

She turned back for the raider, only to find the kat had already ended him.

"Of all the monsters in the Deep!"

Mordan raised her head.

Was Marsh referring to her?

No, Dan. Never you. You are not a monster.

The kat raised her lips imitating a snarl and showing Marsh what her enemies saw just before they died.

Marsh laughed.

You are not a monster to <u>me</u>.

The kat relaxed and then slammed a paw down on her victim's head. Marsh looked away.

Thanks, kat. <u>Not</u> *what I needed right now.*

"Me neither," Roeglin added and Mordan lifted her head, surveying them both with a look of disdain as she flicked her tail in derision.

"Thanks, kat."

Henri laughed as he came over.

"Looks like she told *you*," he said, and looked at where Kearick and his escort had disappeared.

There was nothing there now unless she counted the usual display of shrooms and rock.

"He got away."

Roeglin laid a hand on her shoulder.

"We'll find him."

"*Oui*," Henri agreed, "and when we do, we'll tear the little shit into pieces too small for his momma to put back together."

Marsh remembered that Henri had worked for Kearick and had lost a brother in the same attack she'd rescued the kids from.

"We'll burn the pieces just to be sure." She turned to Roeglin. "We go back?"

He shrugged.

"*Oui.* There's nothing to find here."

Dan, walk with me. The locals aren't happy I brought you to their cavern.

The kat showed what she thought of that in a long rippling snarl that rolled through the cavern.

To everyone's surprise, the snarl was answered in kind.

Henri snapped around to face the dark. Mordan tensed, her tail lashing from side to side.

Stay with me, Dan. We don't want to kill anyone's friends.

The kat gave her the impression that if the creatures now stalking around the base of a stalagmite were anyone's friend, then their *friend* had better stop them before they did something everyone regretted.

"They're wolves, Dan."

"Biggest Deeps-be-damned wolves *I've* ever seen," Henri muttered, drawing his sword and holding it loosely by his side.

The lead wolf stalked forward, and Marsh saw that he had a point. The wolves *were* a lot bigger than usual, and heavier set, their fur thick and long and surprisingly unmatted. Someone clearly cared for them. Before she could pursue that idea any further, Roeglin spoke.

"There's another mage." His quiet murmur was pitched for their ears only, and the kat hissed.

She didn't have time for another mage. She had too many opponents as it was.

"He's a mind mage," Roeglin added, "and he's influencing the wolves."

"Isn't that something you can do something about?" Henri growled.

"I can try, but I don't think the wolves want to attack. I think they're being pushed."

"Enough talk," Henri said. "You deal with the mage. We'll try to keep the wolves from eating you." He sighed, sheathing his sword. "I could do with a really big stick about now."

"Pull one from the shadow," Marsh told him. "It's just like the fire you call to your blade, but darker."

"Fire, huh? How does that go again?"

"Just don't copy Marsh," Roeglin told him. "The locals are already annoyed with us. They don't need any more reasons to add to the list.

Hear that, Dan? You can't kill them.

This time the kat hissed at *her.*

She would try, but she didn't like the way the front one was looking at her. In the time before the raiders, such a look would have been worthy of death.

Just not today, Marsh begged, and the kat's tail flicked. *Please, Dan.*

The kat would try.

Suddenly the wolves surged forward, all focused on Roeglin. If Marsh had needed proof someone was messing with their head, she had it now. Roeglin was not the greatest threat, and wolves weren't stupid.

Beside her, Roeglin sank to the floor, his face contorted with effort. For a moment, Marsh was tempted to try to help him, but that would leave Henri and Mordan facing odds of three to one. With a sigh, she brought her hands inwards, gathering the shadows, then pushed out, sending the resulting wall into the wolf pack.

Much to her dismay, she heard several yelps as they tumbled away from her, some crashing into shrooms and others into rocks.

"I thought you said we couldn't hurt them."

"I can fix what I break."

"Can't you fix what we break too?"

This time, Mordan turned her head to look at Marsh. Apparently, the big human had a point. Couldn't Marsh fix what Mordan broke?

"Not funny, Henri, and no, I can't, Dan. You break things far too well."

Even as she spoke, Marsh saw the wolves getting up and shaking themselves off. At least she hadn't hurt them too badly. She'd also given them someone else to concentrate on.

"Fine by me," she said, drawing the shadows together again.

This time it was harder, and she could feel fatigue nibbling at the edges of her mind. Henri looked concerned.

"Don't push it too far, girl. I'm not carrying you back."

Marsh waited until the wolves had almost reached them, then pushed the shadows over them. This time she pushed harder. Better they suffer a few bruises than force either Henri or Mordan to stop them. At her feet, Roeglin groaned.

"Deeps, but he's strong."

Marsh remembered what the mage had said about him not being the only mind mage in the world, and remembered he'd never claimed to be the strongest.

"*Merde.*"

Henri glanced at her.

"Do what you need to do. The kat and I can hold them."

Marsh doubted it, but she didn't have time to argue. She was about to kneel down beside Roeglin when she thought of something. The shadows formed a wall. She didn't need to use them to knock the wolves aside. Wolves couldn't climb.

"I'm such an idiot."

"Yeah, and?"

Henri didn't have to sound so much in agreement!

Marsh scowled, but the wolves were already picking themselves up, so she had to move fast.

"Get in close," she said, "unless you *like* being stuck in shadow."

Henri crowded in so close he was a line of warmth up one side of her body. The kat, sensing over their link what Marsh had planned, pressed herself against Marsh's legs, her chest forming an arch over Roeglin's kneeling form.

As soon as they were in position, Marsh pulled the shadows together once more, then she closed her hands as though she was gripping the edge of what she'd gathered. In her mind, she could feel the shadows in her fists. Slowly, she stretched her hands apart thinking of pulling the shadows into a wall, of the base of it firm against the ground, the top taller than her head. A wall curving around them, thick enough to stop any wolf and too high for them to leap over.

When she'd pulled her hands as far apart as she could manage, she let go of one edge and turned in a circle, pulling the other around them until the two edges met. Once they were touching she let go, then she crouched beside Roeglin. It was better than having her body fall down when she was mind-walking somewhere else.

Now all she had to do was figure out how to get into Roeglin's head. How had she done it with Monsieur Laberge? Her mind shied away from the memory. Sure, it had been funny at the time, but it had been embarrassing too, and some memories were better not to have.

Normally Roeglin would have laughed as she thought that, but he didn't. It gave Marsh a vague idea of just how much trouble the mage was in. She had to hurry, but she didn't know how.

Taking a deep breath, she thought about thinking what Roeglin was thinking, of feeling what he was feeling, of seeing what was really going on inside his head. At first, nothing seemed to happen, but Marsh pushed away the fear that Monsieur Laberge had been a lucky guess.

She *had* been inside the merchant's head. She *had* seen what she had seen and known he was telling the truth. She *could* do this. After all, Roeglin was in *her* head all the time. All she had to do was find the connection and follow it back, just like she did with Mordan.

Taking another breath, Marsh focused. This time it didn't take her long to find her connection to Roeglin and shift along it into his head. What she found when she did was terrifying.

The other mage had noticed her wall and given one last command to the wolves. From the glimpse she got of his thoughts, Marsh knew it was because the man was sure the pack would turn on him otherwise. Marsh wondered how she could make that happen, because what he was doing to Roeglin was unforgivable.

He'd managed to corner her friend in his own mind and was raining a storm of lightning down on Roeglin's kneeling form. For his part, Roeglin had created a sort of defensive shield over himself, and the storm was beating against it with all the ferocity the other mage could muster.

Marsh looked for the raider mage. When she found him, she'd end his lightning once and for all. She'd end him too if she could. Was that even possible from inside someone else's head? There was only one way to find out.

Seeing it was impossible to reach Roeglin, she studied the storm. It had to be coming from somewhere. There had to be a connection linking the two mind mages. All she had to do was find it and slide from Roeglin's mind into the other mage's.

She snorted.

Yeah, right. That was *all* she had to do.

Don't you da—

Hush, Ro. Momma's busy.

Momma's gonna get her butt kicked when I get out of here.

You couldn't kick a kitten's butt. Now, be quiet.

Well, hello, <u>Mommy</u>!

That wasn't a voice she knew. Marsh looked for the

source. She couldn't find it, but the storm trying to beat its way through Roeglin's shield diminished.

Can't do more than two things at once, can you? Marsh teased. *Why don't you step over here and pick on someone your own size?*

Roeglin groaned, but Marsh ignored him. He could roll all his eyes all he wanted, but he needed the break.

My own size? The strange mage sounded amused. *How about this, then?*

At his words, the storm coalesced into a single solid form, and Marsh realized that it *had* been the mage...or whatever passed for him inside someone else's skull. The form grew, becoming a giant, and Roeglin screamed.

Kick him out! Kick him out!

Underlying his words was the idea that she had kicked him out of her own head so many times, she should be more than able to kick the foreign mage out of his. The man had a point.

Get out!

Marsh remembered what it was like to boot Roeglin out of her head and tried the same. The only problem was that she wasn't in her own head, and she had no idea how to do it for someone else.

Work it out fast.

How could Roeglin sound like he was gritting his teeth?

There was no reply to that, so Marsh tried again. This time she decided she needed to be at least as big as the giant.

No!

The sheer panic in Roeglin's voice stopped her.

Find another way.

Find another way?

Marsh stared at the foreign mage. He still needed a connection to do what he was doing. It was like when she found herself in Mordan's head...

Dan!

The kat was beside her in seconds, inside Roeglin's head.

Outside, Marsh was sure Henri was staring at a suddenly-collapsed kat and cursing a blue streak, but she didn't bother looking out to be sure. They had more important things to do.

Under his dome, Roeglin stirred, lifting his head to study the giant standing above him. He didn't look too good, or like he knew what he was going to do next. Marsh hoped the shadow wall was holding. She took a heartbeat to think about it, discovering she was kneeling with one hand on Roeglin's back, the other outstretched to keep the shadows in place.

It was also enough to show that Henri was standing over them both. Mordan was lying at his feet, and she'd been right—Henri *was* cursing a blue streak. It might have been entertaining to listen to, but she had to deal with the menace in Roeglin's head.

Apparently, Roeglin had something to say about that. Well, of *course*, he did.

Call for help.

What?

Call Gustav.

He wanted her to do *what*?

You heard.

Yeah, she heard all right, and what she heard and what she had to do were two different things.

Ask Henri.

"Henri?" She hadn't meant to say that out loud. Marsh sighed. Well, seeing as she was here..."Call Gustav."

"And just how in the Deeps-misbegotten fornicating depths am I supposed to do that while you're sleeping on the job?"

Marsh let that go unanswered, following the connection back to Roeglin. She found the other mage had been busy while she'd been gone...and that not everything was working the way he intended.

For one thing, he obviously hadn't dealt with an angry hoshkat, before, and Mordan was busy bringing him down to size. The kat's mental presence was clinging to the front of the enemy giant, her forepaws wrapped around its neck as she tore at its throat with her jaws and raked at its belly with her hind claws.

Dan! Marsh cried, and ran forward.

In the distance, she thought she heard a wolf howl, but there was no time to see. No time to check if her shadow wall was holding. She was sure Henri was shouting as well, but he wasn't trying to shake her back into her body so she could only assume that he was holding his own. Drawing her sword, she slid around the giant's feet, hacking at the back of his ankle as she did so.

It was an old soldier's trick. Your enemy couldn't chase you if he couldn't walk. Of course, he couldn't run away either, and Marsh had no idea what that meant for a mind mage trapped in someone else's head.

Nothing, as it turned out.

As she pivoted and brought the blade across the tendon running down the back of his other leg, the giant screamed and vanished.

Get...out, Roeglin ordered, his voice weak.

Well, there was gratitude for you. Marsh might have argued, but Mordan grabbed her by the scruff of the neck and yanked her back into her own body. She had the brief impression of being dumped and pressed against the ground by an outsized paw, then the kat was gone, vanishing down the connection between them as though it was the most natural thing in the world.

Perhaps it was...like the dryness in her mouth and the rampaging headache threatening to split her skull in two. A groan leaked out before she could stop it and she forced her eyes open, then lifted her head.

19

OF WOLVES, KATS, AND MIND MAGES

The first thing she saw was the back of Henri's legs. He was standing in front of the kat, his hand outstretched as though that would stop the wolves from tearing him apart. Mordan was lying on the ground behind him and only just starting to stir.

The wolves saw the kat's first twitch of movement and stalked one step forward.

Henri kept one hand outstretched but dropped his other hand to the hilt of the sword.

"Don't make me," he said. "I don't want to have to hurt you, but I will."

The wolf took another step forward, its ears pricked, its tail stiff and straight behind it.

Marsh found she'd folded over her knees, one arm draped over Roeglin's shoulders, her free hand on the dirt beside her. She pushed to her feet...or she tried to, but her legs wouldn't cooperate. She couldn't even get her feet under her.

"Henri..."

"Not now, Marsh."

At the sound of her voice, the wolf stepped two more paces forward and stopped, one paw raised. A snarl rippled out of its throat as Mordan rolled onto her feet to stand beside Henri. The kat lowered her head and flattened her ears, her tail lashing the air as she growled in reply.

Mine, came clearly through her connection to Marsh.

"Did you call for help?"

"I yelled."

Marsh guessed she couldn't ask for more than that.

Henri took his hand off his sword and reached back for her. She noticed he kept his other hand stretched toward the wolves.

"You know that's not going to stop them, right?"

"You know that's not helpful, right?"

He had a point.

"Why'd you stop?"

"Stop what?"

"Yelling."

"Are you kidding me? Have you seen what came the last time I called? And they don't like me shouting. They stopped when I did."

They had? Well, at least she knew the reason for that.

"The mind mage isn't controlling them anymore. They're probably wondering why they were attacking us."

"Wolves don't need an excuse."

"You met many?"

"You could say that."

Marsh remembered what she'd been told about Henri preferring the surface and why he'd still been guarding caravans underground. Lennie. Right. And Jorge.

"You gonna take my hand or what?" Henri sounded impatient.

The answer turned out to be "or what," because, when Marsh reached for Henri's hand, the wolf pack growled. Not just the leader, but the whole pack as one. Even Mordan flinched.

Marsh studied the wolves. Standing would put her above them and possibly make her a threat. She needed to make them see she wasn't before the wolves decided to make sure the four of them weren't a threat anymore.

"Crouch down," she said.

"You are out of what's left of your tiny little mind!"

The lead wolf barked two short, sharp yaps and Henri raised his hand in placation.

"Are you sure about this?" he asked.

Marsh wanted to tell him she wasn't sure about anything, but she really needed him to do what she asked.

"Just do it."

Henri hesitated, but the wolves didn't move.

"Please, Henri. They don't know why they were attacking us, and you're the only one standing."

"No, I'm not."

Well, *merde.*

Dan, you need to lie down again.

I am not beneath them.

Please, Dan. I need Henri to live.

The kat tilted her head as though assessing how Henri was standing, then, before Marsh could say anything to warn him, Mordan backed up two steps and swept her paw across the back of his ankles. He came down hard, landing on his back on the ground beside her. Before he could do any more than draw a breath to shout, Mordan pivoted, circling swiftly around them so she could stand with one forepaw on Marsh's back and the other on Henri's chest.

Her roar echoed through the cavern, and its message was clear.

These humans were *her* humans, and she would shred the fur of any wolf who tried to harm them.

Looking at the pack, Marsh thought the kat might have made a mistake, but she didn't say a word. She didn't dare move. The leader of the wolves took a step toward them, and the pack followed.

Marsh felt the kat's weight shift, but Mordan didn't move. The wolf took another step forward, his eyes never leaving the kat. He came close enough to sniff Marsh's head, and she held her breath. When he turned his attention to Roeglin, Marsh tensed, but Mordan's presence was strong in her head.

Be still.

The wolf looked from the mage to the kat, and the kat growled. The wolf backed away, circling around until it could sniff the toe of Henri's boot. This time when Mordan's weight shifted, it was because she looked down into the guard's face and growled.

"Deeps-be-damned-and-dusted bossy bitch," he muttered, then gasped.

Marsh tensed, but Henri was still alive. She could hear him swearing under his breath, too softly for her to make out the words. She figured the kat would be insulted if she actually gave a damn. The cursing became a shout of outrage, followed by every filthy word she'd ever heard uttered, and she didn't have to ask why.

She could see.

The wolf had lifted his leg and was drenching Henri's boots with a thoroughness that could only be admired—like his accuracy. It stank, but he didn't hit her or Mordan or Roeglin with a single drop. The spreading puddle was another matter, but one they could deal with later. As a sign of utter contempt for the kat's posing and Henri's defiance, the wolf had just said it all.

When he was done, he turned his back on them, making a show of flicking dirt behind him before taking a few more steps and stretching. It was a view Marsh could have done without, but she was grateful when he trotted into the shrooms, taking the pack with him.

Mordan stayed where she was until all sound of the wolves' passing had faded, then took her paw from Marsh's back and nudged her away from moisture seeping out of Henri's boots. Marsh tried to move but failed, and the kat nudged her again, this time sliding her head under Marsh's hand.

Did her pride need energy?

Marsh scratched the kat's head.

"Deeps, yes, I need the energy."

"And me." Roeglin's voice was barely a whisper.

Marsh wanted to say he was first but knew she couldn't. If she tried to use her magic for anything but replenishing her reserves, she'd sleep where she knelt. She sniffed. That would be unthinkable.

Focusing carefully, she accepted what Mordan was offering and took just enough to allow her to focus on the broader spread of natural energy around them.

"Thanks, Dan. I can do it from here."

"*Oui.* Thanks, Dan," Henri mimicked. "Can you get your claws out of my chest now and let me up out of this puddle of piss?"

The sarcastic resentment in his voice made Marsh laugh and lose her concentration. The kat moved and Henri scrambled up off the floor, taking several steps away from them to shake out his boots and fuss with his trouser legs.

"Unbelievable," he complained, stomping his feet. "Un-shroom-shaggingly-believable!"

He glared at Mordan.

"Next time, don't help."

Mordan stared at him, then walked over to stand in front of him, looking up.

"What?" he demanded, and the kat rose up on her hind legs and slammed both forepaws into his chest, pushing him backward.

He stumbled, tripped over the rock behind him, and went down into a cluster of brown noses.

"What in all the shroom-shagged shadows was that about?" he shouted, hauling himself out of the oozing mass of crushed fungus.

Marsh looked away and tried not to burst into howling laughter. She managed to choke it down to a muffled snort, which Henri was too busy swearing to notice. Taking a deep breath, Marsh tried again. The energy was still there, the cavern more alive than any of the tunnels they had passed through.

Careful not to draw too much from any one source, Marsh took what she needed and focused on Roeglin.

"Tell me when you think you can walk enough to make it back to the shadow mages."

He managed the barest of nods and Marsh cautiously directed the energy into him, using her ability to read life to direct the flow to the parts of him that glowed dullest.

"Enough," he managed a few moments later and rolled slowly to his feet.

Marsh rose too, and Henri pushed off the rock he'd been sitting on.

"Tell me we're going back to somewhere I can get a hot bath, a warm towel, and a clean change of clothes."

Roeglin shook his head.

"We've still got a mind-walker to catch."

Henri rolled his eyes and made a helpless gesture with his hands that took in his wet clothes and boots, but he didn't argue.

"Which way?"

Roeglin frowned, his face going blank.

"He's heading toward the mines. They had a camp between here and there."

"What about the wolves?" Marsh asked. "Won't they be hunting him too?"

"They will once they figure out he's alive."

A howl split the air.

Henri cocked his head to one side and stared at Roeglin.

"You want to try to beat them?"

"I'd like to, but none of us are in any condition to outrun them."

"We going to try?" Marsh asked, walking in the direction of the howl.

Roeglin followed her.

"*Oui.*"

"For the Deeps' sake!"

Henri followed them, his boots making squelching sounds at every step.

Marsh almost felt sorry for him.

He was *protecting us,* Roeglin reminded her in her head, where Henri couldn't hear it.

True.

One man facing down a pack, and he didn't draw steel, Roeglin added. *That shows more courage than I'd have thought.*

Or a spectacular lack of sense.

Roeglin snorted, and Henri reached over and clipped Marsh over the back of the head.

"I don't have to hear you to know you're talking about me."

Marsh's face warmed, and Henri laughed.

"Gotcha. Now you owe me *two* dinners."

Marsh pretended not to hear him, instead tweaking the shadows to show her what was hiding among them and calling on nature to show her the life around and ahead of them. To her surprise, the mage wasn't far ahead—and neither was the pack. He had scrambled up onto a rocky pillar, and the wolves couldn't reach him.

"You!" he said when Marsh and Roeglin emerged behind the pack.

Uh oh.

That was all Roeglin had time to say before he collapsed.

"Ro!"

The mind-walker laughed.

"And now I have his name."

Mordan growled and leapt for the rock, but the mage scrambled higher, and the kat's claws missed him.

Roeglin gasped and Marsh knelt beside him, getting ready to slide inside his head.

"Oh no, you don't!" Henri grabbed her by her collar and hauled her to her feet. "I'm not doing this alone. Next time you can get pissed on too."

Marsh wanted to argue that there were more important things, but Henri was right, if a little off the mark as to what they were and why. Half the pack had turned to face them. The other half was dividing its attention between the mage and Mordan. As the pack leader approached Henri went to draw his sword. Marsh reached out and slapped her hand over his.

"Don't."

"Whatever you're going to do, do it fast."

"I've got this," she told him and stepped forward.

The wolf laid its ears back and snarled at her. Behind her, Marsh heard Henri shift, and she held a hand behind her signaling him to stop whatever he was about to do. The wolf caught her gesture and snapped at the air in front of her. Marsh turned her head making sure she wasn't looking it directly in the eye but watching in case it attacked.

It was hard.

These wolves were bigger than the ones near her cousin's home, but they were still animals like the kat, and the krypthund...and the moutons.

Merde. I am going to have to look it in the eye, she realized. *At least to make initial contact.*

Slowly, she raised her head, aware of the wolf's pitch-black eyes watching her every move. When she'd lifted it far enough, she met its gaze.

We come in peace, she told it and pictured the mage on the outcrop. *Your enemy is our enemy. Look and see the truth for yourself.*

If the wolf was like the kat...

She felt her world split as the pack leader accepted the connection she offered and pulled her in. Inside his head, she found he was even bigger than it seemed on the outside. He stalked around her, his nose touching her as he whiffled up and down the length of her body.

Hey!

He snarled in reply and came back to stand in front of her.

What made the little human think it was ever going to be allowed to leave?

Marsh arched an eyebrow at him.

Like that, was it? Well, it was like this...

You are interfering with our hunt.

That was not the reply the wolf was expecting.

Your hunt?

Our hunt, Marsh confirmed, indicating Mordan. *Our pride, and our hunt. We seek our cubs and the parents of our cubs.*

She managed a credible snarl of her own and continued.

They have taken our cubs, our pack, and our pride. We must protect our territory and get our pride back.

The wolf's ears pricked.

You speak like someone who cannot decide if they are wolf or cat. He paused. *You do not sound like a man.*

Marsh had no answer for that, but the wolf continued.

Yet you cross our territory like it is your own.

Man claims this cavern.

The wolf's lip curled.

Man's opinion is nothing. The pack is all.

Marsh regarded him.

You work with the mages.

It was a guess, and she pictured the leader of the shadow mages and the woman as she thought it. The wolf's ears folded sideways and he looked sheepish.

We have made the mages pack.

Marsh thought of Roeglin, Henri, Gustav, and the others. She pictured Mordan.

We are pride.

She pictured the wolves from Downslopes.

We are pack.

The wolf's ears pricked at the sight of the Downslopes wolves and his nostrils flared as he studied her scent. Marsh tried once more.

May we cross your territory? And secure it from those who would bring it harm?

He stared at her as though considering her proposal.

The pack must be safe.

While Marsh was pondering what that might mean, the wolf kicked her out of his head. She landed in her own as he turned snarling and snapping at those around him, and the pack turned its attention to the mage on the pillar. Mordan growled, and Roeglin screamed.

"Watch him," Marsh told Henri and knelt beside Roeglin, trying to connect to his mind.

She found the way in, then discovered it was blocked.

There was no way for her to get in and defend him from whatever the mage was doing. Marsh focused, trying to find a way past the blocks that one of them had put in place. If she could save him, she'd ask Roeglin about those later. In the meantime...

She rose to her feet, calling a dart to her hand and hurling it at the mage on the pillar. It fell short, striking the pillar below him and dissipating. The mage didn't seem to notice.

He was pressed back against the rock, his eyes closed. A faint smile played across his lips as though he was enjoying whatever he was doing inside Roeglin's mind. Marsh walked through the wolves, relieved when they moved aside to let her pass. When she got to him, she was going to throw him right into the middle of them.

She scrambled up the rocks, reaching the first ledge, and looked back. Wolves and kat were watching her with something akin to anticipation on their faces. Henri had turned his back on them and was keeping watch on the cavern.

He'd drawn his sword and moved back from the shrooms to give himself room to react to anything that might come bursting out of them. Roeglin was curled on the ground behind him. Roeglin... Marsh reached for the next ledge, the one that would put her just below the mage. She froze when something whirred past her, then dropped back to the ledge she was standing on and took a firm grip on the rock as she turned to survey the cavern below her.

Something else whirred past her, and the mage above her gave a short, sharp gasp.

Marsh refused to let him distract her from her search and soon found what she was looking for: Gustav.

Standing in a gap between the callas, he sighted on the ledge above her one more time. Marsh resisted the urge to wave and went back to climbing. The least she could do was drag the body off its ledge.

It didn't take her long to get to where the mage had gone, and Marsh carefully peered over the edge of his perch. One look told her that Roeglin was safe. Gustav's aim had been devastatingly accurate, and two dark quarrels protruded from the mind mage's chest.

Marsh reached up and grabbed him by the boot, trying to pull him down, but he was too heavy. She looked back at Gustav and saw he was no longer alone. He'd been joined by several of the local shadow mages. Seeing Es standing beside him should have been enough to warn her, but Marsh still fought against the dark vines of shadow that stretched out of the cavern's ceiling and wrapped around her.

By the time she'd registered they weren't hurting her, they'd wrapped around the mind mage's body and lowered them to the ground. The wolves stepped smartly to one side to give them space, but only Devin's shout stopped them from rushing in to take their vengeance.

"Leave it!"

Marsh ignored the wolves. As the vines disappeared from around her, Marsh hurried over to Roeglin, worried that he hadn't moved.

"Ro?" She shook him. "Ro?"

When he still didn't move, she knelt beside him and tried to calm her fears. He was still breathing, so he was still alive. All she had to do was reach him. Taking a deep breath, she placed her hands on his back and reached for his mind.

She was relieved to discover she was no longer blocked, not so relieved to find his mind quiet.

Ro?

Did he need healing? Did he...

There's no need to shout. Now get out of my head. I need to sleep.

Marsh felt a nudge, as though he'd tried to kick her out and failed. It would have been funny if he didn't sound so tired and bruised. She left, catching herself in a sob of relief as she surfaced, finding it almost second nature to draw a little of the surrounding energy and guide it into Roeglin's head. As she did, she drew on her nature magic to look at him and used the way his life force looked to guide her healing.

By the time she'd finished, Gustav had come to stand beside her.

"Is he okay?"

Marsh nodded.

"You got to him in time."

"Another mind mage?"

"*Oui.*" Marsh heard the fatigue edging her own words. "Just needs to rest."

"He's not the only one."

From the way Gustav said it, it wasn't a question; it was an order.

"When we get back to camp. Henri has to be sick of carrying me by now."

"Henri's got his hands full carrying Roeglin," Henri said,

coming to stand over her. "He'd just leave your ass here for the wolves to look after."

The wolves...Marsh couldn't help smirking. Henri's boots stank. He nudged her with the toe of one.

"You still owe me dinner."

"How many's that now?" Gustav wanted to know.

"Three."

"Two," Marsh argued, struggling to her feet.

Henri placed his fingers against her shoulder and pushed her over.

"Misbegotten son of the Deep!"

"Three."

Marsh glared at him and got back up. This time he swept her feet out from under her.

"*A la putain!*"

She didn't let him get away with it though. Reaching out, she wrapped her hands around his boots and yanked him off his feet. This time she was able to get up and move out of grab range before he stood. He said nothing but stooped to scoop Roeglin off the ground and swing him over his shoulder.

Gustav rolled his eyes and turned to the local mages.

"We need to talk."

20

OVERNIGHTING WITH THE SHADOW DRUIDS

They overnighted with Dimanche's shadow mages and learned that the group worked with more than just the shadows. Many of them had an affinity with the plants and fungi that grew in the cavern. Others could speak with the creatures that lived there and a very few could call the insects, drawing clouds of glitter-winged color to dance in the air around them or carpets of dark-carapaced menace.

Marsh shivered when she saw the latter but couldn't help being fascinated.

"Do you want to learn how?" Es asked, coming alongside her as she watched one of the younger mages demonstrate their control to an elder.

"Do we have time?"

Her answer came from Gustav.

"Leclerc! We need you."

Es sighed.

"Another day," she said, "but if you want to try it, start

with the shroom beetles. Their energy is easy to pick out from everything else."

Marsh hadn't thought of the beetles as possessing a different form of energy to other things. She wished she had time to ask more, but Gustav bellowed again.

"Leclerc!"

"Thank you," she managed, hurrying to where the Protector captain was sitting with the mercenaries and the shadow mage leaders.

Es followed and took her place beside Devin. As soon as they were settled, he started.

"These raiders," Devin began. "Where do they come from?"

"I don't know. They come through portals they open in the shadows, and I have yet to find their home."

"When will you know?"

"When the caverns are secured, I can begin looking for them."

He nodded and looked over to where Valerie and Luka were sitting.

"This is who you chose for the defense of this cavern?"

Marsh shook her head.

"I did not choose them. They volunteered."

Devin didn't look impressed.

"Their interests are compromised."

Valerie stirred.

"Not anymore. Once we're done here, we're informing the Gaeblers their contract has been terminated."

"And we're doing the same for the Piermonts," Luka added.

"They will issue bounties," Devin told them.

Valerie and Luka stared.

"They have done it before," Devin added as though that proved everything. "Surely you knew that?"

Valerie pressed her lips together and nodded.

"We refused a number of bounties," she said. "I do not know who took them."

"And you did not intervene," Devin interrupted as though that made her just as guilty as those who had.

Valerie blushed, and Luka gave her a look of disbelief.

"You warned them?"

The mercenary leader swallowed and her face paled.

"When we could, we warned them. There were some, though…"

Her voice caught and she bowed her head, letting the words trailed away. When she raised it again, her face was firm. She glanced at Gustav.

"By swearing to defend the cavern and all in it, we can do better."

Devin studied her.

"You want to atone."

She shook her head.

"There is no atonement for not being able to stop what was done. We can only try to stop it in the future."

"You know that when you terminate the contracts, you won't be told of the bounties."

"We'll know of them. Maybe not as soon as we might have, but soon enough…and this time we'll be able to see who takes them."

What she'd do with that information, Marsh didn't know, but it was clear the mercenary leader had something in mind. Luka laid a hand on Valerie's shoulder.

"It is the same for us." He turned to Devin. "We could do with magical support."

Devin didn't answer straight away. Instead, he looked at where Roeglin lay at the edge of the fire, Mordan stretched out beside him. Seeing that the shadow mage was still unconscious, Devin looked at Marsh.

"How does it work for the Monastery?" he asked. "Do you retain your independence?"

"We retain our independence," she said, "but I am not the best person to ask."

She glanced at Roeglin, then at Gustav.

"Jump in if my understanding differs from how it really is," she said, and then continued. "As I understand it, we have an alliance with the Founder of Ruins Hall, and now with the Protectors in Kerrenin's Ledge. We train any of their people who show magical potential and help their troops discover any magical ability."

The look on Devin's face said he was interested, so she went on.

"Our mages fight in their units and come under their command while they're in those units, and the Protectors must look after them as if they are their own men. In return, the Protectors look after the route between our caverns and allow us to recruit or take in any who either don't want to join them or are too young to do so. We also provide a sanctuary for their families."

"And in the future?" Devin pressed. "How do we know the cavern leaders won't use these forces against each other?"

"They've never used force against each other before," Gustav put in.

"They've never had a trained force at their disposal before," Devin snapped back, "so I'll ask it again. How do we make sure that doesn't happen?"

This time Marsh indicated Gustav should answer.

"The Protectors will become an independent force with the sole goal of protecting the Four Caverns," he said, "just as soon as the caverns are secured and the raiders chased to their source. When that happens, the Founder of Ruins Hall will work with the Kerrenin's Ledge Council to help the Protectors from their caverns combine into one independent body."

Devin's lip curled in disbelief.

"I can't see that actually happening, can you?"

Gustav shook his head at the words and looked the mage in the eye.

"It will happen," he assured him. "As much as I have served the Founder since he survived Chaumont, I am happier to serve the Caverns."

That was news to Marsh. She didn't know what Chaumont was or where, or what had happened there, but she knew he'd been with the Founder for a very long time. The look on his face was both determined and closed, as though he kept some powerful emotions at bay. When he spoke again, it was to address Luka and Valerie.

"Will you have the support of the Five?"

"We already have the support of one of them," Valerie answered. "Whether the others will agree is not certain."

Gustav frowned.

"Can you sustain the force without them?"

This time Luka replied.

"It depends on the other companies."

"You mean mercenaries?"

Luka shrugged.

"If you like. The thing is, if we can convince them to join us as part of the Defenders, the rest of the Five won't have a choice but to support the Defenders if they want to stay clear of the raiders."

"That will only work if they're not working with the raiders," Marsh added, and everyone turned toward her.

"What do you mean?"

"I mean that the Piermonts and Kearick both asked about the mages here, then the raiders attacked. It can't be a coincidence."

Devin turned to Luka.

"Is this true?"

"We were asked to see what groups of magic users there were in the caverns," the mercenary admitted. "Our understanding was that the Piermonts were seeking to hire those with skills in animal handling and to help them in the development of fodder shrooms. We never suspected..."

Devin held up his hand and looked at the other mages gathered around the campfire.

"We need to decide what to do next." He hesitated. "You're going to sever your ties to them?"

Luka licked his lips and nodded.

"We are canceling our contracts with them effective immediately."

Devin studied him, his eyes dark with contemplation. Finally, he addressed Valerie.

"Can you vouch for him?"

Marsh caught the rapid flicker of Valerie's eyes from the shadow mage to Luka and back. To her, it looked like the mercenary leader was assessing her choices, but the woman's decision was clear.

"I will vouch for him," Valerie said. "Together, our forces form the basis of the Dimanche Defenders. We are in the process of renouncing all ties to the Five. Assisting you took precedence."

Devin studied them a few heartbeats longer and stood.

"You are welcome to stay the night," he told them, "and we hope you will join us for breakfast in the morning."

As a way of telling them not to leave, it was a subtle as a brick, but neither of the mercenary leaders took offense.

"Agreed."

They fell into silence, watching as the mages and druids withdrew past a line of carefully interwoven calla. The shrooms drew her eyes, and she studied the way they grew.

"Do you like it?"

Es had come to sit beside her.

"I...yes. Don't you have a meeting to attend?"

Es smiled.

"I'm here to supervise."

"Keep an eye on us, you mean?"

And why would you be telling us that?

Exactly.

Roeglin was more awake than he appeared.

Because you are not the only ones who can walk minds...Es's clear voice interrupted.

"Sons of the Deep!"

Marsh's exclamation drew the attention of everyone around the fire and all eyes focused on Es. The mage held up her hands.

"Hey, don't look at *me* like that. I'm just doing my job."

"You're as subtle as a rock to the head," Henri muttered, his comment meant to be heard. "Ouch!"

Izmay punched him in the shoulder. Es shrugged and turned back to Marsh.

"So, you want to know how it's done or not?"

Marsh focused on the shrooms once more, recalling the time she'd seen the rock mages from the monastery's cavern shape fungi into overnight rests.

"Yes, like that," Es agreed, and Marsh kicked her out of her head. "Hey!"

Roeglin snickered.

"Just show her how to shape them. No more games." He winced. "And stay out of *my* head, too."

"No," Marsh said, and Es shot her a puzzled look.

"What?"

"No more magic today. What can you tell me about the Danets? They have steadings around here, don't they?"

Es frowned.

"I only know of two families by that name. One left for the Deeps several months back. The other used to farm shrooms and moutons out near Devastation's Hollow. They vanished a couple of weeks back. If we hadn't heard the moutons, bleating no one would have known. Why do you ask?"

Marsh shook her head, her heart sinking.

"Can you show me?"

Es's eyes grew wary.

"Tomorrow, maybe. Once the Council has decided."

"Decided what?" Gustav asked, but Es only smiled.

"That I can't discuss."

Gustav smiled in return, and he stood.

"Show us where you want us to sleep," he said, and Valerie and Luka rose with him.

Marsh caught Roeglin watching her, his expression shuttered.

"You got space in your corner?" she asked. "Because the kat looks like she needs company."

"Oh, sure," he managed. "The *kat* needs company."

He left it at that, and Marsh looked around for her pack. It took her a couple of moments to realize she hadn't brought it. She wondered where Roeglin had gotten his bedding, and remembered the druids making sure he was wrapped warmly when they'd settled him in his corner.

I'll share...

Marsh blushed, and she fumbled to find an answer.

"It's okay. I'll sleep with the kat."

Across the fire, Henri sputtered, and Izmay gave a startled bark of laughter. Marsh felt her face heat further.

"Not what I meant," she muttered, refusing to look in their direction.

Instead, she crossed over to the kat and settled down beside her...on the opposite side to where Roeglin was lying.

Fine! I know when I'm not wanted. I'll let you hang with Gustav tomorrow.

As if that was any different.

Marsh pillowed her head on her arms and closed her eyes, trusting Mordan to wake her if anything came that was likely to harm her. She did not expect to be woken by two very familiar voices the next morning—three if you counted the fact Brigitte was trying to catch up with them both.

"Marsh!" Aisha's tone was one of sheer hell-raising delight.

"Aysh!" Tamlin's was one of utter frustration.

"Apprentices Danet!"

And Brigitte sounded more exasperated than normal.

Before Marsh could respond to any of that, however, Scruffknuckle arrived. He bounded over to her and set his two front paws on her shoulders while he washed her face with joy. Marsh was still trying to push him off her when Aisha reached her.

"Marsh!"

The child came to a skidding stop beside her, bouncing impatiently on her toes as Marsh hurried to disentangle herself from the oversized pup and the blanket that had been thrown over her in the night. As she did so, she became aware of the sound of voices and the movement of a large group of people nearby.

"When did you get here?" she asked, getting to her feet.

"Just now!" Aisha giggled. "I found you!"

Her happiness was infectious, and Marsh laughed as she lifted the child from the ground.

"You did, but how did you know I needed finding?"

"You not in town. Master Ennermay asked."

"Master Envermet's here?"

"Well, I would hardly be anywhere else."

His voice made Marsh jump and her face colored as Aisha turned in her arms to face him.

"See? She's here," the little girl told him, sounding very pleased with herself.

Marsh was surprised to see a faint smile curve the man's lips.

"Yes, she's here. Have you had time to say hello?"

Aisha nodded, and Master Envermet indicated where Brigitte was waiting a few strides away.

"Then you'd better go back to Brigitte and see what she wants you to do next while I speak with your guardian."

"Kay."

Aisha flung her arms around Marsh's neck, giving her a brief hug before wriggling to be put down. Marsh set her back on the ground, and Master Envermet watched the child run past him. When she was gone, he still didn't focus on Marsh. Instead, he glanced to one side.

"Tamlin..."

The shadow captain didn't add anything to that, just stepped back so Marsh could see where Tamlin had been quietly waiting, one of the hoshkits by his side. She didn't wait for the boy to move but went to him.

"Hey," she said. "You been okay?"

Tamlin rolled his eyes and wrapped his arms around her waist. When he replied, his voice was gruff.

"We're fine. Thanks for asking. We'll catch up later if you've got the time."

He released her and stomped back to Brigitte, leaving Marsh staring after him with her mouth hanging open.

He really missed you, Roeglin told her, his voice soft in her head, *but he also knows Master Envermet needs to talk to you, and he resents that. He doesn't want to get in the way, but he wants your attention too. We need to make some time for you to spend with them.*

Silently, Marsh agreed, fighting down the sudden surge of sadness as she closed her mouth and forced herself to look at Master Envermet.

"You needed to see me?"

"We expected to meet you in town, but Master Leger did not contact me as planned. We were worried. Have you been able to find anything on the children's relatives?"

It was not the greeting she was expecting, but Marsh quelled the urge to tell him she and Roeglin were fine, thank you very much, and how nice it was of him to ask. Roeglin caught that thought and laughed in her head where Master Envermet couldn't hear it.

And you wonder where the boy gets it from.

On the outside, he was as serious and silent as anyone could wish. Marsh fought down the desire to stick her tongue out at him and answered Master Envermet's question instead.

"Captain Moldrane..." she began, but stopped when Envermet frowned. "We met Valerie when we arrived and had to save one of Dimanche's leaders from an angry mob. After that, we learned Kearick was heading for the shadow mages here and went after him."

"You didn't expect the mages to be under attack?"

"We thought it might be a possibility after Luka told us the Piermonts had also asked about them."

"And Kearick?"

"Gone. He had an escort, and we couldn't get to him in time."

"Hmmm. And the relatives?"

"The druids tell me their farm was found abandoned."

She didn't explain what that meant. Master Envermet had seen enough abandoned farms to know. Marsh saw his lips compress and he turned to Roeglin.

"You were injured."

It was not a question, and Roeglin's eyes widened. It was almost funny to watch him realize Master Envermet had checked on them before checking in with them. After a moment's pause, the shadow mage answered.

"There was another mind mage."

"Powerful?"

Roeglin blushed.

"Stronger than me."

"How did you defeat him?"

"Captain Moldrane put a crossbow bolt through his chest."

It wasn't enough.

"And?"

"And Master Leclerc and the kat helped me."

Master Envermet's brows rose.

"The kat's a mind mage now?"

"I believe Master Leclerc can explain that better than I can."

Marsh rolled her eyes, but Master Envermet would not be deterred.

"And?"

"I... It's hard to explain."

"Try me."

"I knew Roeglin could get into my head, so there had to be a connection between us, just like the connection I have with the kat."

Envermet nodded and signaled for her to continue.

"I just found the connection and followed it into his head, and tried to deal with the other mage when I got there."

"And the kat?"

"I needed help, so I called her, and she used the connection between us to follow me."

Marsh hoped Master Envermet wouldn't ask any more questions because she couldn't explain what she'd done any better than that. It was a relief when the shadow captain nodded. He gestured at the campsite.

"And why are you still here?"

Marsh wanted to tell him it was because they'd just woken up, but thought he might take that the wrong way. She was still wracking her brains for an appropriate response when Roeglin replied.

"Valerie and Luka's forces form the basis of the Dimanche Defenders, and the local mages are deciding where they stand based on their discovery that information from Luka might have been used by one of the Five to guide the raiders in their attack yesterday."

As a way of saying Valerie and Luka might be in trouble and why, Marsh couldn't have put it any better. Well, not without using a lot more words. Master Envermet frowned.

"Did they do it knowing they were helping the raiders?"

"No. It was just a contract Luka's people received from their patrons. They believed the reasons they were given."

"Do they still work for these patrons?"

"No. Both Luka and Valerie are terminating their contracts as soon as the local mages give them permission to leave."

"Messy," Envermet said. "We'll need to speak with them."

He looked around, pivoting slowly until his eyes fell on Es.

"I need to speak with your leaders."

Es looked him up and down, assessing the way he was dressed and the expression on his face.

"I'll see if they are ready," she told him. "You will need to wait here."

Master Envermet followed the direction of her hand as she gestured toward the space around the fire.

"Will they be long?" he asked as Devin appeared in the gap between the interwoven callas.

"No," the local mage answered. "We are here. The wolves spoke of your arrival. You are welcome to join us."

"My men…" Envermet began, but Devin interrupted him.

"My people will take care of them."

At his words, Master Envermet looked around, and Marsh followed his gaze. The mage was true to his word. Two of his people were standing beside Gustav, obviously discussing what to do next. As if sensing their attention, Gustav looked in their direction.

"He wants your permission to break formation and put them on standby," Roeglin said, his eyes flashing white. "The Keepers have offered breakfast and somewhere they can rest while they wait."

"Keepers?" Envermet asked, and Devin nodded.

"You have your Protectors, and Dimanche will soon have its Defenders, but we have been this Cavern's Keepers since before the Five arrived."

Envermet regarded him with a skeptical look.

"There don't seem to be enough for you to have been around that long…"

"It's a big cavern with many branches, and this is just an

outpost for the mines." Devin gestured toward the fire. "Shall we?"

Envermet moved as directed, speaking to Roeglin as he went.

"Tell Gustav yes, and that he's in command until I say otherwise."

Again Roeglin's eyes turned white.

"Done," he said seconds later, and followed Envermet to where the rest of the Keepers' leadership had gathered.

Marsh went with him, noting Luka and Valerie's arrival as she took her place beside him.

NEGOTIATIONS, ALLIANCES, AND COMBAT

When they were all settled, Devin began.

"The people of Dimanche know us as the shadow mages that live in the cavern, but we call ourselves the Cavern Keepers." He looked at Gustav. "Just as the Protectors are dedicated to the security of the Four Caverns, we are dedicated to the welfare of this one." His gaze traveled to where Valerie and Luka sat side by side.

"For that reason, we wish an alliance with the Dimanche Defenders, and will work with them in the same way that the Protectors work with the Deeps Monastery."

Before either of them could reply, he returned to Gustav and Master Envermet.

"We would also like to negotiate alliances with the Ledge, the monastery, and Ruins Hall. I take it you can help us do that?"

"Roeglin," Master Envermet said, "we need your assistance."

Marsh stifled a sigh, trying not to think of how long it had been since she'd seen Aisha and Tamlin. Beside her,

Mordan stretched and yawned before leaning against her. The kat would also prefer to be spending time with her cubs. Instead, they were both trapped here while their pride discussed its friendships.

Marsh supposed that was one way to put things. She rested a hand on the kat's shoulders and listened to the negotiation, although it was hard not to let her mind wander. Mordan rested her head on her paws and dozed. It seemed like an age before the alliances between the three groups were settled. By then, Marsh had also started to wonder just exactly how Aisha was able to find her.

The more she pondered it, the more curious she became about how the little girl was managing it, because as magic went, having a way to locate another person would be incredibly useful...and she didn't mean just for finding her friends.

Being able to use magic to track where Kearick had gone would make finding the children's parents much easier too. Right now Marsh didn't have a clue on where to look, especially now their relatives had been taken as well. Her heart sank. She had to tell them that too. It was not something she was looking forward to doing.

Pay attention. Roeglin's voice intruded on her mind, and Marsh realized she'd closed her eyes.

"Before we embark on the next leg of our journey," Master Envermet was saying. "I believe Master Leclerc has some unfinished business in this cavern that she must attend to. Then we will move to secure Ariella's Grotto."

At the mention of her name, Marsh found all eyes turn to her. Her mind raced, trying to make sure she knew exactly what she needed to do. She didn't want to forget to mention something she'd have to do later. Who knew what she'd be allowed to add once this meeting had ended?

"Master Leclerc?" Envermet prodded, and Marsh took a deep breath before she began.

"When I came to this cavern, I had two tasks. The main one was to assist Master Leger and Captain Moldrane with negotiating the establishment of a division of Protectors in this cavern. The other was to make contact with the remaining family of the two children I rescued from a shadow monster attack on the way to Ruins Hall."

She gestured to the group around the fire, conjuring a smile as she did so.

"I see you have managed the first one without me. The second task, however, has changed."

She heard a gasp from the shadows crowded at the base of a nearby outcrop and flicked a glance at Roeglin.

Of course, the little brats were listening...

"Excuse me," she said, turning toward the shadow.

Help me, she asked Roeglin, because Tamlin's grip on the shadows was at least as strong as her own, and who knew what Aisha had learned in the meantime?

Stretching out her hand, she made a grasping motion, attempting to drag the shadows away from the base of the rock. She wasn't surprised to find that they stretched and fought and did not part to reveal what lay beneath them. It wasn't hard to imagine Tamlin holding onto the shadows and pulling them closer around himself and his sister.

From the other side of Roeglin, Marsh heard Master Envermet sigh.

"Apprentices Danet, come here."

Four simple words and the shadows did what Marsh

wanted them to, sliding aside to reveal empty stone as Tamlin and Aisha stepped out from among them to come and stand before the shadow captain. He sighed and looked them up and down.

"What have I told you about listening in on conversations that are none of your concern?"

Tamlin lifted his head and stared defiantly at the shadow captain. Aisha mirrored his stance and look inch for inch.

"This conversation concerns us very much," the boy replied, completely omitting the fact that the negotiations between the Defenders, Keepers, Protectors, and Shadow Mages that had gone before didn't fit nearly as well.

Master Envermet frowned.

"And it was one I wanted Master Leclerc to have with you in private."

Tamlin shrugged. Aisha, mimicking him, copied the gesture with careful accuracy. The boy folded his arms and tapped his foot, his face defying Envermet to continue. Aisha mirrored every move, right down to his expression. By the time they were done, Marsh was having trouble keeping a straight face.

Master Envermet caught her biting her lip and sighed, waving the troublesome pair in her direction.

This time they didn't argue. Tamlin stalked over to Marsh and looked her up and down.

"We're not happy with you either," he told her, then sat at her feet and leaned against her shin.

"Yes, bad Marsh," Aisha added, following her brother's every move.

Marsh realized she was staring in drop-jawed surprise

and closed her mouth. It didn't help when she saw the small smile tugging at the corners of Master Envermet's mouth as he resumed his seat.

"Go on, Master Leclerc."

"I..." Marsh took a breath, all too aware of the two newest members in her audience. "I still need to go out to the Danets' farmstead to confirm their absence, then I need to return to the Deeps Monastery to formalize my guardianship of the children."

Tamlin snorted and, catching the look on Marsh's face, explained.

"It's not like you'd have had to do anything else," he scolded her. "Even if my uncle and his family had been at home, Aysh and I wouldn't have agreed to stay. It wouldn't have been safe."

It was like the kid had thrown a bucket of cold water over her.

"Why not?" she asked.

"Because they felt the same way about magic as Nettie's parents. You wouldn't have liked them."

If what the boy said was true, Marsh would have done more than not like them. She might very well have given them to the raiders, herself.

No, but you'd have kept the children, Roeglin told her. *I'd have seen to that. I'm sorry...*

Marsh brushed his apology aside and frowned at Tamlin. "Why didn't you tell us?" she demanded since the boy had known one of her tasks was to find his relatives.

Tamlin shrugged.

"Because it wouldn't have mattered what I said. You'd

have still had to come and see for yourself." He glared at Roeglin. "Isn't that right, Master Leger?"

"Yes, it is. That part hasn't changed."

"And you'll be coming with us when we check out your uncle's place," Marsh told him.

She'd meant for it to be comforting, but the boy fixed her with a rebellious stare.

"Too damned right, we will."

Marsh risked a glance at the gathered leadership as a small voice rose in echo.

"Damned right!"

An equally defiant wuff followed, and Scruffknuckle strolled out from the shadows to lie down beside them. He was followed by a hoshkat kit that hissed at her as it passed.

Marsh rolled her eyes, catching the quickly smothered grins and chuckles around the fire. Struggling to maintain her dignity, she nodded to Master Envermet.

"Beyond that, I still have to continue my investigations into the raiders so that we can focus on finding them once the Four Caverns are secure, and I believe I have obligations to the Protectors and the Monastery, as well."

It was the best way she could think of to signal that she thought she'd covered everything and it was time for him to take over, and she was glad when Master Envermet took the hint.

"This is true," he said, and turned back to the others. "My business here is to clear the caverns of as much raider influence as I can and to assist the local Protectors or Defenders in establishing themselves. I am also authorized to leave a training contingent if it is required and to establish an outpost for the Monastery, but I think you already have allies who can fill the same role. Once we have assisted in securing the cavern and making sure it is protected, we follow Masters Leger and Leclerc to the next of the Four Settlements. Dimanche is the next to last to require our assistance."

He paused looking at the faces of the leaders before him.

"How may we assist you?"

Marsh blinked. She hadn't realized they'd come as far as they had, but it made sense when she thought about it. The Defenders were established, and very few details remained to be sorted out. She watched Devin stand to answer Master Envermet's question.

The druid glanced around at those gathered, making sure he had caught their attention. His mouth curled upward as his gaze passed over the two children sitting at Marsh's feet. When it had returned to Master Envermet, he began.

"While I understand the Defenders need to formalize their paperwork, I accept they are here to stay." He dipped his head in acknowledgment to Valerie and Luka and continued. "As such, I propose that our first task be to investigate the Piermonts to see if they are in league with the raiders and how far their operations are compromised, and that we do that today."

Luka and Valerie did not disagree.

"How soon do you need us to be ready?" Valerie asked, rising to her feet.

"Is a half-turn sufficient?"

"It is more than enough," the mercenary leader told him. "With your permission…"

Devin nodded assent, and everyone rose from around the fire. The mercenaries and local mages headed in opposite directions, and Marsh could only assume that they knew exactly where they were going. She followed Master Envermet, conscious of Roeglin and the children moving with her.

Scruffknuckle bounded around them in barely contained delight, and the kit stalked by Aisha's side. Marsh frowned.

"Where's the other one?"

"You didn't know?" Tamlin's voice was full of exaggerated surprise. "What a shadows-hung surprise!"

Marsh glared at him.

"We haven't had a lot of time to catch up," she reminded him, trying to keep a firm grip on her temper.

"And whose fault is that?"

Marsh opened her mouth to respond and found she really didn't have an answer for him. It wasn't the boy's fault she'd been busy, but it also wasn't her fault either. It was just the way things were.

"Look, I—" she began, only to have Roeglin cut her off.

"Not fair, Tams. You've both got jobs to do, and they've taken up a lot of time. She'll spend more time with you once we get back."

"When?" the boy demanded. "Before or *after* she goes chasing down the raiders?"

The bitterness in his voice was sharp enough to cut, and Aisha reached up and laid her hand on his arm, her small face full of concern. Marsh didn't give the little girl time to speak.

"Before," she told him. "Even if it's just a day. We'll take the time to catch up."

"Wow, a whole day," Tamlin snarked, but he didn't sound as upset as before.

Marsh noticed that Roeglin was surprisingly quiet, which was odd. Usually, the shadow mage had a lot more to say.

You're on your own with this one, he told her. *I can't help you.*

Not even a little bit?

You're doing fine.

As they reached where Gustav was waiting near their troops, Marsh hoped so. Apart from her uncle and cousins, the kids were the only family she had, and she didn't want to lose them.

Not going to happen.

Thanks, Ro.

They were formed up behind the local mages and druids well before the half-turn was up, and jogging out across the cavern shortly thereafter. As they left, Marsh noticed a small group of mercenaries split away from the group and head back to town, Kels leading them.

"Where are they going?" she wondered.

"Back to Shameless," Valerie said from behind her. "We've got contracts to cancel and contracts to write up, and neither are doing us any good unwritten. I figured Hugh could earn his keep. Luka's sent folk, too. He has to get his people moved into new quarters and make sure his patrons know they need to find someone new."

"Won't they be upset?"

"Yup, but they'll be fine. The way Luka and I look at it, we're still keeping their people safe as part of our duties to the cavern. We're just not giving their safety precedence over anyone else's. The sooner they come to terms with that, the better."

They jogged on in silence, with Marsh stretching her senses out into the cavern to get a feel of the life they passed. She also kept tabs on Mordan, Scruffknuckle, and the kit, noting how the three of them ran together on the edge of the formation, their forms sliding in and out of view between the rocks and shrooms.

They followed the trail back to a turnoff that led them closer to the cavern's center, then swung away toward its outer perimeter. Marsh lifted her head as the air changed, becoming less earthy and more...something else. Ahead of her, Master Envermet noted the change.

"You didn't tell us the cavern breached the surface."

"The Piermonts chose it because there's an outlet into a valley in the Desolation, and they have enough open spaces for the horses to graze."

"The horses?"

"*Mais oui*. The horses, and the donkeys. For making the mules. You didn't think the Shades-cursed creatures grew on trees, did you?"

"No, but I wondered why they were so hard to come by."

"That's how they build their business. They control the supply of mounts in the caverns. Always have."

From the sound of his voice, Devin didn't approve of the monopoly, but before Master Envermet could continue the conversation, Marsh heard the sound of fighting and the leaders signaled for their troops to stop.

"Marsh," Envermet called as Valerie, Luka, and Devin called several names of their own.

Marsh hurried to join Master Envermet, and he signaled her to fall in with the rest of the scouts assembled before their leaders.

"Go and see what's going on and report back," Devin said, and the leaders nodded their agreement.

This time, Marsh was not the only one to fade into shadow and vanish into the dark. She traveled with several other scouts who did the same, and they fanned out from their mercenary counterparts, who moved quietly forward, using all the stealth available to those without magic.

It didn't take them long to reach the battle and Marsh took in the scene with a practiced sweep of her eyes, knowing Roeglin was seeing what she saw and relaying it directly to Master Envermet and Gustav.

Raiders had breached the gates of the compound surrounding the Piermonts' house and stables, and the clash of weapons came from within and around its walls.

Circle round to the back so we have an idea of the layout, Roeglin ordered, and Marsh knew Gustav or Envermet had requested the information.

She did as she was told, stepping from the glow of a patch of brevilars to the darkness surrounding the base of a pillar that had been built in the Times Before. Once there, she scanned the walls again and took another step to reach the rear of the compound, except she didn't. The walls were built into the side of the cavern, which was split to reveal an opening beyond them.

Marsh remembered that the raiders had tried to take Mika's Outlet, and how they had cleared the farm of all witnesses of their activity. She guessed that it was exactly what they were trying to do here. The fact they could take control of the Four Caverns' sole supply of transport as well was just an added bonus.

Marsh vowed that she would not allow that to happen. She might not agree with the Piermonts' monopoly, but that didn't mean she wanted to see that monopoly passed on to the raiders. Focusing on a patch of shadow close to the top of the wall, she slid through the shadows to gain a vantage point from above.

When she emerged, she could look down into the field on the other side of the wall, and she realized just how large a force they were facing.

The raiders had breached broad stone gates leading out beneath the rift into the surface world.

They sent a second force from the outside, Marsh relayed. *I see at least a hundred men.*

We'll be evenly matched unless Luka still has men trying to keep the family and livestock safe.

Marsh scanned the grounds again.

I see two...no, three battle sites, she began, then had to stifle a yelp of surprise when Mordan stepped out of the shadows to stand beside her. She also noticed just how large the kat had gotten, and wondered how she could have missed her increased size before.

You've been busy. Now focus! Roeglin didn't seem interested. *I'm interested, but I'd rather know how the damned beast can shadow step, which, by the way, is a trick I need to learn.*

I could just ask you to figure it out for yourself, but we're kinda busy, so here.

She gave him the concept as she understood it and turned back to studying the skirmishes playing out below her. Mordan watched with her, studying the scene with a hunter's intensity.

We could start there, the big kat suggested, highlighting where a cluster of mercenaries in the dark blues and reds of Luka's outfit were just maintaining their control of a set of stables.

Marsh studied the scene, noting that the raiders and mercenaries seemed evenly balanced in numbers and equipment.

It wouldn't take much to tip the balance, she agreed, hearing war cries and shouts of surprise drifting from the front of the compound. *Ro. We're going to try and even things up here.*

His reply was short and unexpected, and nothing like the protest she expected.

Meet you in the middle.

Well, if that wasn't permission for her to go and wreak havoc, she didn't know what was. As soon as she felt Roeglin refocus somewhere else, Marsh turned to the kat.

What's the plan? she asked, because she was sure Mordan would have one.

We strike from here. The kat highlighted two patches of shadows and the closest raiders.

It wasn't much of a plan, but Marsh got it. They'd come out of the shadows hard and fast and kill every raider in the way of them meeting at the main entrance to the barn. She figured that the kat knew Luka's men wouldn't leave them to finish that particular piece of business on their own.

A quick scan of the battlefield confirmed that the rest of the raiding force was so busy with battles of their own or pushing for the main homestead that they probably wouldn't intervene.

Ready, Dan? she asked, and the kat stepped into the closest patch of shadow and vanished.

THE BATTLE AT PIERMONT'S PONIES

Marsh waited long enough to see which end of the line the kat appeared on and shadow-stepped to the other end.

That could have been done better, she thought, dragging a dart from the shadows and hurling it into the raider nearest her when she emerged.

From the other end of the line, a man screamed, the sound ending in a reverberating crunch. The raider next to the one Marsh had struck looked torn, as if he couldn't decide which way to turn. Behind him, another man screamed, and the kat roared. In front of him, Marsh pulled flickering shadow to her hand. All color drained from his face, but he raised his sword.

Marsh pulled her hand back, preparing to flick the lightning around her opponent, but she didn't get the chance. The man dropped to the ground, a crossbow quarrel protruding from his throat. Marsh sent the lightning into the next man instead, only to watch him fall to another bolt just before it hit.

At the other end of the line, Mordan screamed in outrage, and Marsh felt her gut twist with worry. She looked toward the kat, seeing raiders block more quarrels with their shields as they repositioned to face the new threats. The move also blocked Marsh's view of the kat, but it didn't matter. On the other side of the cluster, one of the men suddenly dropped out of sight with a startled cry that rapidly descended into terrified screams.

The men closest broke formation to attack the kat and were promptly downed by a small swarm of crossbow bolts. Marsh advanced on the men closest to her, pulling a spear from the shadows and trying to stab past their shields. As she did, she heard the barn doors open and shouting as Luka's mercenaries broke cover to join the melee.

The fight didn't last very long after that. Marsh found the gap she was looking for and the raider went down. Instead of pulling the spear free, she left it to dissipate and drew a second one from the dark. Mordan took another raider and bounded out of reach of his companions' avenging blades. Two mercenaries filled the space she had taken while Marsh took down another attacker.

When he fell, she found herself facing men in Luka's colors, and as hard as it was, she released her sword to the shadows.

"Kat your familiar?"

Marsh had no idea what a familiar was, but the kat was definitely hers. She figured she could claim that and ask for specifics later.

"Yup."

The speaker looked around at his comrades.

"Hear that, boys? Kat's on our side." He looked back at Marsh. "Where to next?"

Relieved she wasn't going to have to fight them or find some way of proving her friendship, Marsh studied the battlefield. In the end, she pointed to the nearest skirmish.

"Let's clean up out here, then head inside and see if there are any Piermonts left to protect."

"Or rotisserie the bastards. Let these scum-sucking surface-dwellers in through the back like they were allies, then barricaded themselves in when the mongrels turned. Left the rest of us out in the cold."

"We'll get to them. Luka will have to decide how he wants to deal with it."

"Luka's here?"

"He came for you."

This caused an exchange of glances between them and brief warlike smiles.

"Hear that, boys? The boss is here. Let's not let him down!"

His statement was met with a soft chorus of "Hoo-ras" and they jogged briskly toward the fight Marsh had indicated. Marsh found her place next to their leader, pulling another blade from the shadows as she ran. She'd only gone a few strides before Mordan bounded over to run beside her.

The kat's appearance drew gasps of surprise from some of the men, but none of them made a move against her. Marsh couldn't blame them. She hadn't realized just how big the kat was, but she now reached Marsh's chest in height. Her size and the fact she was covered in blood made her seem fiercer than usual.

They took the raiders in the next skirmish by hitting them hard in the flank, the kat's roar as they attacked causing enough distraction for the beleaguered mercenaries to turn the battle in their favor.

"Road Guards!" they cried, their shout echoed around the cavern.

Marsh didn't stop to ponder what it meant. She turned with the others toward the next skirmish...and the next...and the one after that. At each one, they added more men to their small force until the raiders were breaking from battle and trying to flee rather than face them.

When they had killed every last one of them, the Guards broke through the barrier blocking the back door to the Piermont's mansion, racing through the corridor connecting front to back just as Gustav kicked his way through the front door.

"Upstairs!" he roared, and Marsh led her force up the nearest set of stairs.

She heard Gustav's force following as she breached the first-floor landing.

"This way!" one of Luka's men yelled, grabbing her arm and pulling her along the landing to a door at one end.

He stopped as he reached it and turned the handle, surprising them all when the door opened easily and they could step inside.

They were too late.

Marsh knew it as soon as she'd crossed the threshold. This room had been some kind of meeting hall, with a row of tables along the front of a slightly raised dais and a horseshoe wedge of tables arranged around the edges.

The Guard leader jumped over the nearest ones and

Marsh went with him, aware of Mordan surging ahead of them as more mercenaries followed them over the tables and across the room. In front of them, the room's back wall was torn in two as if it was the backdrop for a stage play. A portal formed, and two great paintings ended in jagged edges as the marble-floored room of an ancient building stretched beyond the mansion.

"Stop them!" Marsh cried even as Mordan leapt for one of the mages standing to one side of the rift.

The mercenaries charged forward but the raiders split into two groups, half moving forward to meet the charge, and the other half manhandling a small family of merchants through the portal and into the marbled halls beyond. As the last man in that group stepped after a protesting merchant, he signaled the retreat.

"Fall back!"

Immediately those who'd turned to stop the mercenaries began moving back toward the rift. Some had almost reached it when Mordan ended the life of one of the mages keeping it open, and Gustav charged through the door. He took in the situation with a sweep of his eyes and put a crossbow bolt through the forehead of the other.

Without their focus to keep it in place the rift snapped shut, and the raiders renewed their struggle, fighting for their lives. Luka's men gave no quarter, and Valerie's people forged their way to the front to help them end the life of every last man or woman who had opposed them.

Mordan used her claws and teeth to take down as many as she could, and Marsh worked her way around the melee in order to fight at the big kat's side. When the last raider had fallen, she stopped and stared at the carnage, then lifted her gaze to look for Master Envermet.

He was standing at the back of the hall with Gustav and Devin. The three of them waited as the two mercenary leaders moved among their troops, Luka introducing Valerie and both leaders letting the mercenaries stationed at the Piermont's compound know that they were all part of one team and that the contracts were no more.

"Couldn't be otherwise, could it, sir?" asked the man who'd met Marsh outside the stables. He gestured at the space the portal had occupied. "We lost them to the raiders."

"They'd lost us before that, Quentin. We were coming to terminate the contract."

Quentin tossed March a wry look.

"And here we thought, sir, that you were coming just for us."

Luka smiled.

"Once we saw the raiders, Quint, you were our only concern."

Quentin grinned at Luka.

"Of course, we were, sir."

"Of course," Luka assured him, and the men around them laughed.

As Valerie and Luka crossed to speak with Devin, Gustav, and Master Envermet, Marsh turned to inspect Mordan for any wounds, running her hands through the kat's blood-slick fur. She had just reassured herself that the kat was uninjured when someone came to stand behind her.

"So," Quentin began, "how exactly did you get a kat to agree to be your familiar?"

Marsh straightened.

"You said that word before," she commented. "What do you mean by 'familiar?'"

"It's an animal that has a bond to you," Quentin answered. "Does she?"

Marsh thought about it.

"I suppose so." She shrugged. "I don't know about bond, though. We sort of just have an agreement. I help her get her kits back from the raiders, and she keeps me alive to do that, then we go our separate ways."

She knew she was wrong the moment she said it, both from Mordan's rumbled growl of protest and Quentin's mocking smile. Those, and the feeling in her gut. The kat was going to stick around. She almost missed Quentin's next words in the sudden surge of joy.

"Not how it works, I'm afraid. You might have started out with an agreement, but you earned the kat's respect and she's bonded to you. She's not going to leave you when your bargain is done."

As if to confirm what the man was saying, Mordan swept a paw across the back of Marsh's ankles and pulled her to the ground, then she laid a paw on Marsh's chest.

"See?" Quentin grinned. "She's making her claim right there."

Marsh didn't know about claim, but she did know the kat's paw was heavy, and her backside hurt from landing on the floor. She stared up at Quentin.

"You want to tell my familiar she can let me up now?"

"Nah," he said, turning away and moving toward his leader. "You're the one with the bond. *You* tell her."

"Everyone's a smart ass," Marsh muttered, wrapping both hands around Mordan's paw and trying to lift it clear.

"Everyone," she repeated when the kat let her get it a couple of inches off her and pressed it right back down.

She lay there for a moment and glared at the big beast.

"Roeglin wants to see me," she said, and the kat regarded her with a contemplative stare. "He really does."

The kat stood and looked around. If Marsh hadn't known any better, she would have said the creature was looking to see if what she'd said about the shadow mage was true. That thought was confirmed when Mordan stilled, staring intently at the mage in question. When it became clear that Roeglin was busy listening to the discussion going on between the leaders of the cavern, the kat turned her attention to Marsh, cocking her head to one side.

Diversions aside, the heads of their pride were busy. Did Marsh want to go and see what the cubs were up to before they were tasked with something else?

Marsh nodded.

Let's go, she agreed, and Mordan lifted her paw away so Marsh could scramble to her feet.

They snuck out of the hall and found the children in the stables, Tamlin watching as his sister moved from one stall to the next, soothing the frightened jennies and mares, her small voice reassuring them that they were safe now and that the "bad mens" would not hurt them. Marsh came to stand beside the boy as Aisha laid her forehead against the lowered head of one of the female donkeys, the jenny closing its eyes as the little girl stroked its face.

The moment was lost as soon as Mordan slipped into the stables, the big kat's presence startling every donkey or horse who caught her scent.

"*Merde!*" Aisha exclaimed as the jenny knocked her off her feet and backed up, trembling, against the end of the stall.

The little girl turned and glared at the kat, her hands on her hips.

"Dan! You bad, bad kitty! Go sit with Perdemor."

Perdemor? Marsh wondered, but understood as soon as Mordan turned to lie down beside her kit, which was sitting next to a very quiet Scruff. *Perdemor is the kit's name?*

"Now I hasta start again," the child grumbled once the kat was settled.

As much as she wanted to intervene, Marsh decided it would be better if she stayed quiet and let Aisha work. The little girl's eyes flared green, and she approached the jenny again. Once she had the animals settled, Aisha came over to Marsh.

"What happen next?" she asked, sounding almost as grown up as her brother.

Marsh thought about that for a minute.

They couldn't leave the animals at the compound, she realized. With the Piermonts gone, the poor creatures would be food for every predator in the cavern, as well as any that came in from the surface, and those that weren't eaten would probably starve to death.

"I'll ask Captain Envermet," she said as the door to the stables opened.

"It wasn't my decision," the captain said, having caught her question, "but I'm glad I found you here. Gustav and the others were ready to tear the place apart looking for you."

"Roeglin couldn't sense me?"

"I had him speaking to the Master of Shadows, and the others didn't want to wait. It seems your headstrong habit of doing things as you think of them is contagious."

Marsh scowled. She didn't see how that was her fault. Gustav and the others were fully grown. They were responsible for their own actions.

And you are responsible for the examples you set.

Give it a rest, Ro.

"I can rest when I'm dead," he quipped, coming into the barn, and Marsh thought that that could be arranged.

Nice, he responded, then said out loud, "We need to come back out to investigate the Danets' property. The Defenders and Keepers want the animals secured, and they don't have the manpower to leave them here."

"What about the entry to the surface world?"

"Master Envermet has already spoken to the local druids. They have people who can seal it until there are enough people to man it as an outpost."

"What if the Piermonts are still alive?"

"You mean what if you retrieve them when you retrieve everyone else you've promised to get?"

Marsh's face heated even as she nodded, and Roeglin ignored her discomfort to continue.

"They'll be tried for treason and executed, and their assets confiscated and held until their children reach their majority. The cost of maintaining the value of the herd will be taken out of the sales made in the interim, and those holding them will receive a percentage of the profits."

"Wow," Marsh said, her tone of voice making it clear she wasn't entirely impressed. "That popular."

"Yeah. After what they've done? *That* popular."

"When do we move out?"

"For that, I need Aisha." Brigitte had arrived, and she didn't sound happy.

She crossed over to where Aisha sat with the kit and the pup and crouched down before her.

"You've already made some friends here," she began. "You want to help us move them back to town where they will be safe?"

"Uh huh."

Aisha leapt to her feet, and Marsh wondered where the child found her energy. Only a few short months ago, the girl would have been exhausted after speaking to so many creatures.

And you would have been out like a light if you'd done as much as you've done today, Roeglin reminded her. *Honestly, now, how do you feel?*

"I feel fine." She hadn't meant to say it out loud, and the comment caused several nearby people to turn and look at her.

Roeglin laughed, but Marsh decided to change the subject.

"How many do we have to move?" she asked, indicating the donkeys, mules, and horses being led out.

Some were saddled, others were tethered in clusters.

Roeglin shrugged.

"A lot, but it's better than having the raiders get a hold of them."

"They'd have left them behind, wouldn't they?"

"One of the teams we sent out after the battle caught a small group of raiders coming out of the other barn. Each one had a string of animals tied to their saddles."

Marsh thought about that, trying to work out the implications, but gave up when Master Envermet called for their attention.

"Defender Captains Brandt and Inglis need your assistance," he shouted. "Do as they ask until I say otherwise."

Having directed their attention, he stepped back and let Luka and Valerie take over. Before too long, the Piermonts' breeding stock had been gathered together and was being led out of the compound toward Dimanche.

OF KATS, KITS, AND HEALING

It took them until well into the night to reach Dimanche and find stabling for the Piermonts' breeding stock, their activities drawing the attention of the other four families. Valerie sighed and rolled her eyes when the first of them arrived at Shameless.

"Looks like it's going to be a long night."

Marsh saw Envermet glance at Gustav and Roeglin and stifled a sigh of her own.

I'm putting the children to bed, she said before the shadow mage could open his mouth, her tone defying him to deny her. Mordan snarled to emphasize the point.

Figuring the kat had said it all, Marsh ignored their stunned looks and went to find the children.

Behind her, she heard Gustav's voice raised in a soft murmur and Roeglin's quiet reply, but she couldn't make out the words. She could imagine, though—and she didn't care.

Tams? Aysh? she called, reaching out for the pair with her mind as she hurried back toward the stables.

Of all the places they might be, that was the most likely, since Aisha would insist on seeing her new friends settled before she'd let herself be put to bed. Of course, that could also be the five-year-old's way of avoiding bed, which would explain why Aisha wasn't answering her.

Brigitte?

Who's that? Marsh? The woman sounded shocked, and Marsh realized she'd never used her mind to speak to anyone besides Roeglin.

It's Marsh. Where are you?

She'd reached the back door and opened it by the time Brigitte's answer reached her.

Up two floors, about halfway along the corridor to the left.

Marsh was about to pull the door closed again when a flurry of movement at the gates leading into the rear court-yard caught her eye. She hesitated, trying to see who it was, but, before she recognized anyone, Mordan bounded past her, knocking her out of the doorway.

"Hey!"

She landed hard on the cobbles, feeling bone crack and muscle tear when she put her hand out to break her fall.

"Sons of the Deep's dark-assed britches! Dan!"

She tried to ignore the pain as she rolled to her feet, but agony lanced through her and she shouted in pain and dropped back to the cobbles. Crouching by the wall, she sucked in several fast breaths trying to get the pain under control and was surprised when the kat came to stand beside her.

"It's a pity you can't fix what you broke," she muttered, leaning into the big beast's side.

Feelings of apology washed over the link between them,

the kat's concern for her covering something else. Marsh figured she'd ask Mordan what it was just as soon as she could think straight.

The kat nudged her.

Did she want to borrow some of Mordan's strength for healing?

It was a good suggestion, even if Marsh didn't think she could concentrate enough to get the magic to do what she needed.

If not Marsh, then who else?

The kat's concern was palpable, along with her anxiety that Marsh be healed enough to deal with the next problem to arrive.

There was another problem?

The kat nudged her again.

Borrow my strength.

"Deeps, Dan. Quit pushing!" But her protest was drowned out by the small wall of noise that ran past them, Scruffknuckle barking excitedly as he led the way.

"Scruffknuckle!" Aisha's childish treble followed in a wail of annoyance and protest.

"Aysh!" echoed over the girl's cry, coming in two tones of sheer exasperation.

"What in all the Deeps is going on?"

Mordan growled, her impatience palpable, and Marsh rested her good hand against the big kat's side. The pain was still there, but with her arm still, it had died down to a dull, persistent throbbing. The steady beat of it echoed through her skin, making it hard for Marsh to concentrate. She tried to ignore it, focusing instead on gathering the energy she needed to make it go away.

She was relieved when she felt it flow into her, even if it was hard to direct it where it was needed. Every time she thought about where she needed it to go, she noticed just how much she hurt and almost lost her grip on it. It was easier when she just directed it toward the hurt and asked it to fix whatever was wrong in her arm.

It became impossible when she felt bone shift back into place and she yelped, losing control of the magic. Squeezing her eyes tight shut against the pain, Marsh waited for the pain to subside, feeling the magic slowly fade as it completed the task she had set.

"You done yet?" came from the doorway when she had been still for several heartbeats, and Marsh recognized Henri's voice.

"Yeah, I'm done," she answered, taking her hand off the kat and pushing to her feet. "Why?"

"Your kids are wreaking ten kinds of Darkness over by the gate, and we've got guests."

If that was Henri's way of telling her to get her tail over to where Tams and Aisha had headed, Marsh didn't think much of it, but she went anyway. When she arrived, Aisha was crouched beside two kits, and Scruffknuckle was prancing around them in sheer, unadulterated delight. Tams stood beside Brigitte and the druid chief from the tunnel leading to Dimanche. He smiled when he saw her.

"Marsh." His gaze shifted to include someone arriving behind her. "Gustav, Roeglin, and Master Envermet, I hope I haven't come at a bad time."

He turned his head as though taking in the activity around the courtyard.

"Things have changed since I was here last."

"You could say that." Valerie's voice cut across Gustav as he was about to reply. "Alois. What brings you here?"

The druid shifted his attention to the mercenary leader and he gestured to indicate Gustav, Master Envermet, Roeglin, and Marsh.

"There was talk of setting up a group to protect this cavern. I seek an alliance."

"You'd be foolish to turn him down," Devin said as he and a small contingent of druids and shadow mages joined them.

Valerie's eyes shifted as if she was only just noticing how many of them were gathered in the Shameless' open gate.

"Let's take this inside," she said, and glanced at the children. "And get them back into bed. Reunions aside, they have work to do in the morning."

The look on Tam's face said he was wondering who'd died and put Valerie in charge, but the mercenary leader ignored him, turning instead to lead them back into the waystation.

Marsh watched them go, noticing that Roeglin didn't go with them. Instead, he cocked his head to one side and regarded Aisha with serious eyes.

"You know you're not going to change his mind, don't you?" he said, and the little girl pouted.

The druid had taken a few steps after Valerie and the other leaders, but now he returned.

"Is there a prob—" he began as Mordan roared.

Before Marsh could react, the big kat had pounced, knocking the druid from his feet and standing over him. The kit Aisha had been petting let out a roar of his own, cannoning into his mother and batting at her with his paws. His attack made Mordan yowl in protest and she spun around, swatting the kit to one side and pinning him to the ground.

"Dan!" Aisha shrieked, getting to her feet.

She might have run over to intervene except that Tamlin leapt forward, lunging out to grab his little sister before she could take a single step. The child shrieked in frustration, and Marsh heard several startled oaths from the inn's back door.

Hurried steps followed, as did the hiss of steel as swords were drawn.

"Hold!"

Gustav's voice rolled over them, and Master Envermet echoed him.

"Hold!"

Marsh had to resist the urge to freeze. She turned her head just enough to catch sight of the two captains standing between the mercenaries and the druids, their hands raised slightly before them as they tried to calm the men and women in front of them.

For their part, the mercenaries and Alois' druids had paused. Some were in the middle of drawing their weapons, and others looked about to dive in and tackle Mordan.

Dan? Marsh asked. *What are you doing?*

The kit is mine! the big kat said, snarling to emphasize her claim.

The kit in question looped himself around her paw, scratching at his mother's foreleg and trying to bite it.

He doesn't agree, Marsh pointed out.

He has made a poor choice.

What choice? Marsh asked, but Alois spoke before the kat could answer.

To Marsh's surprise, he was talking to the kit.

"I told you we should have asked your mother first."

The kit stilled long enough to hiss at the druid and went right back to trying to tear his mother's leg to shreds. Looking at the damage it was doing with his claws, Marsh winced. She was probably going to sleep for a week after putting all that back together, and she was already tired from mending her arm.

Mordan rumbled softly, and Alois shifted his gaze from kit to kat. His eyes flared green as he tried to catch Mordan's eye, but it was a few long heartbeats before the kat lowered her head and consented to speak with him.

Marsh tried to join them but the kat bunted her out like an afterthought, keeping her eyes on Alois's face. Around them, the entire courtyard seemed to hold its breath.

"He could have chosen worse, Dan," Marsh told her, but her only response was that the kat's tail twitched faster.

She stretched a hand toward the kat, only to have Mordan lift her lip in a half-snarl. The kat neither moved her head nor looked in Marsh's direction though, and Marsh waited, glad to see the kit had finally exhausted himself and now lay still but defiant under his mother's paw. Marsh saw the blood running down Mordan's foreleg and hoped she'd be able to do something about it soon.

The silence stretched around them for several more heartbeats, then Mordan sat, lifting her paw from Alois's chest so the druid could scramble to his feet. After a moment's hesitation, the kat also took her paw from on top of the kit, letting him roll to his feet. Instead of trotting over to Alois, though, the kit gave a plaintive mew and rose onto his back feet to put his paws on his mother's shoulders. He mewed again, anxiously nuzzling her face.

At first, Mordan didn't respond, but the kit gave a pleading chirp and the kat relented, swiping a paw under him to knock him off his feet before thoroughly washing his face and head. As soon as she was done, the kit bounded over to Alois and sat by the druid's feet, his tail curled around his forepaws. Alois laid a hand on the kit's head, and it purred.

Mordan looked at Marsh and raised her bleeding foreleg, but Marsh put one hand on her hip and cocked her head.

"Oh, so *now* you want my attention," she began, and the kat waved her paw again.

"I can do," Aisha interrupted, but Tamlin held her back.

"You can go upstairs to bed," he told her. "It's late, and you'll be grumpy in the morning."

"Will not," the little girl protested, adding, "Kat hurts. I fix."

"Nuh-uh," Tamlin told her. "*Marsh* fix."

"But..." Aisha tried, only to find her brother guiding her gently but firmly back to the inn, Brigitte following.

"No," Tamlin insisted, and Aisha pouted but allowed him to steer her inside.

Marsh watched them go. As soon as they were beyond the walls, she shuffled over to Mordan and rested the kat's foreleg across her knees to inspect the wounds. They were deep and would fester if she didn't treat them, but they weren't as bad as she feared. Marsh sighed.

"All right," she said. "Let's do this."

No "let's" about it, Roeglin snarked. *You're on your own with this one.*

His presence reminded her that she wasn't alone—and that she had an audience.

Fantastic.

Roeglin chuckled and Marsh sent him a mental finger before focusing her full attention on the kat's injuries.

"Trust you to pick a fight with something that's got claws as sharp as yours," she grumbled, and was surprised to catch a flash of a kat's butt in her head.

"Everyone's a smart ass."

Focusing again, she called the energy in her surroundings, drawing what little she could from the cobbled earth and a little from each of the people gathered around her, but not so much, she hoped, that any of them would notice.

It's still nice to be asked first.

This time Marsh managed to hold onto the energy despite Roeglin's interruption. She didn't bother giving him the finger either, just directed the magic into the kat's leg, asking it to mend the torn flesh and skin. It didn't take much.

"Now that that's done," Master Envermet said when Mordan's leg was whole again, "let's take our business inside. Captain Moldrane, if you would be so good as to assist the Defenders in organizing accommodation..."

"Sir. Leclerc and Leger, you're with me."

THE DEFENDERS ESTABLISHED

The meeting was still going when Marsh, Gustav, and Roeglin returned from helping the Defenders' Quartermaster. Instead of being held in an upstairs meeting room, it had been moved to Shameless' common room, and the smell of roast meat and freshly baked shroom bread wafted out of the kitchen. The tables had been rearranged into a large square, and the rest of the Five Families had arrived.

At least, Marsh assumed the four groups of important-looking people were representatives of the Five Families. She was only sure of Monsieur Laberge, who was sitting quietly at the end of the table and watching as the other three groups argued with Valerie and Luka. One, a big man wearing a leather tunic dyed dark green, banged his fist on the table.

Cutlery jumped and clattered and the table stilled.

"I don't care if you pay the penalties!" he shouted. "I need the guards. The raids are becoming—"

"Enough!"

The man stopped, his mouth hanging open as he looked at Devin. The Keepers' leader didn't give him a chance to say anything more.

"The raids are worse," he said, and the man closed his mouth, listening as the mage continued, "but a dedicated guard service won't keep you safe. The size of the force that overran the Piermonts' stud would take out your usual guard force in less than a half-turn."

"A half... We'll just hire double!" the man declared, and returned his attention to the head of the table.

Valerie shook her head.

"No, Monsieur Gaebler. As much as I'd like to say my people could handle any threat the raiders could offer, I will not lie. The Vanguard could not have taken the force down without the help of Luka's Road Guards or Devin's Keepers." She nodded toward where Master Envermet and a small contingent of shadow guards and protectors sat. "Or without the Ruins Deep Protectors and the shadow mages."

"What are you saying?"

"I'm saying that what I saw was an organized fighting force that was much larger than I thought possible, and that I think what we saw was just a small portion of something much bigger." This time Valerie nodded at Marsh. "Shadow Mage Leclerc will be searching for it once the Four Caverns are secured."

The big man's eyebrows lifted and he followed Valerie's gaze, studying Marsh like she was a mule up for inspection. Marsh lifted her chin and cocked her head, making it clear she was studying him just as hard—and that she wasn't impressed by what she saw.

Way to make friends and influence people, Roeglin murmured, and Marsh had a hard time holding Monsieur Gaebler's gaze.

In the end, the big man shrugged and turned back to Valerie.

"What makes you think she's fit for the job?" He glanced at Captain Envermet. "Or that she'd give us an honest report on what she found anyway?"

Marsh opened her mouth to respond, then caught the look on the shadow captain's face, relaxing back on her heels and giving him a slight nod. She saw his mouth quirk and he stood. At first, it looked like he might leave, but he didn't.

"Almost two months ago, Marchant Leclerc was nothing more than a courier."

Marsh might have protested that, but Roeglin slipped his hand into hers and squeezed her fingers. The unexpectedness of it startled her to silence and Master Envermet continued.

"She would have been the sole survivor of the last caravan to attempt the journey from Kerrenin's Ledge to Ruins Hall if she hadn't rescued two children as she fled. The rest of the caravan could not be saved, although all that was found afterward were the carcasses of the mules they left behind. There was no trace of the men, women, or children with that caravan when the area was searched. The trade goods had been left intact and the mules slaughtered, but the people? It was like they'd vanished."

Monsieur Gaebler shifted restlessly in his seat.

"And your point, shadow mage?"

From his tone, he didn't hold mages in high regard, and his opinion was carried over to any mage he encountered.

"My point?" Master Envermet asked. "My point is that Marsh survived and kept two children alive for a week while she navigated her way through unfamiliar caverns to return to Ruins Hall, and on the way, she rescued the last remaining family in Leon's Deep and brought them to safety. My point is twofold. The first is that if anyone can find the source of the raiders and get our people back, it is her. The second is that the raiders are part of something *much* bigger, and the Four Caverns need to work together if they are going to survive it."

"And how does establishing what amounts to four private militias do that?" Gaebler challenged.

"Each cavern supports their Protectors or Defenders, as the case may be," Captain Envermet replied. "They make sure they are housed and fed and equipped, and in return," he continued, raising his hand to quell the murmurs of protest that rippled around the table. "In return, those Protectors and their allies secure the caverns by sealing any exits or entrances bar the most essential, then work together to put down every raider incursion they find, refusing to give the raiders a foothold."

Monsieur Gaebler snorted, making his opinion of that idea plain for all to hear.

Unperturbed, Captain Envermet continued.

"Ruins Hall has not had an attack in all the time we have been gone. Prior to that, we were losing people every week, with the outermost steadings and claims being cleared first, and without our knowledge."

His expression turned bleak.

"The Deeps know what happened to those people or if any of them are still alive, but we are sworn to stop any more from being taken."

"Right down to giving your lives, I suppose." The merchant was scornful.

"We'd hardly be an effective fighting force if we weren't prepared to do that, now would we?"

Before Monsieur Gaebler could respond to that, another of the important-looking visitors rose to his feet, demanding an answer.

"And who exactly is supposed to pay for all this *defense*?"

From his tone, Marsh figured he had a fair idea and didn't agree. Master Envermet looked at Valerie and Luka, and both leaders signaled for him to continue.

"I'm sorry, I don't know your name?"

The man was shocked.

"My name? My name, shadow *mage*, is Eamon Freign, and I am the first heir to the Open Skies Consortium."

Open Skies? Marsh tried to process how that made any sense when the man's entire operation had to be based beneath the ground. *Open Skies?* She snorted but turned the sound into a hurried sneeze, ignoring the brief glances turned her way.

You sure you don't need to go to bed? Roeglin asked. *Because that could be arranged.*

You and whose... Marsh began and Roeglin laughed, but not where anyone else could hear it.

I only have to tell you to sleep, he said, and Marsh felt a brief urge to do just that.

You wouldn't!

Don't tempt me.

Marsh might have argued further, but Master Envermet was speaking and she wanted to listen. Pretending she wasn't worried by Roeglin's threat, she paid attention.

"It is a pleasure to meet you, Monsieur Freign. To answer your question, the original plan is for the governing body of each cavern to cover the costs of their Protectors. Once the Caverns have been secured, each force is expected to generate its own revenue from monies earned for protecting the trade routes and operating the waystations."

"Really?" the man wasn't impressed. "And I suppose the current operators of the waystations all think this is a *capital* idea?"

Again his voice suggested he thought no such thing, and the look on his face when Master Envermet answered was priceless.

"We wouldn't know. Every waystation we've encountered except for Downslopes has been completely abandoned." The shadow captain appeared not to notice the man's reaction but continued, changing the subject. "Would you mind telling me what brought you here tonight?"

That got Eamon's attention, and he scowled.

"I...*we*," he corrected himself, indicating the other unidentified guests seated at the table, "heard the Vanguard had returned and wanted to protest their theft of our personnel."

As if his words were a signal, Valerie cut in.

"Our theft?" she demanded. "Your failure to retain your people is not our concern. To the best of..."

Hugh cleared his throat and hurried around the

counter that served as the bar when the common room wasn't being used as a meeting hall.

"Excuse me, Commander. I haven't briefed you on the *new recruits* that came in today."

Valerie closed her mouth, her lips forming a thin straight line. She looked at the ceiling as though seeking either patience or solace. When she returned her gaze to Hugh, her voice was hard.

"We have new recruits?"

Marsh saw Hugh's throat move as he swallowed.

"Yes, ma'am. I believe eight of them resigned from Monsieur Freign's house this morning, and another five came from the Desmarais looms. All of them wanted a more active part in serving the cavern's needs, and were adamant that their skills were better suited to doing that than their current occupations."

"And are they?"

"Are they what, Ma'am?"

"Better suited."

"There are several with experience as caravan guards who were forced to take up alternate employ when the caravans stopped coming, and two who had previous experience in the Battle of Chaumont. I was going to tell you once the meeting was done."

"Thank you, Hugh," Valerie replied, and turned back to the table.

She caught the gaze of the two families, then looked at Monsieur Freign.

"We'll be accepting their service," she told him, forestalling his protest by half-raising a hand. "Your mills won't run if *all* your workers disappear."

"But..." Eamon began as the last leader to keep his silence stood.

"Luka?" he asked, making it plain that Valerie's word wasn't going to be enough.

Luka got to his feet.

"My co-commander's decision stands," he said. "We need men with that kind of experience if we are to keep you in trade."

Silence reigned as both men stared in disbelief and Luka added.

"Or would you rather we left you on your own as we evacuate the rest of the cavern?"

The response was instantaneous.

"You wouldn't..."

Valerie and Luka exchanged looks and turned back to the four leaders.

"We would."

"I have some room."

All eyes turned to Alois, who had been sitting quietly at the end of the table. The four leaders studied him as though they'd never seen him before...which turned out to be the case.

"And you are?" Eamon Freign asked as if Alois had no right to be at the table.

"Allied to the Defenders of Dimanche," Alois told him, "and I will close the route to the surface after they've left in order to protect the tunnels."

He nodded to Devin.

"With the Keepers' permission, of course."

Devin took the cue.

"Without allies to help us protect the cavern, we'll evacuate too, and close the route to Ariella's where we'll take refuge...if it still stands," he said.

Together those prepared to lead the cavern's defense faced the leaders of the four families. As they did so, Master Envermet quietly resumed his seat and Marsh, Roeglin, and Gustav withdrew to lean against the meeting room wall. The silence that followed Devin's declaration lasted for a very long minute, then Monsieur Laberge broke it.

"I would like Dimanche to stand," he said, "but I can only cover a full third of the estimated costs."

The other three leaders were onto him in a flash.

"A third?"

"Who said you could take a controlling share?"

"I don't think so. We can do better. We'll put up half."

"You don't even know the costs."

Valerie and Luka let the argument continue for several minutes, then Valerie raised her voice.

"Gentlemen!"

The word cracked out like a battle command, and all argument ceased.

"No one controls us. Paying more will not get you more favorable treatment than the next person."

"Then what's the point?" Freign demanded.

"Exactly," Valerie replied. "We would be happy if you would each pay a quarter..."

"A quarter!" Freign protested.

"Why not a fifth?" Gaebler demanded. "Surely the Piermonts..."

"There are no Piermonts." Luka's matter of fact statement caused all sound to cease.

A heartbeat later, Gaebler cleared his throat.

"I beg your pardon?"

"I said there were no Piermonts. Weren't you listening when Devin said the Piermonts' property was overrun?"

"Yes, but..." Realization dawned. "Didn't you get them out?"

Gaebler looked from Luka to Valerie and back again and his voice rose.

"Are you telling me they were all *killed*?"

Master Envermet intervened.

"No, but we couldn't reach them before the raiders dragged them through a portal they opened in the back of their..."

"Ballroom," Valerie provided.

"...ballroom," Master Envermet ended. "Are there any more questions?"

The way he said it suggested he was asking if there were any more *stupid* questions, but Gaebler clearly missed the implication.

"Portal?"

"A gateway through shadow from one point to another."

"But...you know where they went, don't you? You *can* go and get them?"

From the anxiety in his voice, at least one of the Piermonts had more importance than just that of a trade partner. Marsh wondered which one, and why Monsieur Gaebler was so anxious. Roeglin choked back a laugh.

Madame Gaebler wasn't the only one having an affair.

Seriously?

At the table, the Four founding families came to a decision.

"What are your terms?"

Monsieur Envermet sat and watched silently as Hugh brought five sheaves of paper to the table. He set one before each of the families and the last one before Luka and Valerie.

"I trust you will find these to your satisfaction," he said, but more to his commanders than the families themselves.

As the leaders fell to reading the contracts, Marsh slipped her hand from Roeglin's and made for the stairs leading up to where Brigitte and the children were quartered. She didn't need to be here for this, and she'd promised to tuck someone in.

25

A TRIO OF TROUBLE

"You're a bit late," Tamlin greeted her when Marsh quietly opened the door.

She had been hoping to see if they were awake and leave without disturbing them if they weren't. She'd even had Mordan let her kit and Scruffy know she'd be coming so they animals would stay quiet, all to no avail. Apparently, Tamlin had been waiting for her...or he was a very light sleeper.

Marsh was betting on the former as she heard a gasp from across the room and Brigitte sat up.

"Who's there?" she demanded.

"Me," Marsh said. "I just came to..."

"You came too late," Tamlin snapped, resentment coloring his voice, the implication that she was always too late clear.

"Not fair, Tams," Brigitte interrupted. "You know she's..."

"There's always something," the boy bit back, "whether it's raiders or getting captured by raiders or running errands for Captain Moldrane. She's supposed to be *our* guardian, not everyone else's."

Since when? Marsh wanted to ask, but she knew when. She'd made the promise the minute she'd dragged them out of the ambush—and she'd made it again when she'd accepted the ruling that they were her responsibility until she found them relatives or had passed them into the monastery's care.

She might have warned them that her duties would take her away and Tamlin might have accepted that to start with, but the boy clearly wasn't happy with it now.

He knows he has no relatives. Roeglin's presence made her jump. *And you promised you'd be their guardian if that was the case. He might not have been so upset at you being away if they hadn't been dragged out on the road, but they were, and now he knows they can survive it, and he doesn't see any reason for them to be separated from you anymore.*

Roeglin's words made Marsh realize that there wasn't one.

Neither do I.

"Sons of the Deep," he muttered, and Marsh was sure he hadn't meant to let that slip out.

Tamlin was at the door in an instant, pushing past Marsh and Mordan to glare at Roeglin.

"No, she's not available. She owes us a month of bedtime stories!"

He didn't say any more, just grabbed Marsh by the arm and dragged her inside, slamming the door in Roeglin's face. By then, Brigitte had lit a lantern and Aisha had emerged from under the blankets, rubbing her eyes until she saw Marsh.

Her small face lit up with delight.

"You came!" She glanced at Tamlin, her expression triumphant. "I told you she would."

Her happiness made Tamlin smile, and he crossed to sit on the edge of the bed.

"Yeah, you did. Move over."

"No," Aisha argued. "Your bed is dere."

She pointed, the gesture as much a command as what she said next.

"You sleep."

Tamlin sighed and rolled his eyes.

"Fine," he told her, "but tomorrow she sits on *my* bed for storytime."

Aisha scowled, and Tamlin scowled right back. The little girl crossed her arms over her chest and pouted.

"Fine!"

Marsh looked at Brigitte and the shadow mage laughed.

"Yes, I brought your cookies," she said as if that was the question Marsh had been about to ask, and she added, "They like adventure stories the best. You must have heard plenty when you were growing up at Hawk's Ledge."

Since Marsh had been about to protest that she didn't know any stories, she figured Brigitte must be a mind reader.

No, but she knows what they wanted. They've been talking about "storytime with Marsh" ever since they left Downslopes. Tamlin started it to keep Aisha happy.

He had? Marsh didn't know whether to hug or strangle the boy. Given he was watching her as he climbed between the sheets, she decided not to do either. Storytime, right?

She searched her mind for one of the funnier tales she'd

heard as a child. It surprised her to discover just how many of the merchants' stories had stuck.

That one, Roeglin told her as she tried to decide, then he knocked at the door, opening it before any of them had time to reply.

"Someone said cookies?"

He slipped into the room, shutting the door behind him and making himself comfortable at the end of Tamlin's bed.

"Fine," Tamlin grumbled, and Marsh began.

Aisha was asleep before she had finished and Tamlin's eyes were closed, but he laughed at the end, and she knew he was still awake.

"You got another?" he asked, his voice thick with sleep.

"Not tonight, I don't," she replied. "You're on rations."

"You owe us..." he murmured, but he didn't open his eyes, and he didn't protest when she got to her feet, Roeglin mirroring her movement.

Brigitte handed Marsh her cookies and pushed her toward the door.

"Go on," she said when Marsh hesitated. "They'll be around to bug you in the morning."

Roeglin led the way out into the corridor.

"We'd better get moving," he murmured. "Master Envermet is going to—"

"Be very upset if you don't get your asses downstairs," Gustav finished for him, appearing at the top of the stairs as Mordan and Marsh emerged.

Marsh hastily closed the door behind her, reflexively shushing the captain as she did so.

"Downstairs," he ordered, the command sounding a lot less fierce when delivered in a hoarse whisper. "Now."

Marsh ate her cookies on the way.

When they arrived in the common room, she saw Hugh carrying a huge sheaf of papers out of the room and into an office behind the bar.

"Oh, good. You're back," Master Envermet greeted them. "I'll be leaving a delegation with the Defenders and heading back to establish the waystation in the morning. The children—"

"Will be traveling with me," Marsh told him, defying him to say otherwise.

Master Envermet stilled and crooked an eyebrow.

"Are you a mind reader, Master Leclerc?" He sounded amused and continued before she had a chance to respond. "I was going to *suggest* that you might like to add Master Petitfeu and the children to your group, since the children still need to inspect their relatives' property and the three of you need to return to the monastery to formalize their adoption."

Marsh felt her spirits rise, but then he paused, and Marsh waited for the sting that had to be in the tail end of his orders.

Suggestion, my ass, she thought but didn't say out loud.

As expected, Master Envermet did not disappoint.

"You'll take the road to Ariella's Grotto and offer our alliance and assistance to them before completing your journey. Once I have the outpost established, I will be following."

So, not a straight run back to the monastery then. What a surprise.

"Captain Moldrane and his team will accompany you, and I will follow once I have helped Alois decide how much of the Piermont's breeding stock can be resettled in his cavern and how much will need to be pastured at Downslopes."

He caught the surprise on Marsh's face and apologized.

"If I didn't need your team to lay the groundwork at Ariella's, I'd have sent you and the children back that way so you could spend some time with your cousin and your uncle when you passed through the Ledge, but there is no time. I'm sorry."

That hadn't been what had surprised her, and Marsh was about to ask why the stock had to be moved when Master Envermet told her.

"The Defenders will be taking over the Piermonts' breeding operation as a means of supporting themselves, and Alois says he has the space to stable them, which they don't have here. Should any of the Piermont children be retrieved from the raiders, the Defenders will keep what they have earned up to that point and hand the animals over."

It was much the same as Roeglin had said, but Master Envermet wasn't finished.

"Once the trails between here and the monastery are clear, you'll be free to look for the raiders' home. I want you to think carefully about what you're going to do with the children then."

Marsh was still trying to work out whether he was warning her or trying to tell her it would be all right for the children to go with her when he gestured toward the table.

"Dinner," he said. "I'll see you in the morning before you leave."

It was both order and dismissal, but he didn't wait for her to acknowledge either. Instead, he seated himself beside Alois, and the two were soon deep in conversation. They paused long enough to accept their meals, and Devin joined them, then Roeglin poked her on the shoulder.

"You going to eat or just watch it all disappear?" he asked, indicating the table.

Marsh decided the man had a point and led the way to an empty space.

"You're not going to join me?" she asked when they reached it, and he hesitated.

He glanced down at her, his expression distracted.

"I...yes. Excuse me..."

Marsh watched as he turned away, noticing his eyes had turned as white as a budding calla. One of the servers arrived with two fully loaded plates and Marsh sighed.

"Can you give us a minute?" she asked, then hurried after the mage before the server could respond.

She left the man standing with a plate in each hand and a very puzzled expression on his face.

"Ro?" she called, but the mage kept walking, speeding up as he headed around the bar and toward a side door.

"Well, Deeps-be-damned," she heard Henri grumble, followed by the rattle of downed cutlery and the man's heavy tread. "Anyone touches this while I'm gone, and I'll use their head to scrub the latrines."

Some of the Defenders snickered, but others caught the sincerity in his voice and eyed him warily. Still others decided something was up and wanted to know what it was. Chairs scraped and Gustav sighed.

"Dinner can wait. Those two need minders."

Minders? Marsh thought. *I'm perfectly fine. Only one of us is out looking for trouble.*

Usually that would have elicited some response, but Roeglin kept moving.

He didn't stop, but walked out the side door and into an alley that ran alongside the inn.

"Wait," he said, his voice carrying undertones of compulsion and command.

Marsh looked to see who he was speaking to and saw three figures at the end of the alley. Two had started to move away, and a much smaller third had hesitated briefly before running after them.

"Wait," Roeglin said again, and Marsh heard some of the footsteps behind her come to an abrupt halt.

She might have laughed, except she was trying too hard to keep moving. She decided she really was going to have to get him to teach her how to ignore that kind of command.

Again, Roeglin left that thought alone.

Funny. Usually he'd be telling me not a hope in the Deeps.

Marsh's brow furrowed and she hurried after him.

"Please wait," he called, and Marsh realized that not one of the three figures they'd seen had stopped at the sound of Roeglin's voice.

They were *all* resistant to magic?

Just when she thought they'd have no chance of catching up to them, Mordan raced past her and then past the people they were pursuing until she was in front of them. Once she was in position, the kat turned and growled. All three figures stopped—and then all three tried to bolt down the street in the opposite direction to the kat.

Again Mordan raced around them to block their path.

Finally, Marsh had had enough.

"Will you just stop?" she called. "We're not going to hurt you."

Mordan gave her hunting cry, a sort of screaming roar, and the trio skidded to a halt. By that time Marsh and Roeglin had reached the street, and the guards weren't far behind them.

"What about her?" one of them asked, wrapping her arm around the smaller figure and pushing it behind her, away from the kat.

"She's just asking you to stop," Roeglin said. "You'd know that if you bothered to ask her.

"A beast of the earth?" The tallest figure, a man, asked, stretching a hand toward the woman and child.

He tried to edge sideways, but Mordan pivoted to face him.

"A hoshkat," Roeglin corrected.

"*My* hoshkat," Marsh added, but Roeglin refused to be distracted.

"Why don't you present your request to Master Envermet yourselves?" he suggested. "You'll find him more accepting than you fear. After all, he travels with me."

Like that would make a difference, Marsh thought, but it did, and the trio approached until she could make out their features.

Judging from the child's face, it was a family. The girl looked to be a couple of years older than Aisha, and she carried the fine-boned features of her mother and her father's dark gray eyes. Now that they were close enough, she could also see that their skin was slightly darker than her own and their faces more angular, as if their ancestry was slightly different.

As she studied the trio, the guards' footsteps thundered over the cobbles as they ran past Marsh and Roeglin, cutting off the trio's options for escape. Gustav came to a halt beside them.

"Why don't you join us for a meal?" he asked, the tone of his voice more order than invitation.

The parents exchanged glances, but the girl stepped forward. She looked Gustav up and down, reminding Marsh more of a miniature commander than a child. Her eyes flared briefly white, then she spoke.

"You'll do." She turned to her parents. "Mama, Papa, we'll go with them. Dinner is waiting."

"I beg your pardon!" Gustav's voice was full of outrage, and the man and woman crowded protectively close to their child.

"Mina!"

"What have we told you about asking permission?"

The girl rolled her eyes and extended her hand to the captain.

"Let's go," she said, "before the others eat your meal."

"Do that one more time, child, and I'll put you over my knee," the captain rumbled.

"And I'll let him," the girl's father responded. "You've been quite rude enough!"

With the situation under control, Marsh reached out

and wrapped her hand around Roeglin's wrist. He started and glanced at her.

I can hear them, he said, and laughter rolled through them.

They both looked up to see the father of the group smiling at them.

"You weren't meant to," he said. "We were just trying to get Mina to go somewhere safe."

"And you?" Roeglin asked. "Where were you going?"

The man's face darkened, and Gustav interrupted before he could reply.

"We can discuss it inside," he said. "Our dinner's getting cold."

"It's probably getting eaten," Henri added darkly. "I'll have some scrubbing to do."

26

TRAVEL PLANS

It turned out that the Defenders were smarter than Henri gave them credit for. Not only was his dinner still untouched, but all their meals were being guarded by a handful of the men he'd fought beside. He glared at them suspiciously.

"What did you do to it?" he demanded of the man standing beside his seat.

"Nothing!" The mercenary looked horrified by Henri's suggestion, then his face took on a crafty look. "Why? Did you want me to?"

Henri didn't reply but took his seat, still scowling, and Marsh saw the others do the same. Gustav led the little girl and her family over to Master Envermet. Seeing they were being taken care of, Marsh crossed to where the server was standing beside their places. The relief on his face was almost comical.

"Sorry about that," she said and surveyed their plates. "Anything we should know about?"

His surprise *was* comical.

"N-no!" he stammered, looking shocked.

Marsh brushed past him and sat.

"Thank you," she said, not complaining when her first bite was cold. That was Roeglin's fault.

Hey!

If the boot fits.

What have I told you about thinking with your mouth full?

You and whose army?

I don't need an army.

Lucky you, because you don't have one.

Is this conversation private or can anyone join in?

They both started, but Marsh recognized the voice of the father. Turning in her seat, she saw the family being shown to a table and tapped Roeglin on the shoulder.

"Come on," she told him. "You dragged them into this. We'd better not abandon them now."

She picked up her plate and led him over to their table.

"Mind if we join you?"

The woman gestured at the spare places beside them, and Marsh and Roeglin sat. Mordan had followed them and wormed her way under the table, making the family gasp as she bumped against their legs before stretching along the floor at everyone's feet. For a moment they all sat tense and stiff, then Mordan started to purr.

The little girl's eyes flashed green, and she stuck her head under the table. Marsh heard the kat grumble a moment later. It was a happy grumble and the purring resumed, continuing when the little girl emerged from beneath the table, her eyes alight with joy.

"She says we can travel with them to Auntie Lemma's!"

The father raised his eyebrows and tilted his head in surprise.

"Oh, she does, does she?"

He looked at Marsh.

"You're going to Ariella's?"

"How did you know?"

"It's where Lemma lives, and your Master Envermet suggested we approach you and Captain Moldrane to see if we could accompany you."

Marsh studied his face and saw no hint of guile. Only hope.

"We've been stranded here ever since raiders took the last caravan. We were hoping another one would come through here on the way to the grotto or the Deeps Monastery." He gestured toward his daughter. "Mina has the gift. We figured if the druids at Ariella's couldn't help us, the shadow mages might."

"What about the mages here?" Marsh asked and the man looked away, his eyes evading her gaze.

"We have family in the Grotto. The mages have been very kind, and we appreciate that, but they are not family."

"They could be," Roeglin told him, "if you wanted."

The man sighed.

"I know, but if I have any chance of making a home, I would rather make it with family."

Marsh frowned.

"Why did you run then?"

The man ducked his head, his skin darkening with embarrassment.

"We were afraid of being forced into service," he said, and his wife nodded.

"We know our gifts are rare, and how useful they could be in a war…" She paused with a faraway look on her face, then blinked it away. "We didn't want to risk that."

It made sense in a weird kind of way, but it made Marsh wonder why the woman would even be aware of it.

"You ran into shadow mages in the caravan, didn't you?"

It was a wild guess, but it hit the mark. Both adults drew a sharp breath, but the little girl just sat straighter and gave her a very solemn nod.

"They said they wanted me to go to a special school, and they looked a lot like the shadow mages that lived here. I thought they felt bad and I told Mama and Papa, and we made sure they couldn't find us. It was hard. There was one who could sense us. We had to hide in a basement and sleep for two whole days!"

They'd what?

"I bought a sleeping draught from one of the local druids. Said I had nightmares from the tunnels or something. They warned against us taking too much unless we wanted to sleep through a full cycle. I made sure I bought enough to make that happen."

Marsh shot an alarmed look at Mina and the woman favored her with a small, sad smile.

"We weren't *that* desperate. I made sure we had the dosage right for her to sleep lightly and wake early. Hers is not so much a gift of the mind but one for things that grow." Her eyes shifted to the spot where Mordan lay and her smile broadened, "and things that walk, as much as we try to deter her. The other mind mage was not looking for her. She watched over us."

That had to have been a big responsibility for a small child.

"We didn't sleep for longer than she could bear, did we, Min?"

"No, Papa, but you *did* sleep a long, long time."

From the child's tones, it was clear that what her father thought of as "no longer than she could bear" and how long he'd slept were a fairly close match. Marsh kept that thought to herself, though. She thought of the mind-walker she and the wolves had cornered and wondered if they were one and the same.

Before she could ask, however, the man answered.

"Yes. Is he..."

"Gustav put a crossbow bolt through his heart," Marsh told him, and both adults breathed a sigh of relief.

She didn't know what they had to be relieved about. For all any of them knew, he'd already sent word back that Mina's family existed. Maybe his encounter with her, Roeglin, Henri, and Gustav had put an end to all that. If they were lucky, he'd been the last raider alive to know the family existed.

In the end, she shrugged the thought aside. Even if he *had* gotten word back, the last place the raiders knew the family had been was Dimanche—and she was sure the Keepers and Defenders could secure it between them. No raider was going to get into the cavern to find out where this family had gone—especially now that they had to worry about getting more than one cavern back.

She doubted they had a force large enough to take care of Ruins Hall, Kerrenin's Ledge, Downslopes, and Dimanche all at once. Any one of these settlements could now hold its own against a force like the one that had taken down the Piermont's stud...and now they could call for help.

That idea stopped her cold.

They could call for help a whole lot better if they had mind-walkers in every town. She sighed. It would be nice, but there just weren't enough. Of all the magic she had seen, the ability to get into someone else's head or even just speak with them was the one she'd seen the least—and that included fire magic.

Once the Protectors had seen it, most had acquired it to some degree. The same wasn't true for those who'd seen Roeglin at work. Besides the possibility that Master Envermet *might* be starting to develop the ability. She just couldn't be sure.

She didn't say anything to the parents, though. It wouldn't be fair to pressure them to act as relays when it would mean they would have to be separated from each other. She thought of Tamlin and Aisha asleep upstairs, and how she wasn't going to let her duties keep them apart anymore. If she wasn't willing to let that happen, then she had no right to ask that of anyone else.

Thank you.

The woman's voice made Marsh jump, and she kicked herself for not being more careful. She was so used to Roeglin being the only one able to step into her head that she hadn't even thought of the others. Her face heated with embarrassment but the couple only smiled.

"It's okay," they said, and the woman added. "My name's Elise, by the way."

Marsh's blush deepened. It wasn't the first time she'd

forgotten to ask for names or to properly introduce herself.

"Marsh," she said, and indicated the shadow mage. "Roeglin."

"Felix," the man answered, "and Mina you've already met."

"And you really are willing to take us to Ariella's Grotto?" the woman pressed.

"Yes," Marsh told her, and Roeglin nodded his agreement.

"And will you be setting up a force of Defenders there too?"

Marsh frowned.

"We'll be asking them to set up their own force, but we'll help them if we can. Master Envermet usually helps with the training if they need it, and I believe he's leaving a liaison team in each cavern."

"But how do they communicate?" Elise asked. "If you don't have mind mages, how can they call for help if they need it?"

Roeglin smiled.

"We do it the old-fashioned way; we send runners."

"Through the tunnels on their own?"

"Usually with a small escort. It's better now we've secured the main tunnels."

"Speaking of which," Felix began, "the tunnel to Ariella's. Has it..."

"No," Roeglin told him. "We'll be scouting it for Master Envermet's force, and he'll secure and clear it. Our priority is reaching the Grotto and making sure the settlement holds until the Protectors can reach it."

"We can help with that," Felix said and tried to stifle a cavernous yawn. "In the morning..."

"Which is far too close," Roeglin told them, pushing back his chair. "Do you know where you'll be sleeping?"

Marsh had mirrored his movement and stopped. She didn't know where *she* was sleeping either. She looked at Roeglin, but he answered her before she could speak.

No, I haven't a clue.

He'd just started to scan the room when Master Envermet cleared his throat.

Marsh gasped. The sound had come from directly behind her. Pivoting quickly, she caught the faint remains of a smirk curving his lips, and he spoke.

"The five of you need to speak to Hugh. He has your room assignments."

Marsh followed the direction indicated by his hand and saw Shameless' former owner waiting at the bar, a large ledger open in front of him. Shortly afterward, she was standing in front of the open door to her room and biting her tongue. It would have been rude to ask what they'd done with all the rooms.

Mordan looked up at her and back at the room. The single bed took up two-thirds of the space, and the kat wanted to know what Marsh was unhappy about. The small cave was perfectly defensible.

She twitched her tail and leapt up onto the bed, stretching out along the wall and leaving barely any space for Marsh. Marsh decided the kat had a point. A bed was a bed, and she was tired...and her pack would fit quite well at the end of the room.

She stepped inside and pulled the door closed behind

her, taking just enough time to take off her boots before stretching out beside the kat.

"You're too big for this," she complained, and the kat replied by showing her that there was plenty of room on the floor.

Marsh wriggled under the covers and curled onto her side. She was too tired to argue.

OF FAMILIES AND FAMILY SECRETS

The next morning came far too soon. Marsh was woken by the sound of bells ringing loudly...inside her head...where only she could hear them. Her startled shout drew a snarl from Mordan, who was on her feet and facing the door before Marsh had cleared the covers.

From outside the door came the sound of a triumphant little voice.

"In dere!"

You got it, kiddo. I am "in dere," Marsh thought, pulling on her boots and scooping up her pack before opening the door.

"Good morning," she said, trying for cheerful.

It wasn't hard. She could feel the grin lighting her face as soon as she saw them. Aisha leapt forward and wrapped her small arms around Marsh's waist and Tamlin stood beside Brigitte, looking very much like he was trying not to do the same.

Marsh picked Aisha up and walked over to the boy.

"Morning hug," she told him, and did exactly that.

Judging by the look on Brigitte's face, she'd done the right thing.

"We getting breakfast?" she demanded, letting go of the boy.

"You bet the Deeps we are," he said and led the way along the hall.

As Marsh followed him, she saw Roeglin and Gustav emerging from a room two doors down. Gustav gave her a brief wave and wrapped his hand around Roeglin's arm.

"We'll save you a table," he called over his shoulder, and Brigitte hurried after him.

"I'll make sure they don't forget."

Watching them move swiftly down the hall, Marsh wondered what the two of them knew that she and Roeglin didn't. She looked at Tamlin, but the boy seemed relieved to see them go, and Marsh had a sinking feeling that something was up and she wasn't going to like it.

Her fears seemed well founded when Tamlin stopped her just before they entered the common room.

"We don't need to go to my Uncle's place," he said. "There won't be anything there, just emptiness. It wouldn't feel right. We'd feel like we were spying."

Marsh looked from him to Aisha and caught the girl's solemn nod.

"Not good," the child told her.

"Okaaaay..." Marsh told her as Roeglin slipped back into the corridor. "The kids don't want to go to their uncle's place."

He shrugged.

"It would mean we could head straight for the Grotto. There's no need to check on the abandoned farms on the way out. The Keepers have that under control." He caught Tamlin's eye. "Are you sure? You don't need to see for yourselves?"

Tamlin stood straighter.

"I'm sure. The Keepers wouldn't lie, and we don't need to be reminded of what my uncle was like. Going there would just... It would remind us of things that were said. My father..." His breath caught, and he took another before continuing. "My father refused to back down, and my uncle said a lot of things."

This time when his breath caught, he closed his eyes and tried a different approach.

"Why don't you take a look for yourself?"

"Are you sure?"

"Yes. Marsh, too."

Marsh didn't want to see the memory. She could recall the hatred in Davide's eyes when he spoke of children—children!—with magical gifts, the crisscross of stripes on Nettie's back because she'd been able to manipulate shadow, and the prejudices she'd encountered in Mika's Outlet. She didn't want any more memories of that kind.

That wasn't enough to stop her from taking Roeglin's hand on one side and Aisha's on the other.

"You don't have to come," Tamlin told his sister. "Someone has to keep guard."

"Dan, Scruffy, and Perda will watch. I come too."

Tamlin sighed but took his sister's other hand.

"Ready?" he asked but didn't bother waiting for their reply, which was a good thing since Marsh didn't think she'd ever be ready.

A new voice, the uncle's, met her as she followed Roeglin into Tamlin's mind.

"You'd be better off putting them both out in the Desolation and leaving them there!"

"I'll pretend you didn't say that."

"No need to pretend. It's what we'd do if any of ours showed signs."

Seeing the look on Tamlin's father's face made Marsh feel both better and worse. It was one thing to lose a brother, but to lose him while he still lived and breathed? That had to be hard.

"You can't mean that."

"I know a good place. There's a canyon. You could just put them over. They wouldn't be coming back from that."

Marsh wanted to say she'd seen enough, that there was no need for Tamlin to share anymore, but the memory continued.

"No." The reply was soft, but it echoed like a shout.

"He was shouting in his mind," Aisha said. "It was loud. I made it so I couldn't hear. See?"

She was right. Their father *had* been shouting, his inner voice a single wordless scream even as he tried to reason with a brother he had loved like life itself.

The children's mother had picked Aisha up and carried the little girl away, but it hadn't blocked her father's pain. Only she had been able to do that. At least she hadn't heard what the uncle had said next.

"I can do it for you if you like."

Only Tamlin's presence had stopped his father from attacking his uncle. The man had noticed his son and taken Tamlin's hand.

"We're done here," he'd said, and led the boy away.

Their departure had not stopped either of them from hearing the uncle's parting words.

"Don't come back until they're gone."

Marsh saw that it had been the first time Tamlin had ever seen his father cry. The boy hadn't meant to share that last thought, but it had slipped through as he ended the memory.

"You can get out of my head now," he told Roeglin. "Take her with you."

Marsh hadn't wanted to leave. She hadn't wanted to stay either, but she'd caught the sadness threatening to overwhelm the boy and didn't want him to have to face it alone. Roeglin dragged her out anyway, but he couldn't stop her from kneeling to wrap her arms around the boy and hug him tight.

Tamlin let her hold him for several heartbeats, then shrugged her away.

"I'll be fine," he said, catching Aisha's wide-eyed look.

"Dat was a very bad man," she declared before turning to Marsh. "We not go dere."

Marsh hugged her too.

"No," she agreed. "We won't go there...will we, Roeglin?"

"No," he confirmed. "We won't. We'll go straight to Ariella's instead, okay?"

"What's this?" Master Envermet's voice made them all jump, and Marsh wished she could put a bell on the man.

Several bells, if that was what it took to stop him from sneaking up on them.

"We're not going to the uncle's farm," Marsh told him. "It wouldn't be good for the children."

If he was upset that she was giving him orders again, he didn't show it. Instead, he looked at Roeglin.

"I trust you can explain."

Roeglin caught Tamlin's eye, and the boy nodded.

"I can show you," he said, but Master Envermet raised his hand.

"Get them fed first," he said, and almost smiled. "I know a certain young lady who is horrible if she doesn't eat first thing in the morning."

"Am not!" Aisha argued before Marsh had time to wonder who he meant.

Funny, Roeglin muttered, *so do I.*

He led the way into the common room before she could respond, and Brigitte and Gustav waved at them from a table next to one of the walls. Marsh headed toward the pair, saying nothing as Roeglin drew Master Envermet aside, his eyes turning white as he shared what Tamlin had shown them.

"You stay here while we get food," Gustav told her as soon as she had the children settled.

Marsh might have argued but Tamlin was tugging on her sleeve, so she nodded taking a seat beside him.

"You still need to get them," he told her. "When you go and get my parents, you still have to try and get my aunt and my cousins. My uncle too, if he's there."

That last bit was added reluctantly, but Marsh understood.

"I will try," she promised, hoping it was one she could keep.

Gustav and Brigitte returned as Roeglin joined them at the table. He didn't sit down, but returned to the servery with the other two to bring the last of their meals. Breakfast was a silent affair, and they finished quickly.

"The others will have the mules ready," Gustav said when he saw they were done. "They ate early."

"And the family?"

"Was up before I was," the captain answered, sounding disgusted with himself, "*and* they didn't wake me."

He sounded so put out that Marsh almost laughed. They left the room together, discovering that the team hadn't let Gustav down and that Mina and her family were already mounted. Henri and Izmay came over leading three mules apiece, and Marsh couldn't help but notice that the two of them seemed comfortable together...more comfortable than just as comrades in arms.

Master Envermet appeared from the direction of the stables as they were preparing to ride out and Gustav stopped beside him.

"Yes, sir?"

"The order stands, Gustav. I just came to say goodbye." His gaze traveled over the children and he nodded to Brigitte. "I'll miss these two."

"Bye. Miss you, too." Aisha's little voice drew the shadow captain's attention, and he paused to smile at her.

"Why, thank you, Apprentice. Be good for Brigitte and your guardian, won't you?"

"Yes, Master Ennermet."

"And you, boy."

"Yes, Master Envermet." Tamlin's tone was solemn as he replied.

The shadow captain stepped back, letting Gustav lead them through the gate, but he had one more thing to say.

"Try to keep out of trouble, Leclerc."

Marsh rolled her eyes, relieved she had ridden past and he wouldn't see.

"Yes, Master Envermet."

Roeglin snorted, and Marsh was very glad to leave the inn behind. She was gladder still when they reached the outskirts of town and the calla shrooms rose in dense clusters around them. It was good to be on the road again.

What made it better was the fact Tamlin and Aisha were riding to one side of her and Roeglin was riding on the other. While the shadow mage's presence was nothing unusual, it felt right to have him there. The children just made their family complete.

That thought stopped her, even if the mule kept moving. Family? The children, yes, but since when had she started thinking of Roeglin as family?

When he didn't respond to that, Marsh breathed a silent breath of relief. She needed to sort that out—and what he was, since she didn't think of him as a brother.

Yeah. She pushed the thought away to deal with later. Much later. First, they had to get to Ariella's, then to the Deeps Monastery. After that... She glanced at Tamlin, unexpectedly catching his eye. The boy smiled, happiness lighting his face. Marsh returned it, then surveyed the cavern around them, her smile slowly fading.

As good as it was to be with them, she still had work to do.

"You got the lead?" she asked, and Roeglin held up the rope he'd attached to the mule's bridle.

"Ready when you are."

Marsh took a deep breath, focusing on the shadows and

trying to feel what they touched while seeking the hidden things to which they were connected. As soon as she was aware of the spaces they linked, she called on the natural magic of the world around her, using it to show her what lived and lurked among the shrooms and rocks and blending the results of both magics together.

It was easy, and she realized just how much stronger she'd become in the past few weeks. She knew she could probably open her eyes and not lose the sense of what surrounded them but didn't want to risk it...She wasn't *that* confident yet. Even so, she was able to keep hold of that sense as her mind drifted to just how good it was to have her family with her, even if it wasn't her "natural" family, but one she'd chosen for herself.

What made it better was the idea that she was helping another family reunite. Mina, Felix, and Elise deserved to be with their relatives too. The thought made her sigh. It would be good to get them safely to Ariella's Grotto and see them with the ones they loved.

Roeglin snorted.

And the chocolate has nothing to do with it, right?

Chocolate? Marsh had forgotten the chocolate. Now she remembered. Ariella's was where they grew the cocoa beans that made up her favorite drink. How could she have forgotten the chocolate?

You know? she told Roeglin as her mouth watered. *I hadn't even thought about the chocolate.*

He made a sound of disbelief.

You? Forget chocolate? Not a hope in all the Deeps.

Marsh rolled her eyes. Trust *him* not to believe her. The

chocolate was important, sure, but having a family? Nothing could compare.

She forced herself to refocus on her scan, pushing Roeglin to the back of her mind so she didn't lose her awareness of the life around them. Family was important.

She almost couldn't wait to be done delivering Mina and her mother and father and making sure the Grotto would stand. Not just because she could then adopt Tamlin and Aisha for real, but because she could also begin the search for where the raiders had taken their parents and her own.

She didn't fear losing either of them if she succeeded but looked forward to making her little family larger. After all, keeping Roeglin in line was a full-time job.

Hey!

AUTHOR NOTES - CM SIMPSON

APRIL 10, 2019

Well, the end of Book 4 is here, even if the last ten thousand words came hard and slow, and I thought they would never get written. THANK YOU for coming on this journey with me. It has been one of the bright points in a fairly tough twelve months.

You see, what I didn't know, when I first answered Amy's call for submissions, was that my mum had been diagnosed with terminal cancer. I found out shortly after Amy gave me the news my submission had been accepted.

Being told I could write Marsh's journey was exciting and wonderful...and the news from home was its exact opposite. At that stage, mum wasn't expected to make Christmas, let alone be around for the end of this book—and she certainly wasn't meant to be there to be happy when you guys decided to make *Trading into Shadow* a best seller. The fact she was has just made this journey so much more memorable.

As I type this, *Trading Close to Light* is about to launch, I've just passed a bi-annual rental inspection, am preparing the application for full-time homeschooling registration, and learned that the chemo mum had, which was meant to be a last-ditch extension of a few months, now means she has two more years she wouldn't have had.

It's been a long nine months, with a lot of change, and 2019 is almost a quarter over, but my mum is still around, and feeling a lot better than she has in a long time, and that is a memory that, for me, will forever be entwined with the memories of writing Marsh's adventures.

I have been told that books provide readers an escape from the real world and the things that trouble them there, and I hope this one has been a good place for at least some of you to escape to—I know it was for me... even at its most difficult to write.

Now, with the fourth book of this series at an end, I find I will miss you guys... and I will miss my characters, too, for however long I am away from them. Their adventures continue, albeit without me looking over their shoulders—and I hope you have enjoyed reading this part of their journey, as much as I have enjoyed writing it.

I look forward to seeing you in the future, whether it's to travel with Marsh for a little while longer, or to adventure with another character in another world. Peace be with you – and all your families – wherever you may be.

THANK YOU for not only reading this story but these *Author Notes* as well.

(I think I've been good with always opening with "thank you." If not, I need to edit the other *Author Notes*!)

RANDOM (*sometimes*) THOUGHTS?

Fans are (effectively) what everything is about for us as writers, and business people. Many of us are older - in our 30's to 50's (a couple higher, maybe one or two lower) and the fact that readers love us enough to spend their time, money and support investing in our characters means a LOT.

The first fans that supporting Death Becomes Her, encouraged me that I had 'something there... now get it edited!' and went on Facebook and encouraged me with kind words started something that has touched tens of thousands of lives.

And I'm not even bringing in the hundreds of thousands of readers - I'm just talking authors and those who are in the Indie Publishing business.

How did you do that?

By supporting our books. From there we support more authors coming into the business by providing encouragement, wisdom, and support.

EVERYTHING started with fans - so thank you from the bottom of my heart for being the catalysts for what we do.

NEW FEATURE - FAN NOTES!

Suicune - Woden, Texas - Over 30,000 books in his lifetime (damn dude!)

(Why? Note my comments from above - because Fans are the BEST!) - Here are the questions and his answers.

His favorite series or character (apparently, I need to ask about an order or preference) are:

The Kurtherian Gambit, Protected by the Damned, War of the Damned, War of the Angels

If you made up an LMBPN Character, what would be three attributes you would use? (For Example, Bethany Anne is Justice, Family (including friends), and Coca Cola. Brownstone is Keeping it Simple - Respect - and BBQ):

Honesty, fulfilling promises, willing to take responsibility.

Tell us a few short sentences about yourself, and your reading hobby (When did you start reading, why, how much do you read and preferred genre's etc. (as ideas)):

As soon as I wake up and after my breaks to play games and I now like Sci-FI and urban fantasies.

You can have my <what?> before you can have my reading time?

Car (Holy Shit! - Mike.)

Place you have loved to read the most in your life - best memories (mine was as a teenager at my grandparent's house under the featherbed on cold days.)

Any place that I have power for or can get my hands on a book.

AROUND THE WORLD IN 80 DAYS

One of the interesting (at least to me) aspects of my life is the ability to work from anywhere and at any time. In the future, I hope to re-read my own *Author Notes* and remember my life as a diary entry.

Cabin in the Sky(™) Las Vegas, Nv USA

I'm banging away at my keyboard wrapping these notes up for tomorrow's release wondering if any of you fans would like to have a word or two in the back of these books? We typically write between 350 to 600 words about ourselves, what we are thinking or what we are doing.

—- I finished up these notes in the Pizza Bar (Five50 - Aria Hotel)

FAN PRICING

$0.99 Saturdays (new LMBPN stuff) and $0.99 Wednesday (both LMBPN books and friends of LMBPN books.) Get great stuff from us and others at tantalizing prices.

Go ahead, I bet you can't read just one.

Sign up here: http://lmbpn.com/email/.

HOW TO MARKET FOR BOOKS YOU LOVE

Review them so others have your thoughts, tell friends and the dogs of your enemies (because who wants to talk with enemies?)... *Enough said ;-)*

Ad Aeternitatem,

Michael Anderle

Colleen Simpson Social

Amazon author page:
https://www.amazon.com/C.M.-Simpson/e/B0086QFGFO
Blogspot:
http://cmsimpson.blogspot.com.au/
Facebook:
https://www.facebook.com/CMSimpsonWriter/
Pinterest:
https://www.pinterest.com.au/cmsimpsonauthor/
Twitter:
https://twitter.com/simpsoncolleen1
Mailing List:
https://mailchi.mp/
718baa508302/cmsimpson_newsletter_signup

Michael Anderle Social
Website:
http://www.lmbpn.com

Email List:
http://lmbpn.com/email/

Facebook Here:

https://www.facebook.com/OriceranUniverse/
https://www.facebook.com/TheKurtherianGambitBooks/

* 9 7 8 1 6 4 2 0 2 1 9 9 8 *